A Pocket Full of Regrets

A NOVEL BY

ANJEL REYES

A Pocket Full of Regrets

Copyright © 2025 **Anjel Reyes**

First published in the Philippines in 2025 by 8Letters Bookstore &
Publishing
Lapu-Lapu City, Cebu
www.8lettersbooks.com

Cover Illustration by **Dane Reyes**
Edited by **Tamara Prastalo**

This edition is independently published by the author in United States of
America in 2025.
Contact: angrey012@outlook.com

ISBN

979-8-9998020-0-2

Trigger Warning

This book contains topics that may be distressing to readers that includes but is not limited to mentions of sexual assault and harassment, abusive behaviors, gender discrimination, mentions of rape, religious and cultural conflict, and homophobia. Reader discretion is advised.

If you or someone is experiencing emotional distress or any related themes on this book, please do not hesitate to seek support. You are not alone. For immediate help, kindly reach out to the following resources:

Philippines

- **National Domestic Violence Hotline**: 0917-899-8727 (text only) or 155-LOVE (for voice calls)
- **Commission on Human Rights (CHR):** (02) 928-5656 / (02) 928-1913
- **Barangay (local neighborhood office):** Local Barangay offices can assist with sexual harassment complaints and provide immediate support.

United Statess

- **National Domestic Violence Hotline (USA):** 1-800-799-SAFE (1-800-799-7233)
- **National Sexual Assault Hotline (RAINN):** 1-800-656-HOPE (1-800-656-4673)
- **National Suicide Prevention Lifeline (USA):** 1-800-273-TALK (1-800-273-8255)
- **Text Crisis Line (USA):** Text HOME to 741741
- **Emergency Services:** Call 911 for immediate support.

If you are not within the Philippines or the United States, please contact your local emergency services or seek help from a local mental health professional or helpline.

Your well-being is a priority, and there is someone ready to support you.

To us,

who have been told that we do not have a place in this world

because of who we are and who we love,

I'll see you by the rainbow and we'll have the time of our

fucking lives.

Prologue

TEN YEARS AGO

"ARE YOU a good kisser?"

As our friendship trio tradition dictated, we were all now lying on the floor as the rolling credits of our comfort movie, *Princess Diaries,* played in the background. It was Nico's turn to host the slumber party after Halloween night, and with the ever-rebellious spirit that he had acquired after dressing up as a drag version of *Darth Vader,* he was so proud to present us the cans of beer that he was able to hide from his parents.

And one can of beer down, here I was, running my mouth already. "You know, the mind-shattering, foot-popping, love-struck eyes, kinda kiss that will make you forget all your worries away."

Nico scoffed as he sat up and took another sip on his beer. "I can't wait to go to college and meet some real college *men*," he made a show of frustration by removing and throwing the bald cap he used for the costume. "The boys in this town don't know anything. They think spreading spit on my face is enough for them to be called a 'good kisser' and assume that's enough for me to give them the..." He opened his mouth in a wide O, and starts to...

My eyes widened as realization dawned on me. "EWW!!" I threw the pillow in his face. "WE DON'T NEED TO SEE THAT!" Nico laughed. "Just telling you what it is. That's it for us gays my age here in this town." He shrugged his shoulder and went for another sip. "How about you, Adi?" he returned the question back with a suggesting tone. "Have you smooched anyone in school?"

Nico put down his beer to give his full attention to me. "Has the golden child, Adalia Reia Castillo, ever gone behind her parents' back and defied them to… hmm… kiss a boy?"

Even if I wanted to, I couldn't hide the blush that ran up to my ears as Nico pouted his lips, kissing air. I tried to cover my face, but he was faster as he grabbed my hand and held it in place.

His expression was a mask of disbelief, astonishment, and of course, excitement. Not that it was unexpected—it was not every day I defied my parents and lived to tell the tale.

"Remember Sam?" I finally confessed. He nodded eagerly. "So, after their basketball practice last Friday, I was still in school, prepping to go home. He caught up to me when he was walking back to the locker room to shower, and we just started chatting, until we reached their lockers."

Nico's eyes widened at first with anticipation but slowly morphed to apparent concern. The realization of what he had assumed dawned on me. "No, no!" I waived. "We only kissed. I really don't know how it happened." His shoulders visibly relaxed out of relief.

The whole thing was a blur, and it didn't even last for two minutes. I could only remember that he pulled me to the locker room and whispered that he had always found me cute and wanted to kiss me. And before I could even answer, he had his face lowered on mine already. "But as soon as I realized what was happening, I ran out and left him there."

"Probably with blue balls," Nico muttered. "So, how was it? Was it everything you imagined?"

"Why would I be asking you if you were good kisser if it was?" I grunted and plopped back down on the floor. "It was just… wet." I made a disgusted sound to show my disdain. "Can't believe I lost my first kiss to that."

"They think that by opening their mouths and shoving their tongues inside, make them a good kisser," A quiet voice quipped. I turned to the other person in the room with us, whose eyes were glued to her phone screen; fingers swiping up as she casually browsed videos—not a care in the world.

"How about you then, Lexie?" I asked, now curious. I couldn't remember any time she'd talked about anyone she was interested in, let alone anyone she has kissed.

I eagerly turned to Nico with a huge grin on my face, expecting that he would back me up on my faux interrogation, knowing he was always keen for new gossip. But to my surprise, all I saw was tight-lipped smile with a waiting gaze turned to Lexie.

"Kiss someone?" Lexie continued to browse her phone. "Yeah, I've kissed a few here and there."

My mouth almost dropped in shock from this news. She had never mentioned anything to me about kissing anyone. *How? And when?* She was with me almost every time we were at school.

I glanced at Nico to see if he had the same thought process as I did. But based on his reaction, or the *lack thereof*, he knew.

A slight pang of hurt thudded in my chest, realizing that I have been left in the dark from something as monumental as this. But instead of focusing on it, I pushed it down and pulled up my overeager face, seizing this opportunity to know more about Lexie's love life.

"Who did you kiss?" I never imagined Lexie kissing someone would give me a feeling of unease. "And who is the best?" The over-the-top excitement in my voice could have given it away.

Lexie finally stopped scrolling and set her phone down. She grabbed another can of beer to open, and the sound of frizz was the only thing we could hear before she continued, "I've kissed boys from our school… The last one was Archie from the volleyball team." I put my hand in my mouth. *I've never even seen them talk!*

"But the best…" She took a sip as she contemplated, the seconds ticking by with anticipation. "…would probably be Brittany. She taught me what to do with my tongue."

Lexie dropped this bomb as if it wasn't the most mind-blowing thing she has revealed. "Oh, don't act like it's a big deal that I kissed a girl. You two are the only people who know I'm bisexual. It was a kiss. Most of them happened in dares but…" She glanced at Nico, as if a silent communication was passing through them.

Left in the dark. *Again.*

"Some of it were a type of experiment," Lexie finished in a quiet voice. "Besides, I even kissed Nico here for a dare." She made a show of gagging while Nico hit her with a pillow.

I could clearly see that there was something going on between the two that I was not aware of. And that hurt more than not knowing who Lexie kissed. I could feel my chest tightening as the banter in front of me unfold.

"Kiss me then," I said out of unfounded insolence and envy.

"I dare you to kiss me, Lexie." I snatched a can of beer and opened it rather aggressively than I intended to. Nico stopped midway from tackling Lexie and turned his head so fast, I thought he would do the *Exorcist* out of shock.

"You don't know what you're saying, Adi," Nico was the one who disproved. He sat back down and faced me; apprehension now clearly painted his face. "You're drunk and this is the alcohol speaking." He tried stealing the can from my hand.

"What's wrong?" Ignoring Nico and daringly eyed Lexie, "You said you kissed Nico, right? Will it be a problem if you did it with me, too?" I flashed my carefully crafted smile. "I just want to be *in on the fun.*"

I've always thought that Lexie and I were closer than they were—that she had no secrets from me, even her most embarrassing ones. I was the first one to be friends with her, not Nico. But this revelation had shaken something inside me that wasn't sitting well enough for me to accept it as it was. Maybe it was the alcohol speaking, but the confrontation felt good as I nudged this feeling on.

Lexie and Nico glanced at each other. *There it is again.*

After a few moments of awkward silence, Nico stood up and muttered something about showering and removing his make-up. I knew that he was stepping out for me and Lexie, and the guilt had started to blossom its way into my mouth, that I almost apologized out of habit. But the unease in the pit of my stomach was far too greater, knowing that the two people I trust the most were keeping secrets from me.

"You don't want this, Adi." Lexie repeated as soon as Nico stepped out of his room. "Maybe you're drunk and you're not thinking straight."

Irritation swelled in my chest. *Why do people around me keep on deciding what I want or not want? Was I not capable of doing that for myself?*

"You're not my mom, Lexie." I snapped. "I am an adult now, so don't tell me what I do or don't want!" The feeling of being restricted was making me want to go against it more. "Besides, it's not as if you're contagious." In hindsight, it was stupid of me to use this argument knowing that this was a sore spot for her. But my mouth acted even before I could fully process what I said. "Don't worry, I won't turn gay if you kiss me."

Lexie flinched and her eyes darkened.

"I'm sorry," I said a bit too fast, fully knowing it was too late. I knew I fucked up. "I didn't mean that." The remorse has started crawling up my chest, conscious that I said that with the intention to make her feel how hurt I was from being left in the dark.

But instead of walking out or lashing out on me, she closed her eyes for a second and as soon as she opened them, I knew I was a goner. This was not a version of Lexie that I had seen in the five years we have been best friends.

"Yes, you did." She smirked. "You meant it."

She slowly started inching towards where I sat, until we were merely a foot away from each other, now face to face. My stomach was churning, from what—I have no idea. Nervousness? Anticipation? I never had any issues with personal space with my best friends, we were almost attached to the hip at school, always together.

Yet this felt like it was different. Dangerously and magnetically different.

I was immediately drowned by those brown orbs that seemed to stare right at my soul, making me squirm and wanting to take back the angst and insolence I have been throwing—yet curious enough to push through and see what this side of her can do to me.

This is okay… right? It was too late to back out now. *Nothing would change between us… right?*

My heart felt like it was ready to jump out of my chest. I was all bundled up for this autumn night, but I didn't think that the heat was coming from the clothes I had on.

"One last time," she asked, the warmth of her breath now

caressed my face. "Don't let the alcohol think. Is this what you really want?" Her pupils were so dilated under the dark, effortlessly pulling and lulling me into her pool. "Or are you gonna regret this tomorrow?"

I knew I was going to regret it. This was a line I never thought I would cross. But before I could second guess myself, I closed the gap and crashed my lips against hers. She stayed still for a second, surprise painted all over her face. And slowly, as if remembering what had started all of this, her expression transformed into something else as she gently placed her hands on my neck to slowly pull me closer; the touch searing and spreading into my skin. It was as if no distance was still too much between us. She coaxed my mouth open and slid her tongue inside my mouth.

So, this is how you kiss.

It was supposed to be gross—all I could feel was spit in my mouth and face when I did it with Sam. But this… the feeling of her tongue against mine was sending waves of shivers down my spine. It was as if we were dancing to a melody only our mouths could express.

My thoughts were muddled, and I knew right there and then that my rationale had just bid her farewell, leaving me into a mess of pure yearning and overwhelming sensation.

My breath hitched as she sucked on my lower lips, a tingle shooting electricity to all ends of my body, and I could feel the unfamiliar warmth starting to gather in my lower stomach. My eyes have been opened to a whole new territory, unaware of what to do, unfamiliar of all the sensations that were taking over my body; the visceral hunger to get closer, a gnawing feeling clawing its way into my gut.

I now knew why people our age would do anything to steal moments like this. My whole world shook, untangling all the stability that I was carefully taught with my entire life.

And I was ready to fall. Fucking ready to risk it all for a minute more.

An unexpected moan escaped my lips as Lexie deepened the kiss again, my body grinding against hers, as if it has a mind of its own.

More. I could hear my mind whisper.

I could feel my body shudder as her hands found its way inside the back of my shirt. I whimpered as I felt the subtle caress on my bare skin.

But instead of diving deeper to this unexplored territory, it was as if a light switch has turned on in Lexie's brain as soon as I tried reaching out for her face.

She started pulling away from the entanglement that we have become, the space between us now cold with uncertainties. She shook her head as if trying to gain clarity. And when she returned her gaze to me, the corner of her lips pulled up coyly, giving me a glimpse of a Lexie that I never knew existed.

"What do you say," she stood up and sipped the remaining beer. "better than Sam?"

They say alcohol could release your inhibitions and have an excuse for acting stupid. Or was it a way to release your inhibitions so your true desires could surface and give you the courage to act on it?

Despite the bitter taste of knowing how this skill was acquired, I made a show of masking my face into one of satisfaction and nonchalance.

"Brittany taught you well."

PART I

Adi

They say second chances do not come around often.

But it did.

For me, at least.

I thought I deserved it.

I thought the universe owed me something.

After everything that had happened,

Wasn't it fair to ask for something good?

But in the end, it was torture.

To finally accept what I have been denying for the longest time.

Yet realizing that it was all too late.

I lost her.

All over again.

Chapter One

A SWIG from the cold beer bottle in my hand was what I needed after what seemed to be hours of dancing. Even if I wanted to step out, the throngs of body moved as if it was one entity, making it impossible to go against the current. Not like it was any different—I have lived my life like that anyway. Always going with the tides, never against the current. It was what I have been taught—*head down, stay in your lane.*

The liquid felt like a breath of fresh air as it ran its way down my body, pushing down the memories that had started to emerge. I raised my hand to catch the bartender's attention, signaling for one more. She nods in acknowledgement, stepping closer as she handed me the frosty bottle. I offered a sweet smile, the one I have been trying to practice all night in the hopes to catch any eyes that could distract me for the night. She merely turned to the person next to me, already taking her order.

I sighed in disappointment. Even with a woman, it still didn't work.

The thought of putting myself out there again scared the shit out of me but I knew I needed a distraction—a way to step out of my skin and get away from myself even just for a night. And it was by some miracle when Nico had texted me, asking if I wanted to go out Friday night. The reply was sent in mere seconds. It was not as if I wanted to—it was more of a need at this point.

I needed to forget.

I waved my hand holding my card, confused as to why the bartender didn't let me pay for the drink. She smiled and pointed to the other side of the bar, "it was paid for already." I squinted my eyes, hoping to see who it was but the darkness was not of any help.

I stood up and started heading towards whoever this was, curiosity getting the better of me.

Maybe my smile worked, just not with the intended person. I chuckled to myself. *But it's just to say thank you, or maybe the distraction I need.*

The closer I got, the more nervous I was. Despite the liquid courage that was helping me tonight, I could feel the coldness in my palms and the butterflies in my stomach. I have never been the one to be this proactive.

Well, tonight was all about breaking character, anyway.

Closer and closer, I started to see who it was. Pixie blonde hair, pointy nose and lips that were already in smirk, a white button-down shirt, opened so low that it exposed a... black bra.

A woman. I felt my stomach drop.

Duh. I rolled my eyes to myself. *Very good observation.*

Are you sure? We're going to say thank you, that's all.

And before I could convince myself to turn around and just go back to find Nico and Amanda, I pushed myself to walk the last few feet. And now I was in front of *her*.

"Thank you for the drink," I made a motion of lifting my bottle. "I'm Adi... and you are...?"

She straightened up from her seat and leaned closer to whisper in my ear. "Eli," she answered, voice smoky and low. She clinked the bottle in my hand with hers and motioned for me to sit on the empty chair beside her. "You're all alone on a Friday night, Adi?"

My mind went into hyperdrive. *True crimes 101, never let them know you're alone.* I wasn't alone anyway. I just didn't know where the two people I was here with, and what or who they were doing now.

I mustered a confident smile even though deep inside I was already strategizing all the things I could do if this turned out to be a worst-case scenario type. "I'm with my two best friends." I took a gulp to conceal the nervousness. "I needed a quick breather. You know, the dance floor here is not one to mess with."

She laughed. And no matter the danger I was preparing for, the sound of her voice made something swell in my chest. A tiny part of me giddy that I made this woman laugh.

And this is why I'm not going to survive a serial killer.

"I know." Eli smiled. "My best friend did a lot of work to make this club a success. It's one of the best clubs to go to, on a Halloween night here in Vancouver." Oh, her best friend owned the club. Bougie. "And also, the best if you're looking for…" She paused and gave me a suggestive look. "…*something else* for some other nights."

The implication did not go unnoticed. The urge to play along was at the tip of my tongue, but something kept stopping me from acting on it.

She's a woman. I reminded myself.

Was I ready? *Let's not open that door yet.*

So, instead of taking this gorgeous woman up on her imposed offer, I plastered a smile on my face and extended my hand. "It was nice meeting you, Eli."

She shook my hands with an amused grin. "Thank you for the drink and thank you for letting me know where to go if I wanted to look for… *something else* in the future." Before I forgot, I added, "and regards to your best friend. Tell her she's doing a great job with this club."

Eli chuckled. "You know, I am not used to being turned down," And instead of being discouraged, a determined expression was evident on her face. "Definitely a first… for now." She kissed the back of my hand and tipped her bottle as a salute before I stepped away. "I hope to see your gorgeous face around here, again!" she shouted through the distance.

A small smile played on my lips, feeling happy with the how the night was going so far. I never would have thought that a stunning human being, be it may a woman, would give me her time today. Feeling wanted was a refreshing change after enduring a year full of nothing but pain and isolation. And I think I could count this as a win for myself.

I shot a quick text to Nico and Amanda, asking where the hell they were, and what were the plans right after. I was able to settle in an empty couch before receiving a response in the group chat.

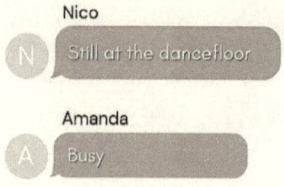

Nico

Still at the dancefloor

Amanda

Busy

I knew what busy meant and I would not interrupt with their shenanigans as long as they were safe. I grinned to myself as the thought of my two best friends getting laid tonight crossed my mind. *At least, some of us are happy in that aspect.*

I leaned my head back and closed my eyes, hoping to rest for a bit. Finally feeling the exhaustion and the effects of the alcohol in my body, the buzz in my head seemed to be overpowering my will to move my ass and just go home.

I have spent my whole week at work, doing overtime if I could and without even resting, went straight away to drinking and dancing. My twenty-eight-year-old body was not getting any younger.

Though energy-draining, it was the distraction I needed. I tried to make myself scarce and only went to Nico's place when it was almost time to sleep. He extended his couch when I didn't have anywhere to go to—it was a small sacrifice to pay, to give him the privacy that I have intruded for a week now.

Thinking of the situation I had put myself in, made me chug the rest of the contents of the bottle in my hand. My fingers hovered on the screen of my phone, ready to send a quick text to the group that I was calling it a night, when a figure approached the table. The man didn't even wait for an invitation when he scooted to my side aggressively without even uttering a word.

He bumped his knee into my thigh, and before I could react, a hand grabbed my arm—the touch too familiar not to recognize. The sleepiness in my body was gone in an instant, replaced with cold utter fear and panic.

"You forgot to turn off your location, hon," he sounded almost feral. "I already gave you a week to bask in the freedom you've desperately begged for, but my patience is running thin, little girl. At least, have the decency to respond to my text and calls." A menacing smile was slowly spreading on his face as if a predator who has finally caught his prey. "You think we're done just like that? Do I need to remind you who makes the decision in this relationship?"

I tried yanking my arm away from him but fully knowing how this usually turned out, I realized there was no point fighting back if I want to leave here unscathed. The difference in physical stature was so vast, I knew he could yank me without even sparing much energy.

So, I settled with the next best thing I thought I could do—I stayed put in my seat, unwilling to give in to the insistent tugs he was doing.

"We're done, Damien." The attempt to imbue confidence in my voice failing as it quivered. "I told mom already. And I also told her that I moved out." I looked at him straight in the eyes even though my whole body was trembling inside. *"We're done."*

It was as if the finality in my voice broke the civility in him that he began hauling me forcefully out of the booth, uncaring of the eyes that were starting to dart in our direction.

That's good. I thought despite the pain that was starting to lance through my shoulder. *Maybe someone would notice and save me from this.* The sad reality of my situation came flooding back to me, making tears brim my eyes.

Because I knew I couldn't do it for myself.

I heard someone shout, but it seemed all muted in my ears. I was lost in the trench of panic and hopelessness. *Maybe I deserved this.* A sob escaped my lips. *Maybe this is karma, finally seeking atonement for how I lived my life.*

Damien continued to drag me from the table, but I tried holding on as I buried my nails at the edge of the leather couch; a last-ditch effort to convince myself that I was not fully giving up on myself.

Despite the blurry vision, I saw the crowd parting and a familiar blond, pixie hair came bounding up on us, followed by a figure I couldn't clearly see.

Eli approached the table and put a hand on Damien's

shoulder. "Sir, I suggest you stop pulling Adi. We can talk about this without anyone getting hurt." The playful tone that she used while talking to me was now replaced with a placating one. "We don't want the authorities involved in this."

"I *suggest* putting your damn hands off me." Every word was laced with venom. Damien let go of his hold on me, making me stumble back on the couch. Eli made a move to reach out, but he blocked their direct line of sight, hiding me behind his shadow. "And who are you to tell me…" he hissed and looked down on Eli, "on how to deal with my fiancée?"

A flash of shock and confusion crossed Eli's face but was immediately gone in less than a second. "Regardless, sir, you are in a private establishment, and we have the right to refuse service and escort out anyone who is being disruptive." Her eyes darted to me, and back to Damien. "Can I please talk to Adi? If she agrees to go with you, we'll escort you out with no trouble."

"No," Damien said without any hesitation. "Whatever I say, goes for her. So, run along to your boss and tell whoever he is, that there is no commotion, and we are all set to go." He turned towards me, his threatening look forcing me to say yes.

I peered around and saw that the people closest to us were starting to gather around as if we were a spectacle to watch. This was not something I was proud of, and I have done my best—anything—*everything*, to keep this part of my life hidden from everyone to see, even from my best friends. But here it was, all in display, for everyone to see.

An audience has already gathered around us to get a glimpse of the misfortune of someone they don't even know, some reaching out to grab their phone, ready to record.

I opened my mouth to give the answer Damien was forcing me to say—the 'yes' to stop this humiliation and at least save face. *It was as if the universe was telling me to suck it up and just go along with it.*

But before I could utter any words, a woman's voice rang out behind Eli. "Eli said you wanted her to say something to *me*?" A tinge of familiarity tried to jog my memory. "I own this club and you're disrupting business. Should I call the cops to escort you out… *sir*?"

I scrambled outside the couch to confirm if I heard it correctly.

And it was.

A woman wearing a three-piece suit stood in front of us, as imposing, despite the difference between Damien and her height. She has both of her hands in her pocket, a sign of ease and confidence, while her face was stoic, bored at most. The long dark mane that used to crown her head was now cut in a pixie, accentuating her strong jawline with the side part slightly covering half of her face.

"Lexie," I whispered before I could stop myself. She gave me a quick glance—no recognition reflecting on her face.

I would be lying if I told myself that that didn't hurt.

Out of all the things that I was expecting that could happen tonight, Alexandria standing in front of me was not in my bingo cards.

You wanted distraction. This ought to do it.

The fear and panic that were plaguing me were replaced by confusion and surprisingly, a sense of calm. As if these two women in front of me could turn the tides around this situation.

I looked over Lexie's shoulder and saw Nico and Amanda fighting their way through the crowd.

As soon as Nico saw Damien, he pushed forward until he was on the other side of the table, pulling me away from Damien. I told him what happened after a year of hiding it from everyone I knew. He finally understood what my ex-fiancé was capable of.

"She's my fiancée," Damien reiterated as he grabbed my arm, pulling me back to his side again. "I didn't allow her to go out tonight, and now I am taking her home." He flashed Lexie a taunting smile. "You know... *lovers' quarrel.*"

Wonder crossed Lexie's face, staring at Damien then finally turning her gaze on me. It was the first time she acknowledged my presence since the commotion started.

"*Adi,*" I almost cried as the familiar voice called out to me. "Is he your fiancé?"

Lexie never broke eye contact with me and it was as if the anchor that I needed to finally summon the courage to say no. Slowly, I shook my head and muttered, "Not anymore..."

Damien turned around, and just like those nights where I ended up black and blue, his eyes were full of rage, making my skin crawl with fear. *I know what happens next.* I closed my eyes and tried to raise my arms to at least protect my face. But nothing came after, just the release of the pressure from my arm.

I opened my eyes to see Damien on the floor with bouncers restraining him down.

Everything seemed to be moving in slow motion. Eli's face was suddenly in front of me, trying to shake me out of my stupor. Lexie was at the back, phone in hand and was walking away already.

Stay, I wanted to call out. But I knew I have given up my right to demand anything from her ten years ago.

Nico and Amanda were up in my face, checking if I was okay, too. Everything seemed so slow and was starting to get blurry. I could feel the nausea and sharp pain creeping at the back of my head, overpowering my senses until I was hunched over, gagging my guts out.

And before I could apologize to the owner of the shoes I was hurling my insides on, blackness took over and I was no more.

Chapter Two

BEEP. BEEP. Beep.

Prying my eyes open to take account of my surroundings felt like a chainsaw splitting my head open; the continuous beeping sound wasn't making it any better either. I squinted my eyes and looked around.

White walls.

Dimmed lights.

And the scent seemed so... clean.

Understanding dawned on me.

What the hell am I doing at a hospital?

My left arm was attached to an IV bag, my clothes replaced with a hospital gown. I tried racking my brain to get a logical sense of what has happened, and as I wished – everything came crashing back to me.

Eli and her offer.

Damien and his grip on my arm.

Eli, stopping Damien.

And…

I almost bolted out of the bed. *Lexie.*

I pressed my palms into my eyes as a wave of nausea hit me. I uttered a silent prayer, hoping it would pass right away. Bad luck though—I already felt something coming back up from my stomach and I knew it needed to get out, one way or another.

Remind me to never drink again. I could see my inner self rolling her eyes. *Yeah, right.*

My eyes darted at the things that were within my reach; the panic rising as the acidic taste of vomit was starting to barge its way towards my mouth. I reached out to the bedside cabinet, hoping to get anything that could catch my dinner.

It was that or the floor.

A momentarily relief left my body as I saw a basin, but I knew the storm was just about to start. Hence, the retching began.

The acidic taste and the smell of alcohol overpowered the hospital room as I emptied my stomach in the tiny basin. Though calling what I threw up dinner was an overstatement. All I hurled out was basically the tequila and beer we drank last night.

There was a momentary silence and peace while my stomach started to settle. I put the basin back at the bedside table and had began moving towards the edge of the bed, eager to clean up and remove the stench that was starting to fill my nostrils. I could feel another gag coming up at the back of my throat when I heard the door sliding open.

"Hey," a soft, woman's voice called out. "You should be staying in bed. You're not strong enough to move around yet."

I could feel the fog in my brain from the hang over and it took a few seconds before I was able to put a name to the face. A very gorgeous face at that.

Eli.

The dim lights from the club last night didn't do her justice. She leaned on the door frame like it was the most casual thing to do, her button-down shirt from last night, now replaced with plain white shirt tucked in her green corduroy pants, accentuating that toned arm as it flexed when she waved a hand. She ran her fingers through her blonde pixie, her eyes like green orbs under the fluorescent light, and a natural flush on her cheeks was the perfect cherry on top to make her even more breathtaking.

The thought of this person offering something more to me last night was an ego boost I never knew I needed.

Not that I would accept.

Very good prioritizing skills. I could hear my inner voice scolding me. *You're in a hospital, hooked to a bag, and all you could think about is how gorgeous this woman is.*

14

I smacked myself internally.

She started walking towards me and assisted me back to bed, her gaze flickered to the side and noticed the basin at the table. Her nose wrinkled. "Do you feel okay? Do you want some water?"

I forced a weak smile to mask my embarrassment and grabbed the bottle she offered. Her eyes did not leave my face until I finished everything. I muttered a small thank you as she took the bottle from my hands.

"You remember me from last night, right?" A tentative tone, checking. "The free drink? Was trying to hit on you." Playful, yet still cautious.

I nodded. I didn't dare open my mouth just yet as I feel the nausea had just started slowly dissipating. I sighed and leaned back at the bed, wiping the sweat in my face with my free hand.

Eli offered a small smile. "Do you remember what happened last night?"

She didn't need a verbal confirmation as I grimaced from the memory. The feeling of never escaping the past that I have been trying hard to escape from, clutched my heart like a barbed wire. The mere thought of feeling Damien's touch on my body again made the hair on my arms stand and my skin crawl.

Eli looked at me grimly. She knew what I was thinking. "Mr. Flores was sent to the police station. I don't have any news yet since…" She glanced at her watch. "It's just four AM and my best friend has been dealing with this shitstorm. She hasn't texted me yet."

The comfort of knowing that Damien was at the police station pulled a thorn out of my back. At least, I was safe… *for now*.

"The police will pass by maybe early this morning or afternoon to ask you for questions." She sat at the chair beside the bed. "We have filed a complaint against him and your witness statement could help us." Eli offered her hand. "I know it's hard. But think about it if you want to file charges against him as well. He was taking you against your will. That can be a strong case for attempted kidnapping."

I grabbed her hand and gave it a squeeze. A silent thank you for all the things she has done for me when I was basically a stranger. But facing all these was a bit too soon for me to grasp.

I just got out. One week. And it didn't take long for him to find me again.

I don't want to be involved again. The thought of filing a report against him and possibly seeing him again, stirred the fear that he had unconsciously ingrained on me for the mere one year we were together.

"But that still doesn't answer why I am in the hospital." The thought came out like a question pushed down farther, out of priority. A segue. "Did I bleed anywhere?"

Eli took my hand to her lips and gave it a small peck before releasing it. The touch sending jolts of electricity from my arm to my gut, making me forget the awful past that I was reminiscing for a bit.

That was so unnecessary. I wanted to roll my eyes. But I couldn't lie to myself, the hopeless romantic in me was kicking her feet and giggling her heart out. *My knight in shining armor.*

You wanted distraction. My inner voice reminded. *The universe is sending you two.*

This made me stop from the internal kicks and giggles, the reminder of the other person who helped me last night, blasting me in the face.

"Alex wanted to…" Eli started explaining yet it all fell on deaf ears.

It completely flew out of my mind that Alex, Eli's best friend and club owner, was the same Lexie that I knew. *How is the world so small?*

My mind was suddenly consumed with Lexie's presence from last night—her voice, her new appearance… and how she looked at me so cold as if I was a mere stranger that she was passing by on a busy street.

When I asked if Damien was my karma, the universe literally sent Lexie right then and there, to point out that, *'No, he's not your karma. She is. Pay for what you did.'*

"I'm sorry, I zoned out for a bit." I'd ask Nico about Lexie later. Despite the commotion last night, I was sure he wasn't as surprised as I was when she saw Lexie.

The realization hit me like a ten-wheeler truck, *left in the dark. Again.* The reminder, an arrow striking me directly in the heart. *Until now.*

Eli gave me an understanding nod, probably attributing my mind fog from the recent incident. "After last night, Alex insisted to get you to a hospital. Though there wasn't anything remotely wrong with the findings, she insisted to at least have you hydrated. Once you're done with this bag, you're good to go. Also, the doctor found some bruises in your thighs, and they wanted to check with you if you were hurt before we got here."

Instinctively, I looked at my thighs and pulled the cover to hide them. *Week old bruises.*

"No, it's not from last night." I tightened my hold on Eli's hand, the warmth and comfort grounding me from spiraling. "Thank you. For saving me." My voice shook as tears slowly blurred my eyes. She pulled me to a hug, a reassurance from the frustration, the fear, and the realization that something worse could've happened to me. "Thank you," I whispered again.

"Now, now," she consoled as she drew circles on my back. "Ladies usually cry out because of happiness when they're with me. Don't break the streak, Adi."

I pulled away and tried teasing her despite the mess of tears in my face. "Maybe I'm the exception."

"Maybe, you are." She smirked opened her mouth to follow through the banter, when her phone rang. She signaled that she was going to step out to answer and would be back in a bit.

It gave me time to check my phone and look if Nico and Amanda were able to get home safely, too. Number of messages and missed calls from them as expected, a voicemail from my mom and from an unregistered number that I couldn't forget, even though I tried so hard to. Great.

I listened to the voicemail from my mom. I knew this tone all too well, most especially when growing up. This was the voice she used when she was about to reprimand and tell me how disappointed she was in me. Not that it mattered, because as far as I knew, she always has been.

> *Adalia. We need to talk. Come back home and we'll*
> *sort everything out with the Flores'. Don't disappoint*
> *me. Listen to me. I know what's best for you.*

The pit in my stomach continued to drop. The feeling of hopelessness that I would never be able to escape this cycle was inducing an anxiety attack.

I have escaped. And I promised myself that this was my time to take back control and finally decide what I want to do with my own life.

I clicked on the trash icon, hoping that it was enough to put a stop on the discomfort that had started creeping its way on my mind.

HALF AN hour has passed when Eli came back with a plastic bag on one hand, and a bouquet of sunflowers on the other. *Where the fuck did she get a bouquet at this hour?*

My confusion was squashed when she walked over and handed me the bag, my heart almost leaping when I saw what was in it.

Egg drop soup. How did she know that this was my go-to food whenever I was sick?

Eli beamed at me as she saw how surprised I was with the food choice. "I heard it was your favorite." She winked and started settling at the chair by the bedside.

My empty stomach grumbled as the waft of the soup hit my face. "It is."

It was too early, but my hopeless romantic self was moved. My go-to sick food and my favorite flowers. *Which fairy godmother granted my wish last night?* A comforting thought out of the mess that my life has been. *Maybe something good came out of last night, after all.*

I wanted to scold myself from being swayed by this simple

gesture since this woman in front of me was a stranger at most, yet my stomach felt like it was full of butterflies. A giddy smiled started to spread in my face, unable to contain the silliness of this fleeting emotion.

"Done?" Eli asked when she saw I had stared cleaning up. I nodded as I put away the bowl to the side. She offered her hand as she scooted closer.

What was with her and holding hands?

But who was I to complain? I reached out and took hers. She started drawing circles in my palms, the innocent gesture wiring my body up.

"I'm here to apologize on behalf of the club," she said without breaking eye contact. "Alex's ultimate goal for *Club Tala* was to be a safe space for everyone to just be themselves and not worry about danger when they lose their inhibitions." A small smile played on her lips. "I could remember clear as day when she asked me to work as a marketing manager and a liaison for her. As good as her mission was, my heart broke for her when she mentioned that it was rooted from a bad experience. And she didn't want anyone to experience what she did," Eli continued without noticing the grimace on my face. "She said *Tala* meant a bright star in the Filipino language. Surprising if you ask me, since she isn't of that cultural decent. But who knows?" She chuckled. I couldn't tell if Eli knew that it was me who was the reason for that experience and this was her passive-aggressive way of telling me off.

"Anyways, she meant the club to be that, for people who can't find their way in the dark."

If my guilt from the past ten years, always wondering what happened to Lexie after she disappeared, was not enough—this was definitely a reminder to slap me in the face. *Club Tala* was built up from the pain I had made her suffer.

And yet she still named it after my favorite Filipino word.

I was the root of Lexie's hurting, and I didn't deserve this kindness that they were offering. Not one ounce.

Or how can I assume that this club was all about me when she could have lived a life I didn't know within the last ten years?

Who cared about saving face? I was a horrible human being,

and this was my payment. *Maybe I deserved to be with Damien.* The mere thought of going back to him made me almost sob.

Eli grabbed my shoulders and pulled me towards her, enveloping me in a warm embrace. She tightened her hug, a clutch from all the guilt that was consuming me.

"Thank you," I whispered.

"To fully compensate, we're inviting you to dinner where we can discuss your terms." She offered me her phone. "Here, put your number in so I can send you the details after."

The fear of facing Lexie again made my stomach do somersaults, but I have promised myself that I would make better choices for myself. Maybe it was karma that had sent me in front of Lexie again, and this was the universe giving me a second chance to make up for the mistakes I have committed ten years ago.

I gave Eli her phone back and timing as it was, the nurse came in to inform us that I could be discharged in the next hour or so.

An hour passed before Eli returned, my ID on her hand. "We're good to go. Did you get everything you need?" she asked.

Good to go? "How about the bill for this?" I asked. She apologized again and said that it was the company's responsibility to compensate at least the co-pay for the hospital bill. I didn't know a lot of businesses, but I knew that they could take their hands off this case since the altercation was between two customers. Business owners literally find the tiniest hole to not pay for anything.

Not unless…

Don't make me hope. I whispered to my inner voice. *Remember how she looked at you when she saw you? Even in distress, she acted as if you're a stranger.*

And who's fault is that? I asked it back. *Ours.*

Don't forget that.

And it was time to repent for what we have done.

Chapter Three

THE DRIVE back to Nico's apartment was filled with silence I didn't know how to fill. The sun had just started rising, offering a soft glow to the sky. Eli kept her gaze to the road despite possibly noticing that I kept on glancing at her.

"What is it?" she finally asked. "Spill it."

My life was basically in ruins, my emotional state worse, and the only thing I could hold on to now was my relationship with people. And despite the shitshow from last night, it became an opportunity to build new ones with kind hearts and gentle hands. *Or reconcile old ones.*

"I wanted to say thank you, to you," I started. "You've been helping me out since last night. Can I take you out for coffee?"

Eli stole a glance at me before returning his eyes on the road. A smile was slowly forming on her face. "Adi, is this your way of asking me out on a date?" she teased. "What a good morning it is!"

The panic and embarrassment shot of my body so quickly. "No, no! I... it's to say thank you for all of these." Wringing my hands wasn't enough to push down the mortification.

Eli didn't respond right away, prompting me look at her now, confused face. She gave me another glance. "Wait—," Her brows crunching up closer. "Are you not... gay?"

"I... *no*," I answered too quickly out of habit. "I mean... I'm not sure?"

"No, sorry." Eli's tone now appeasing. "I'm sorry, I just assumed that you were... since you were at *Club Tala* last night and *it is* a lesbian bar. I should have known, considering you were with, who I'm assuming, was a straight man."

I knew it was a lesbian bar. I knew what I would see when I got there. And I couldn't deny that feeling a woman's body against mine in that dance floor brought a lot of intrusive thoughts that I should be pushing down. And my rationale won as usual. Even before my dance partner became too touchy, I was able to get out and get a breather. Because I knew I was not ready to enter that territory just yet.

As ironic as it was, thinking that I got out of a sticky situation, here comes fate taunting me and dangling the person who made me question all my beliefs and values in life, in front of me.

"Uh…" How was I going to answer this? "I don't know yet. I'm still trying to figure things out for now." A tinge of honesty to an entirely whole lie.

Eli smiled knowingly. "No pressure, Adi." She reached out to cover my hand in hers. "Just know that if ever you want to… try something. You have my number." Ending it with a wink.

I gave her an incredulous look. "Are you seriously offering me to have sex with you after we met like what, hours ago?" As much as the implication, I didn't feel a shred of fear in her presence. "Pervert," I tried adding playfully.

She retuned it with a heartfelt laughter—one that tugged something inside my chest, making my lips pull upward, returning the laugh.

"No, no," she tried backtracking, laughter still in her voice. "I mean going out, dates, coffee, travel." She parked the car by Nico's apartment. "Sex is still on the table, though. But let's not start with that."

All of these were making my head reel and my heart swell. Eli seemed a kind person with a sweet heart. I couldn't lie to myself even if I wanted to—the woman was attractive—conventionally attractive.

So, what she was saying was not adding up on my mind.

It was as if Eli took the silence and my confused look at face value when she turned to me. "Look, it may not make any sense to you, but I find you pretty and I like to know you better." She dropped the compliment like she was sharing how mundane her day was. "So, text me when you decide that you're… really not straight."

I grabbed my purse but before I could step out of the car, Eli held my hand to stop me. "Can I give you a bit of a nudge to see?" Her face was a few inches away from me, that I could smell the scent of coffee from her breath.

"What do you mean?" And before I could say anything more, she closed the small gap between our face, giving me a lingering peck on my lips.

And instead of the giddiness I felt earlier, it was as if I was doused with cold water as I sat still, my face in between her hands. She pulled away with an oblivious smile on her face. "Think about that and let me know. There's a lot more from where that came from."

I tried pushing down my anxiety, struggling to hide the panic that was slowly rising. I waved my hand goodbye to send Eli off, hoping the smile plastered on my face wasn't giving anything up. She was about to drive off when she rolled down her windows and called out to me. "I almost forgot. I'll text you the date and time when we can meet. You don't work weekends, right?"

I shook my head, and Eli gave me a nod before driving off.

I straightened my back and darted my eyes at the surroundings if anyone was around.

No one saw, a soft voice reminded me from the back of my mind.

Still ashamed, are we? Fuck you, subconscious.

I GAVE the front door a soft knock before Nico and Amanda burst out of the door with bags under their eyes, clearly up all night. They pulled me in a tight hug before escorting me inside as if I was a fragile human being, going to break at the smallest sign of inconvenience. They sat me down at the kitchen island, Amanda already stirring the cup of coffee she had prepared for me. Based on the coffee maker's content, it seemed like these two have been running in fumes the whole night.

"You both could've slept you know," I smiled at them as I took a sip of the black liquid. "Staying up all night wouldn't make anything better."

Nico reached out his hand across the counter, grasping mine. "Bitch, you think we could sleep soundly while you're at the hospital?" He tried mocking hurt in his face yet failed miserably.

"It was a good thing the staff was there right away," Amanda continued. "I couldn't imagine if they didn't stop him before he could take you."

I nodded along, reassuring them that I was fine and was glad that Damien was behind bars for now. I didn't want to dwell with the incident as much, trying to put it behind me as far as I could—hoping and praying that it would be the last time my path and Damien's would cross.

After countless hugs and reassurances that I was okay at surface level, Amanda decided to sleep over for the day, knowing she couldn't drive in her state. We settled in at the living room, Nico foregoing his bed to join us. We shut all the window blinds and turned on the TV as white noise in the background. And as soon as we hit the pillow, it didn't take more than ten minutes before Amanda's breathing steadied, a light snore coming out of her mouth.

Nico turned around to face me, surprised that I was still awake.

"*You didn't tell me she was back,*" I mouthed to him. And instead of hiding the fact that he knew, he squeezed my hand and gave me a sad smile.

"*She didn't want to be found yet,*" he whispered.

She didn't want me to see her. The pain of realizing the weight of this clasped my heart tightly.

"You can't force her to reconcile, Adi. She deserves a space where she also feels safe."

"*Why do you always leave me in the dark?*" My chest felt heavy as the memories of our younger years flash through my mind—the lingering looks, the silent communication, the messages between the lines between Nico and Lexie—was I the outsider between us three? Was I too naïve to believe that I had a say in who Lexie wanted to be close with, aside from me? Did I have the right to feel that way, in the first place?

Before I could turn to the other side, Nico held me in place, staring at me with an almost reproachful look. *"Stop thinking about yourself for a minute and think about her. This decision was for her, not you."*

That felt like a slap in the face. Because it was true.

The urge to stand up, leave and just run from this reality was too tempting. *It was my fault.* I pushed Lexie out to the point of irreparable and now that she was back, I had no right to force her into anything, and I have no intention to. It was the only comfort I could give from the shitstorm that happened to us before.

The urge to be angry and lash out at Nico was boiling under my skin, ready to come out. But all he said was right, and he was calling me out for my bullshit as he always did. So, instead I turned to face the other way, ignoring the tension that was starting to taint the air. I knew that if I give in to my emotions right now, I might lose Nico to an argument about the past that we both couldn't do anything about anymore.

I closed my eyes to try and fall asleep, hoping the exhaustion from everything that had happened within the last twenty-four hours would pull me in a deep slumber, yet I was barraged with clips of memories that I have long pushed down into oblivion. Seeing Lexie again had opened the box that I have locked in the past decade. And now, it was as if I could hear my mother's voice right beside my ear.

"Is this what you're doing instead of studying?" Mom gestured towards Lexie with full of disgust on her face. *"What did you do to my daughter?! She would have never betrayed me like this!"*

"Mom!" I tried interjecting. *"It's not—"* I did not see my mom's hand coming in, and I definitely wasn't prepared for a slap in the face. I should have felt the pain from falling to the floor, but my mind cannot comprehend that mom—my own mother, just hit me. In the face. Hard.

I was stupefied. I could see that Lexie was about to run towards me when my mom grabbed her in the arms and yanked her away. The vein in her forehead throbbing, as if threatening to pop any moment her anger unleashes.

"What. Did. You. Do. To. My. Daughter?"

Lexie winced as my mom's grip evidently tightened with every word. I have

25

never seen her like this.

"I-I-..." *And before Lexie can even start her sentence, my mom's hand found Lexie's cheek, a smacking sound ringing across the room.*

I was frozen, glued to where I was sitting. I wanted to run to my best friend and protect her. But I couldn't even protect myself from my own mother.

Lexie held her face. Just staring at my mom with utter shock and fear, tears starting to stream down her face. "You are an evil person!" *My mom shouted at Lexie.* "You corrupted my daughter's mind with sin! You will rot in hell!"

Ten years have passed since this incident happen. *'Now tell me what happened, Adalia. Did you consent to what happened?'*

Ten years since I lost my best friend. *'Don't worry, Ms. Grace. I won't disappoint you again. We're just best friends. This won't happen again.'*

Ten years since I lost myself to my mother's control. *'You're not going to see Lexie again! Go to church and confess your sins!'*

I didn't realize I was crying until I almost ate the snot running down from my nose. I haven't thought about Lexie for a long time or rather, I chose not to think about her, knowing that without me, her life would have been better in the long run. She didn't deserve to be treated that way, and I did nothing to defend her. What kind of best friend was I?

Eli's words came back to me. *Text me when you decide that you're really not straight.*

I wasn't sure. Maybe I was not. Was it as simple as that?

But that didn't stop the self-loathing and disgust from eating my being whole.

Liking girls is a sin and I'll make sure you are not tainted with that girl's depravity! And instead of Eli's face, a new yet familiar face appeared in my mind.

Oh, mom, you were right. I'd probably rot in hell.

Chapter Four

ELI'S QUESTION has haunted me the whole Saturday, making me feel quite remorseful as both Nico and Amanda have been trying their best to distract me. Even though I wanted to stay in and rot for the weekend, they forced me to dress up and brave the November evening chill as we walked to the coffee place near Nico's apartment.

The warmth of the café welcomed us when we stepped into an industrial interior, filled with plants and a quiet buzz from the customers inside. Given that this was a twenty-four-hour café, most of the customers were young people who were studying and a few couples who seemed to be on dates.

"Hazelnut latte?" Nico asked.

I nodded and walked away to find a table.

"Look at this," Amanda turned her phone screen towards me. "We just matched and she's asking if we can meet up already." She swiped left and unmatched without even a second thought.

"Why'd you do that?" I was bewildered. I've been out of the dating game for some time.

"I knew she'd only want to hook up," she shrugged as she pulled the red, metal chair and sat down beside me. "And I'm not in that phase right now. *Mood swiper,* you know." She stared at me as if I should know what she was talking about.

And as much as I was curious about what Amanda was saying, my thoughts drifted back to Eli and her offer again. Was Amanda the perfect person to ask? We knew she was bisexual when she joined me and Nico two years ago. She had been very vocal with her types and that she was not looking for anything serious right now. It was no news to us to see her with different partners every time, man or woman. Whenever we ask if it wasn't tedious enough to keep trying to know people every time, she always said, '*Clear and agreed expectations from the start is always the key to make this dating style work.*' She was very open to people she met from the get-go, if she only wanted sex or companionship with them. And more likely she was in the latter phase right now.

But my situation was different. I don't even know what to expect from myself, now that I have entertained the idea that I may like women... *too*?

"Is it that bad?" The burning question finally came out. "To just hook up?"

"Who's hooking up?" Nico came back with trays of sandwiches and coffee.

Amanda pointed a finger at me.

Nico looked at me as if he was gawking at a stranger. His eyes were wide with shock, mouth slightly opened with no words coming out.

"No! I..." Both pair of eyes were burning holes in my face. "I just want to know if hooking up... is okay?"

"Wait. Did you... hook up with someone last night?" Amanda gasped.

The events of last night flashed back in my mind again, making me wince from the reminder of what a spectacle we were – and not the good kind.

As if I had the time to hook up after everything that had happened.

"No," and Eli giving me a kiss was clearly not a hook up. "Eli... she gave me a kiss... a peck this morning when she dropped me off. And she said that if I ever wanted to..." My eyes slowly darted to Nico. He knew my history and I could see in his face that he knew where I was going with it. "Go on dates with her, to just text her. She even offered hooking up." I tried injecting some mockery in my tone, hoping to ease the tension that was starting to wire up in my body. "...Once I figured out if I wasn't straight."

And Amanda, oblivious to my past, was overtly enthused with the news. "Wait, Adi..." She couldn't hide the smile on her face.

28

"You weren't... *straight?*" She looked at Nico, expecting him to join in on the thrill. "I thought you'd only been with men. How have I not known this side of our golden child?" She was so baffled with the discovery.

And there it was, the same question that has been the upheaval of my stability as of late. The urge to shush and cover Amanda's mouth had me gripping my coffee mug tighter than it was.

"Eli dropped you off this morning?" Nico asked, ignoring Amanda, an underlying question unvoiced.

"Yes," I answered and gave him a knowing look. *No, she didn't visit me in the hospital nor drop me off.* I wanted to lie and convince myself that that didn't hurt. *It's okay. I'm okay.*

"Oooh, Eli. The gorgeous blonde," Amanda cooed. I nodded. "What's stopping you then? Is she not your type?"

Eli was more than my type. I could even say she was way out of my league. And even when she offered taking me on dates and even hooking up even though we literally met for just a few hours, I didn't feel that I was in danger despite us being alone in her car. She could have driven me off somewhere and do what she wanted. Yet she didn't. At first, I thought her innuendos were a joke, yet after kissing me this morning, I couldn't figure out which was which anymore.

A sense of safety in a partner was something I had not been afforded to for a long time. And here it was, served in a silver platter yet the hesitation kept on creeping up, forcing me to hit the breaks when all I wanted to do was reach my hand out.

Are you sure it's Eli you want? My inner voice whispered at the back of my mind.

"Or are you not sure if you like women?" Amanda filled the silence.

Or do you like a certain woman? I have to start taking control of this inner monologue. Any more of these subconscious thoughts might push me off the edge of my sanity. *Stop it. Please.*

"I haven't thought about it, really," I answered as honest as I could. "I just broke up with my ex last week and you know how that went." A memory I didn't want to rekindle. "I might give it some time, but I'm not closing myself from any experience now that I'm free."

"So, if Eli asks you if she can kiss you again, you wouldn't say no?" Nico asked. "Or let's say, *not just* Eli but any women or men your type."

I knew what he was implying.

I gave myself a few moments to answer. *What do I want?* I had promised myself that I'll take back the power I have in my life, the moment I stepped out of my ex's door. He was not here to control me. My parents were not here to judge me.

Finally. The decision was all for me to make. But what decision was there to make? If I like men or women?

"I don't know." I hate this. I hated that I was not sure where I was in my life and what I needed to do. All of this was foreign territory and it's making me question everything that I had built for the past twenty-eight years. I was so used to having a concrete plan—a step-by-step process to achieve the goals I have set. If I ever get lost, I always come back to my spreadsheet and look at what I was supposed to do. I always have an anchor to grab onto, when everything's spiraling out of my control. But now everything's in disarray. Almost three decades in this universe and here I was, going back to 'figuring out myself' shit.

"Is it okay to hook up… to make sure if I like… women?"

Nico remained silent while Amanda looked like she was preparing for a speech.

"You know," she started. "I didn't know I liked women until I was twenty-five."

"Uhm. Okay? I don't know where this is going but go ahead." Amanda pretended to smack me in the head while laughing.

"Just listen. I didn't know I liked women because I never acted on my attraction to them before. You know why?" We shook our heads. "I was taught to believe that women were only meant for men. No one else. And it scared the shit out of me whenever I feel attracted to a woman. I start to question myself. *'Is there something wrong with me?'* and *'Am I being punished?'* and *'Am I being tested?'*"

"Then one day I decided, *'fuck it!'* and made out with a coworker who was giving me the signs for god knows how long. I started to accept that maybe this is a part of who I am. Have you ever wondered why I haven't settled with anyone yet? It's because I think I don't know this side of myself well enough yet, and I'm not sure what I want. So, instead of hurting someone with the illusion that I can give a part of myself that I haven't fully discovered, I'd rather be upfront and tell that I am still exploring."

Amanda looked at me, straight in the eyes. "So, go out Adi," she made a grand gesture of her hands splaying everywhere. "Explore. Fuck a dude. Fuck a chick. Settle. Whatever floats your boat. Until you are sure of yourself and what you want." She stood up and made a dramatic bow. "It's your decision, and yours alone."

The decision to take back my power. I gulped. *The opportunity to start over, now in my terms.*

"So, technically just hoe it out until I figure out what or who I want?"

I stood up to get a cup of water and distance myself for a minute. All this talk about Amanda's projected uncertainties to me was making me want to switch from caffeine to alcohol.

Cause it rings to some of your truth. Fuck you, subconscious.

"Okay, lemme have your phone." Amanda had her hand out expectantly as soon as I returned to my seat. Knowing my best friends, I knew this wouldn't be good. The last time they had my phone, Nico had posted a sleeping picture of me on social media when we got a hotel for Amanda's birthday. I could still remember the call I got from my mom, forcing me to take it down for being so provocative.

I was wearing boxer shorts and a crop top.

Amanda saw the distrust in my face and chuckled. "No, I'm not gonna post anything. I just want to see if you have already downloaded a dating app." She grabbed my phone and saw none. "Tsk. Tsk. How are you gonna *'hoe it out'* if you don't even have this?" she reprimanded, giving me the side eye.

She clicked at the orange icon to start the download and as soon as it was done, Amanda started entering my information and photos, taking suggestions from Nico here and there. It felt like we were students working on a group project—except instead of a school paper, it was my dating life.

"We," Amanda said as she clicked on settings. "are changing

your preferences to both men and women. Not unless you're so sure you only like men or women. We'll keep your options open." She handed me my phone back as I saw an image of a woman appear on my screen, an unsettling feeling starting to grow in my stomach.

It was as simple as a click to change sexual preferences in this app. A decade of suppressing this side of me, exposed in just a single click

Chapter Five

SURVIVING MY ex and almost being kidnapped from a club within a span of more or less than a week, probably served as an awakening for me to go out and try to live my life more freely. Twenty-eight years of existence yet I just realized that I have never been happy in a relationship. Being broken up, always being blamed for not being enough, and being cheated became a routine. My bar was so low, to the point that I believed that my last relationship could actually work, and he could be the one I could settle with. But I was glad I have woken up and I finally got out.

And thanks to my best friends helping me swipe all throughout the night, I had decided to dress up and sit in a coffee shop, waiting for my date to arrive. I looked at my phone to check the time or if *she* had sent any updates. But to my dismay, nada.

As the thirty minute mark from when I arrived flashed at my phone screen, I started grabbing my stuff, prepared to go home and just be over it. I felt so stupid, thinking that dating around could actually help me figure this aspect of my life and yet I was stood up on the get go. Maybe friends with benefits was the way to go.

I pulled up my phone to shoot an update to Nico and Amanda, convinced that I would just give up on dating at all, when I heard the chimes as the door opened for another customer.

"Adi?" A breathless woman called out. "I'm sorry I was so late. There was a medical emergency at the train station, and they've stopped the operations from Lafarge to Brentwood. And the buses were not arriving on time. And my phone died as I was trying to call you." And as proof, she showed me her phone screen which was just black.

I was still staring when she offered her hand out. "Grace," she introduced herself. "Let me make it up to you. Did you eat?"

I reached out and shook hers. I smiled. "No, but you owe me dinner now."

Grace was... very energetic. She was the extroverted type to just say hi to strangers and ask how they were. As soon as we sat down at the ramen place we have agreed to go to, she had started a full-on conversation about the server's life story. It was a good ten minutes before we even gave out our orders.

"I'm sorry," Grace said as soon as the server stepped away. "I'm very curious about people and their life stories that's why I tend to ask a lot of unnecessary questions."

I merely smiled as an acknowledgment, not really relating to the sentiment. I mostly kept to myself, and I try not to be a nuisance to the people around me. So, taking their time to ask personal questions was something that never sat well with me. *Never be an inconvenience to the people around you,* was a motto I always try to live by.

"Which is why," she leaned forward and placed her chin on her hand. "Tell me why you're on a date with me right now."

I was caught off guard. At most, I expected her to ask me to tell me more about myself. We talked for about two days, and we have not disclosed anything too personal. I swiped right since she mentioned she likes books and traveling on her profile and that was something I was interested in, too. And to be honest, Grace was someone who probably has a lot of matches in her dating app. Curly long hair framed her small face with a cute button nose, and her blue eyes lined with long lashes. Her lips were coated with a pink gloss, which were accentuated when she pouted or smiled. But other than the similar interest and the physical attraction, I wasn't really sure what I was doing here or what I wanted to get out of this date.

"Uhh... I think you're nice?"

There was a glimmer of surprise in her face and instead of being offended, she threw her head back, laughing at my answer. "Tell me," she teased, her eyes twinkling under the light. "You're new to the dating scene, huh?"

"Was it that obvious?"

Grace leaned back and crossed her arms. I could feel my palms starting to sweat under the scrutinizing gaze. "You're restless. You're quiet. You haven't even got mad and walked out on me when I was obviously flirting with the server. And you keep looking at your phone."

I didn't realize I was that ignorant when it came to dating cues. I even felt more embarrassed that she was overtly flirting with someone right in front of me, and I was just there… smiling.

"It's my first time using dating apps," I admitted, trying to push the humiliating feeling down. "It's my first time actually going out with a woman."

This was met with brows raised out of surprise and maybe intrigue. Unlike the initial energy she had exuded, Grace responded with a 'huh' and stayed quiet until the server came back with our food. Now that I was aware, I observed how Grace was smiling coyly at the server, even tucking her hair as she said thank you.

As we were about to dig in, Grace looked at me and straightly asked, "Are you dating women out of curiosity?" Her words sharp and cutting. "I'd rather you be honest with me, than to waste both of our time."

The one-eighty change in her demeanor caught me off guard. But instead of feeling attacked, I understood where the hostility was coming from.

Was curiosity the right word to describe what I was feeling? The weight of Grace's question made me want to just say whatever she needed me to say so I could appease her.

"I'm sorry," she continued with less angst in her tone. "I had straight people matching with me on these apps merely out of curiosity or just for the heck of it. They don't realize that it was a waste of my time, emotions, and effort to talk and meet with them. Dates ending with 'let's just be friends' are okay, but I hope they were straight forward from the start. I get so emotionally invested easily."

I felt the guilt, knowing that at least once in my life I was one of those people.

"I'm sorry you had to experience that." As much as I was saying this to Grace, I hope my old best friend could hear me, too.

"And no, I'm not here for the heck of it." The comfort of finally being honest to myself was a high. "But I'm trying to go out on dates, to hopefully help me figure out myself more—if I like women to be precise."

Grace smiled at my answer as if she understood what I was going through.

The evening went by fast enough that by ten PM, Grace was waiting with me for my rideshare. I was glad a friend came out of this incident, even giving me advice on how to navigate the dating scene with women. I would consider this a win.

"One last thing," Grace called out. "Let's be honest, we might not be seeing each other again." She pulled me into a hug. "But can I give you a goodbye kiss?" She was about to lean in when I pushed her away by instinct. My skin tingled with terror, my eyes darted at the place we were at, looking if anyone saw us. My heart almost jumped out of my heart with the panic of being seen in public.

I was not ready for that.

I was prepared for Grace to lash out and be mad at me for saying no, but she merely smiled at me knowingly. "I was about to give you *just* a peck on the cheek like friends do. But that should be enough for you to know where you stand with being affectionate with a woman." She jutted out her hand, opting for a handshake. "And just a tip, people, regardless of if they're queer or not, don't want to be hidden as if they're a secret that you are so ashamed of. One closet is enough for us to hide in."

She walked away with a wave of goodbye, leaving me into the realization that she was right. This was a repeat of ten years ago.

I was still ashamed and embarrassed for who I was.

"I'M GIVING UP."

A slumber party at Nico's place to celebrate his promotion was underway when we got into talking about my dating life. Nico and Amanda ended up laughing to the point of crying as I retold the unfortunate dates I had after meeting with Grace.

I matched with a woman from downtown, and when I pulled up for the date, she admitted that she was in a polyamorous relationship and wanted me to be a sex partner. I didn't have anything against it, but it wasn't for me. Another date ended with her asking if I wanted to be a unicorn, and to give myself some credit, I thought she was talking about cosplaying or dressing up as a hobby. I immediately figured out that their unicorn was a thousand miles away different from my definition of unicorn. And most of the other dates, ended up with make out sessions with roaming hands, but nothing after. And then they leave once I tell them that I did not want to have sex on the first date.

Nothing changed from before. Kisses were still sloppy, and I still didn't see the allure of it.

Except for one. Lips that haunted me. *The same fucking one.*

After fits of laughter, Nico grabbed my phone and clicked on the app. "Adi, where are you getting these people? Why are you matching with these women?" The humor was still in his voice. He was browsing through the options when he suddenly stopped at a profile, eyebrows raised. He showed me the screen and to my surprise, I saw a familiar face at the screen.

"Isn't this Eli?" Nico asked. I snatched my phone from his hands and browsed at the profile. As expected, all of her pictures were gorgeous, even showing a picture at a gym, her toned body in display. And as we scrolled towards the 'About Me' section, it clearly stated that she was not looking for anything serious.

My stomach dropped from disappointment. I couldn't deny that after that offer, I had a glimmer of hope that she was doing it to date exclusively. The feeling of being a damsel in distress when I was at the club, and knowing she was the one who came running to save me, still gave me butterflies in my stomach.

Amanda grabbed the phone back and browsed through Eli's profile again, a playful smile spreading across her face. "Adi, I wouldn't blame you for relinquishing your lesbian deflowering ceremony to this gorgeous woman." I almost smacked her in the forehead. "I like femme lesbians more, but I wouldn't mind getting in bed with her, too. But be careful, these types… they don't usually settle in relationships." And Amanda did one of the most atrocious things she could ever do in the duration of our friendship. She swiped right at Eli's profile. "Heartbreakers. But you'll learn a lot." She winked.

The sinking feeling in my stomach dropped. Eli would probably think I was being too pushy and clingy. She already said that she didn't do relationships yet here I was, as if stalking her after a kiss on the lips—not even a make-out, tongues-involved type of kiss. Just a fucking peck and she would think I was head over heels already.

I lunged at Amanda, trying to wrestle my phone out of her hands. She threw it at Nico, hoping to get some help as I squished her under the pillows. The chaos ensued as I stalked towards where Nico was sitting, ready to pull out my WWE moves, when a notification rang.

We all looked at the phone that Nico was holding, our eyes fixated on the screen.

One message flashed: *You matched!*

Chapter Six

> Dinner. 7PM. I'll pick you up at 6PM.
> -Eli

I'VE BEEN staring at this text for a few minutes while Amanda's words of wisdom repeatedly played at the back of my mind. *Hoe it out until I figure what I want.* Was this some kind of joke to invite me after matching on the dating app?

Despite the incredulity of it all, a tiny hopeful voice in my mind continued to plant those curious questions. Could Eli be the person I could do this with? But she mentioned that she was not the type to do relationships. So, could this be just friends with benefits set-up?

I punched a quick text to my group chat with Amanda and Nico.

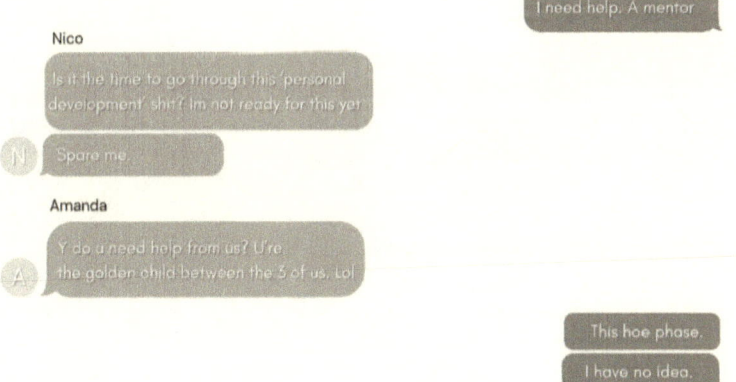

> I need help. A mentor

Nico

> Is it the time to go through this 'personal development' shit? Im not ready for this yet

> Spare me.

Amanda

> Y do u need help from us? U're the golden child between the 3 of us. Lol

> This hoe phase.

> I have no idea.

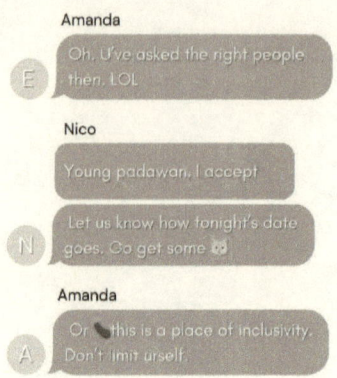

Amanda

Oh. U've asked the right people then. LOL

Nico

Young padawan. I accept

Let us know how tonight's date goes. Go get some 🐱

Amanda

Or this is a place of inclusivity. Don't limit urself.

Oh, I'm fucked.

By five in the afternoon, I was a bundle of nerves with no idea what to wear. Eli didn't say anything about the place where we were going nor what this date entailed.

Date. Was it safe to assume that this was a date? *Well, she asked me out for dinner after matching on the app.*

Damn it. I was so confused.

Half an hour later, I was donning my go-to outfit: a mini black dress and my green and cream loafers. Not too dressy, not too casual either. My brown hair, loosely curled for the night, just fell on top of my waist and I settled into a nude make-up so as not to appear like very 'dolled up,' as young people call it now.

Nico was out with his work friends, denying me of his wisdom that I badly needed right now. I was about to call him to do an outfit check when my doorbell rang. I glanced at my watch and saw that it was ten minutes before six.

Eli's early.

I took a quick panicked peek at myself in the mirror to deem if I looked appropriate enough to go out on a date, but then realizing I didn't have much time if I decided to change anything anyway, so I ran to the door.

I had to take a minute to soak Eli's appearance in. Her opened white button-down shirt, revealed a tight-fitting white undershirt, paired with khaki pants and white sneakers. Her light hair was immaculately messy and when I gazed down, her green eyes were looking at me wide with curiosity.

"You dressed up tonight." Eli gave me an amused smile. The panic must have been apparent on my face, thinking that I overdressed. "No, no, no. My bad. You look good, Adi. If anything, I now feel so under dressed."

"You look great." *Anything you wear looks great on you, for sure.* I wanted to add.

"Come on." Eli grabbed my hand and led me towards her car, feeling a little happy with the physical contact. "We don't want to be late."

We started heading downtown. The traffic wasn't so bad, considering it was a Friday night. I still don't know what the plans were for the evening, I wasn't even sure where we were headed.

"Uhm," I tried to catch Eli's attention. "I appreciate you picking me up for dinner but... where are we actually going?"

Eli took a quick glance, puzzled at my question. "Wait, did I not tell you what we were doing tonight?" I shook my head. "Shit, I'm sorry Adi. I had a lot of things going through my mind these past few days and I thought I already told you. Must have slipped from my mind."

"It's all good," I assured her. "You can tell me now."

"Adi," There was a change in Eli's tone, as if mockingly reprimanding me. "Do you not know stranger danger? For all we know, I might be kidnapping you right now." she said teasingly and winked.

"As if," I retorted. "For all you know, you might be the one who's falling into my trap." Watching too many true crimes shows had me ready for this moment.

Well, not ready enough for me to almost say yes to a lifetime of torment a few days ago. My subconscious reminded me. *Not enough to get out of a situation where I could have ended up being dead just because I was scared of someone.* I shook my head to avoid the direction my thoughts were spiraling into.

"Touche," Eli's voice pulled me out of my reverie. "We're going to the restaurant on top of Queen Elizabeth Park. Have you

41

been?"

"Oh, Palace in the sky?" I remembered the last time I was in that place, and it was a dinner I would very much love to forget. "Yeah, I've been."

Oh, is it a date then?

"Quite a fancy place..." *to have a platonic dinner.* "...for a first date." I couldn't believe I said that out loud.

"I know ri—wait, what?" Eli turned to me in confusion; her mouth still parted. I could feel my face warming up, realizing this evening wasn't what I had expected. I had no words to use as an excuse nor explain my assumption, knowing that I had put myself in this situation. "I'm sorry, Adi, did you think I asked you out on a date?"

Ouch.

"Huh?" I feigned innocence as if I didn't hear what she just said. The embarrassment of assuming this gorgeous woman was actually interested in me—plain, average looking at best, made me want to jump out of the car and hide inside a room and never go out.

"No, I mean you would know if I asked you out on a date," she tried backtracking after seeing my reaction. "Besides, you didn't even tell me your decision yet."

As much as the rejection hurt, she was right. Was it that simple? To decide that *'okay, I'm gay*,'" and throw out everything that I have built and learned from when I was young? And reconstruct myself as if I was a Lego that could just take a pick of the parts that I do not want and replace it with new one?

Eli realized that I wasn't going to answer her question or give her any response. "Alex didn't want to meet at *Club Tala* considering what happened to you last Sunday."

"Alex?" I feigned innocence but the bucket of ice dropped in my stomach had started spreading in my body, making me feel numb by the second.

Eli peeked at me. "Oh. You don't remember. Alex. The club owner. My best friend. Remember when I told you that we'll schedule a dinner with you to talk about the compensation for the incident in the club? It's this. I'm sorry it took so long though."

"Yeah, I remember. It's all good." *Lexie. How could I forget?* If I knew that I was meeting up with her, I would have focused on steeling my mental fortitude rather than spending hours on picking what to wear and make up to splatter in my face.

I started straightening out my dress, thankful that I didn't choose to wear something so formal. "I'm glad you set this up. Thank you." I forced myself to smile at Eli, despite the discomfort of not wanting to be at the same space anymore.

I took out my phone to send a quick update to Nico and Amanda.

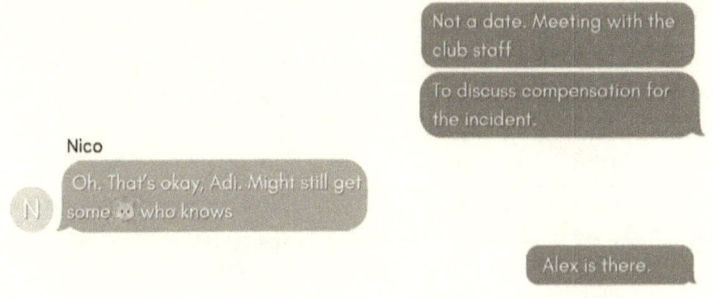

I slid my phone back in my purse and released a sigh.

"Nervous much?" Eli asked. "Don't be. Alex might look scary but she's a sweetheart when you get to know her." An affectionate smile painted Eli's face as if recalling fond memories. "Just don't be late. She hates tardy people. Believe me, I know." Her face scrunched, thinking of better ways to describe her best friend. "She's like an adorable black cat... who's not afraid to scratch you." Eli laughed a little with her analogy. "Yep, she's a cat with claws... Very sharp claws."

So, it was confirmed. Lexie didn't tell Eli yet that we knew each other. Did she want to hide the fact that we used to be best friends? Or has she not forgiven me yet and chose to act as strangers?

"That's reassuring," I didn't mean to sound sarcastic, but Eli's supposed reassuring words did not work the slightest. I couldn't claim that I knew the Alex that I would facing in a bit. The way she looked at me at the club was justified—*we were strangers.*

"HI!" THE hostess greeted us a tad more cheerily after looking at Eli and giving me the side-eye. "Do you have a reservation?"

Eli gave Alex's name, and the hostess enthusiastically guided us to the table in the far side corner of the restaurant by the window. This had been my favorite restaurant because of the city lights view at night, until recently. It could have been a perfect romantic date. But as Eli had pointed out, not tonight.

It struck me again. How foolish I was. The lure to grab a table that we passed by and start smacking my head with it out of sheer embarrassment, was far too tempting. I knew I had no one to blame but myself for assuming.

I was a few steps behind Eli and the hostess. Small talk was underway, yet as small as the talk was, Eli's charm was oozing all over the place. She gave the hostess a small, coy smile and perfectly played the part of someone so interested with what the hostess was sharing, as mundane as having a busy day at the restaurant. Regardless, the hostess was charmed. And her painfully, slow walk to prolong the conversation was a testament to that. Ten minutes might not be enough just to reach our table at this point.

I was stuck behind. Putting one foot after the other in a very painfully slow pace. I have always been a fast walker, and I attribute it to compensating for my small stature of five-foot-three. Slow walkers were my nightmare. And I was probably living it right now. Arguably even worse.

I tried to peek in front of them to get a glimpse of Lexie. Her back was facing us, and all I could see right now was her messy hair, and a black fitting shirt. A complete contrast of what she was wearing a few days ago.

We were a few steps from the table when Eli turned towards me, her look asking if I was okay. I wanted to roll my eyes, but I merely nodded and took advantage of the small space that opened in between them. It was hilarious that I almost ran to pass between her and the hostess, with the scene from *Harry Potter and the Goblet of Fire* during the last challenge of the *Triwizard Tournament*, playing in my mind; their flirtations my maze, and finally passing through them was a win on my end. I could no longer endure the slow walk and be the witness of the obvious flirtations from them both.

I walked up to the table until I was a few steps behind Lexie, the courage that I have mustered all gone as soon as I felt her presence within my personal space.

"Hey," Eli called out as she reached us. "I'm sorry, I was just... Never mind. Alex, this is Adi and Adi, this is—"

"Lexie." My voice barely a whisper. Alex stood up and reached out her hand as if introducing herself for the first time. There was no sign of recognition, nor a tinge of a smile to indicate any emotion.

"Alex," she reiterated. The apprehension in my face must have been so apparent that she had started withdrawing her outstretched hand. Not to appear rude, I tentatively reached out and shook *Alex*'s hand, sending jolts of memories with the barely-there contact. I was feeling warm again, and it was nothing to do with the heater nor Eli's lingering hand at the small of my back.

"Wait, you know each other??" Eli asked, a bit confused. "You didn't tell me you knew Adi." She turned to Alex to confirm.

"It was unnecessary at the time," Alex answered, unbothered. "Given the circumstances that night." She sat down and continued browsing through the menu, as if seeing me again was not a big deal. And as much as that hurt, I understood where she was coming from.

Strangers, my inner voice whispered. *Don't forget.*

"Adi," Eli called for my attention. "Are you planning to just stand there?" I shook my head once, to answer and another, to shake myself back to the present. I scooted beside Eli.

"So, you have to tell me the story how my best friend and this *soon-to-be-mine girl*, know each other," Eli asked jokingly.

I couldn't hide the surprise in my face when I heard Eli's claim that I was soon to be hers—considering the not-so-discreet flirting and asking-the-hostess-out situation, yet that gave me the opportunity to gauge Alex's reaction from Eli's claim. A small part at the back of mind *hoping*.

A muscle in Alex's jaw twitched but she schooled her expression back to a neutral, almost-amused face and met my stare. Alex gave me a daring smile and that tugged something inside my chest that I didn't recognize. It was different than what I felt with Eli—this felt familiar and new at the same time.

I knew that smile.

I missed that smile.

"I didn't know you started dating her, Eli," Alex said without breaking eye contact with me even though she was talking to Eli. "I thought you only liked your women blonde?"

I held Alex's gaze, trying to maintain my composure even though I was on the brink of wanting to run away from this confrontation.

"As I have told Adi," Eli grabbed my hand from under the table, stealing my gaze away. "She might be the exception from all of them." She looked back at me, as if expecting me to affirm what she had just said.

And if she had asked me ten minutes ago, I would have been excitedly saying yes to her, most especially after putting me onto a pedestal as her only exception. But now, all I felt was panic, that my eyes drifted back to Alex, staring at our hands, now on display on top of the table.

I pulled my hand away from Eli's grasp. Alex's eyes met mine, a questioning look on her face.

But I have questions of my own, too. *Did you ever change? Are you the same Lexie that you were before?* I silently asked Alex, as if she would hear me through my eyes. *Where did you go? Did you ever miss me like I missed you?*

Alex held my gaze. "*Yes.*"

The shock had me sitting up straight. Did Alex just respond to my thoughts?

"Yes," Alex answered again, breaking away her gaze from mine to Eli. "We knew each other when we were young."

"She was my ex…" I started. Hoping to finally clear out the air between Alex and me.

"She was my ex-best friend," Alex finished.

Yes. Just bury me alive. I pleaded to anyone who could hear me right now.

Chapter Seven

AWKWARD WAS the understatement of the year. I did not know how I was able to continuously chew and swallow the mashed potatoes and steak with my stomach twisting in a knot. Eli and Alex could be chatting about the most random of things, or the if the world would be attacked by aliens tomorrow—it still sounded like a bunch of mumbo jumbos in my ear. The blood rushing in my head from trying to grasp what was happening right in front of me wasn't helping either.

Alex still maintained her calm demeanor from earlier—a huge contrast from Eli who was talking animatedly with gestures and facial expressions. She cut her wavy black hair into a pixie, tousled style, one side carefully tucked in her ear while the other slightly obscuring the other side of her face; those piercing brown eyes, crinkling whenever she smiles from whatever Eli was babbling about. Her face hadn't changed much except some evidence of aging—gracefully at that.

"Adi…" Eli woke me up from my musing. I snapped my attention back to her, embarrassed that Alex might have seen me ogling her. "As I was saying, it's so exciting that you know Alex! You have to tell me all about your childhood shenanigans!"

I nodded, barely reciprocating the energy Eli was exuding. My mind couldn't wrap itself around the idea that my ex best friend was sitting right in front of me. These last few weeks still didn't make sense. I was still recovering from the thought of being almost kidnapped, accepting that I might really like women, and now this. A blast from the past, a reminder.

At least, one out of the three of us was finding this entertaining.

A few more minutes went on with Alex and Eli conversing about the club, the initial question left hanging and ignored in the air. I maintained my silence, merely sipping on my red wine, gazing out the window at the city lights. My calm outside was the complete opposite of what I was feeling inside. I was barely holding it in, and I hoped the alcohol would help ease my anxiety.

"So, Adi," Eli started after the server filled our glasses with wine. "You both mentioned that you were ex-best friends. What happened?"

Too much for asking for this dinner not to be awkward. I didn't know how to answer the question, or if it was appropriate to talk about this instead of Alex.

"Um…"

"Short version is, we were best friends during high school. I had to leave during college because my university was in a different province. We didn't get the chance to stay connected and fell off." Alex took over the conversation, leaving out one of the most important details of our friendship before—not that she needed reminding of it. I was pretty sure she left that out for my sake than hers.

I suddenly felt a confidence boost coming from the liquid courage. "I tried contacting her though." This elicited a surprised reaction from Alex. "Apparently, she changed numbers and disabled her socials. Maybe she was just hiding from me." I stared back at her and playfully rolled my eyes, trying to ease the tension and downplay the situation.

Eli chuckled and said, "Well, it's no surprise. She was a very hard-to-get woman at first." Eli looked at Alex sweetly. "Right, sweetie?" she added while grabbing Alex's hand from across the table.

Alex yanked her hand back. "Can you please stop? You're grossing me out." She cussed but I could see that it was spoken endearingly as if… *Wait. Is she…. Alex's girlfriend?? But that wouldn't make sense!* She had hit on me multiple times… the drink… the kiss… *What the actual fuck is happening?*

The baffling realization caught me off guard—it was clear that these two were not just best friends. No wonder the two acted as if they were in sync.

"Wait." I grabbed Eli's shoulder to make her face me. "Are you two... *together?*" My thoughts were already running in fumes, and I could no longer take any bombshells of information. This could not be the situation I was currently in. I looked at Alex, hoping to get some confirmation from her. She merely looked annoyed that this question was being asked.

"We were," Eli answered lightly, as if this information was not vital from the get-go. "But we eventually discovered that we both wanted to take the dominant role in the... relationship. Can you imagine the disaster we were during those days?" Eli looked at Alex.

"You were such a pain in the ass," Alex answered very shortly.

"But you liked me. At some point," Eli responded while giving Alex pouty kisses which she responded with an irritated side eye. "So yeah, we dated for a bit but when we discovered *very* shortly that the dynamic would just not work, we decided to call it quits and became friends. And now, best of friends!" Eli shook Alex's arms playfully. "Didn't even last for a month."

My world spun, not knowing what to do with this revelation. Alex did not even know that Eli already kissed me just a few days ago and that I was very much considering delving into an exploration quest with her to determine if I really wanted women.

Why would she care? My inner voice asked. *It's not as if you're an ex... girlfriend.* That was a low blow, even for my inner self. *Fuck you, inner Adi.*

Eli clapped her hands a little bit excitedly, getting my attention back. "Are we all done?" I gulped my remaining drink then nodded. "Good. I'll get the bill."

I was about to protest when Alex shook her head and motioned for me to just stay at my seat. This was the first time we would technically be alone since the last time we saw each other back in high school. And all I wanted was to throw everything I ate up.

"The dinner's on us." Alex waved her hands, dismissing any of my attempts to foot the bill. This was the first time Alex had talked to me directly after the introduction earlier. And it felt uneasy, now that I have her full attention. "I'm sorry to put you in this awkward situation. I didn't realize that you might have not known that it was me you were meeting tonight. I thought you might've recognized me from last time when we brought you to the hospital."

I felt a pang in my chest with Alex's formality. As if I was somehow, really a stranger that she just met, our history be damned. But what Alex said caught me off guard. "You were with Eli when she brought me at the hospital?"

"Yes," Alex answered as she drank the remains of her wine. "I guess it's no surprise she didn't tell you. But yeah, when we took you away from that man, we drove you to the hospital right away. I wasn't there when you woke up 'cause I had to go back as soon as I could. When they've confirmed you're stable, I drove back to the club to deal with the police report."

Alex stared at the glass in her hand. "I went back around half an hour past four in the morning, but Eli said you were still sleeping. Did the food help settle your stomach?"

Oh. My heart didn't know what to feel. The elation of knowing that the Lexie still cared for me, or the betrayal of Eli lying straight in my face to take credit for the act.

She never told you she bought it. My inner voice reminded me. *You just assumed that the gorgeous woman did.*

But she lied. She said I was asleep when we've been talking for a bit already.

"You brought the food... and the flowers?" I needed to hear it from Alex.

She raised her eyes to meet mine and tilted her head. A questioning look on her face. "Weren't you able to eat the soup? I told Eli to make sure you ate. You only threw up alcohol and I know how much that hurts the stomach and throat."

There were a lot of emotions I was feeling, and I don't know which one to address first.

"You could've at least taken a shower at her hospital room before going back to the club," Eli butted right away as soon as she sat beside me again. "Ugh. Poor officers, seeing and smelling you like that."

Alex glared at Eli, oblivious to the storyline that has evolved in my head from that night in the hospital, "I have a change of clothes in my trunk," and rolled her eyes.

"I mean, I wouldn't mind most especially after what you did for me." I discreetly peeked at Alex then returned my gaze to Eli. "But why shower?"

Eli suddenly exploded laughing out of nowhere. Alex looked out the window awkwardly.

"You… you…" Eli tried explaining in between her heaves of laughter. As she finally calmed down, she continued, "You wanted to take your clothes off, saying over and over again that it was hot. Alex tried to stop you because you were taking off your clothes in front her."

Eli winked at me. I could see Alex's ears turning red.

"And suddenly, you just gagged and heaved whatever's in your stomach on Alex's suit, shoes, and car. Then, you lost consciousness."

I could feel the blood draining from my face. I looked from Eli then slowly to Alex, my eyes wide as saucers. My plea to whoever could hear me still stood. *Yes. Just bury me alive right now.*

I didn't know why I stood up, maybe from sheer embarrassment, but I did, and looked at Alex. "I am so sorry." Was sorry enough from all the embarrassment and inconvenience I unknowingly put them through? "Let me pay for the dry cleaning of your stuff. I insist." It was the least I could do.

"It's all good. After all, everything happened in the club, and I should take responsibility for it." Alex motioned for me to sit down. "Eli, it's not something you should laugh at. What happened to Adi was not a joke. That is so insensitive of you." I wasn't expecting that she was going to stand up for me. But then again, I remembered the Lexie I knew and this wasn't out of character.

"And the food and the flowers, did you not give it to her?" Alex continued but now in a probing tone.

Instead of looking as if she was caught in a lie, Eli leaned back and draped her arms around my shoulders. "Come on, man. Don't be a sour pus and ruin a woman's game," she chuckled. "You should've seen her face when she saw the soup, it's as if she's eating for the first time after a hunger strike."

Alex stared at Eli for a few seconds, an unreadable expression on her face, before nodding curtly, leaving the conversation at that.

It was as if an understanding had been agreed on between the two of them without even uttering a word.

"Okay, let's start," Eli straightened up and she pulled out a folder, opening it in front of me. I browsed through the contents, knowing full well that this was an agreement with the compensation they were offering for me. "As you can see, here's our offer to compensate for the incident on the club. We'll give you time to read it and if you want to negotiate the terms, we can meet up again to discuss."

I didn't want to take anything from them, but I let my eyes read the itemized offer out of curiosity. *Five thousand dollars?? For an altercation between two customers that they do not have any business with??*

"Five thousand dollars?" I voiced out. And before I could continue, Eli butted in right away.

"Is it too low? What is your asking price?" She was waiting with a pen on her hand. *Too low?* This was absurd.

"No, isn't five thousand dollars... too much for something that both of you have no control over?" I looked at Eli, then to Alex. "Damien created the ruckus. You've tried to deescalate as best as you can. You didn't have to offer this."

It was silent in the table for a few minutes.

"Too much?" Alex asked in a quiet voice while looking at her wine. "Peace of mind has no price..." She turned her gaze towards me. "Sense of safety has no price..." She held my stare. "And having a place to run to, when all else is shit has no price." She put down her glass and clasped her hands together in front of her. "So, no, Adi, five thousand dollars isn't too much. I'd pay much more to make sure that my club is still a safe haven for queer people."

I lowered my head, feeling embarrassed for being so dense, and I couldn't help but feel that it was a dig on our history, too. I had intruded on her safe space again.

I pushed the document back to Eli. "I don't need compensation," I finally said. "You have already taken care of me that night, and you have put him behind bars. That's more than enough for me."

Eli took the folder and glanced at Alex, as if confirming next steps. When Alex nodded, Eli continued, "We'll put this on the side.

The offer still stands until the end of month. If you ever decide otherwise, just text me and I'll bring you the document to sign."

Alex stood up and began walking towards the exit, ending the conversation at that. I stayed a few steps behind as we walked towards Alex's car.

Alexandria. Why are you back in my life right now?

I observed the two and noticed the differences between the supposed best friends. Aside from the contrast of their physical appearance, the two were emitting different auras too. Eli was imbibing a playful, easy-going vibe while Alex was the quiet, brooding best friend; though both exuded confidence with how they carry themselves—one could see that they're not afraid to take up their space.

"Adi!" Eli called for my attention. They were now standing beside a black sedan. Alex was already getting at the driver's seat, and Eli was standing beside the passenger door.

"You don't mind riding with Alex, right?" My heart wasn't ready for this. But as the people pleaser I was, I smiled and nodded. "I have some... business to attend to." She kissed me at my cheek and started walking back to the restaurant.

Yeah, right. A business with two long legs, blond hair and a curvy body.

Let it go, Adi. I reminded myself. Again. Though the thought of Eli getting it on with another woman didn't disappoint me as much as I expected anymore.

And I probably know the reason why. I released a huge sigh and opened the door. I didn't want to make it anymore awkward than it really was, and as much as I wanted to rekindle whatever Alex and I had, I knew we both need time to wrap our heads around what was happening now.

"Hey," I called out from the other side of the car. "I can just take the transit. I'm guessing you still have to go to the club and Nico's apartment is on the other side of the city. Thank you for dinner and what you did for me back at your club." I closed the door and started walking towards the bus stop. I didn't give Alex the chance to say anything because if she has not changed from ten years ago, I know she would get out of her way to accommodate the people around her, *to accommodate me.* And I didn't want that anymore.

I heard a car door opening and closing, then footsteps following me. "Adi," Alex called out. I didn't stop and continued walking towards the waiting shed, hurrying my steps a little.

"Adi," Alex said my name as if it was a command and that made me stop. I turned around and was surprised to see her just a few feet away from me. She continued walking until she was close enough to tower over me. "Adi," she repeated my name. "Get in the car right now. I will drop you off." The timbre of her voice making me feel a rush of warmth.

"It's okay," I protested. "Nico's place is so far from the club. I will take an Uber if that gives you peace of mind." I took out my phone to convince her.

"Adalia." My stomach dropped from hearing my full name. No one had called me that aside from my parents when they were angry. But instead of eliciting the anxiety I feel whenever my mom called me out, this time I could feel my face warming up. "Stop being stubborn."

There was no way to win this. Or maybe there was, but my subconscious was blatantly ignoring it because somehow, I knew that I wanted to spend time with her.

I did not give Alex the satisfaction of answering, instead I started walking back to where she was parked. Given the differences between our strides, it was no surprise that she was beside me in a matter of seconds.

The drive back to Nico's apartment was the longest car ride I've ever been in. There was only music in the background and silence from both of us. A lot of unspoken words despite our ten years apart.

Was it coincidence that Alex had returned from my life after making the decision to finally get away from my past that had me on shackles until just recently?

Was it coincidence that flashbacks from ten years ago kept repeating on my mind, as if to remind me what an awful human being I was?

Was it coincidence that Alex came back the moment I had

decided to accept myself and started exploring this entirely new territory?

Coincidence or a second chance?

I stole a glance at Alex, her eyes were trained on the road, fingers thrumming against the steering wheel, playing along with the music. I couldn't believe she's right beside me, after long years of waiting to make it right with her.

They say when life throws you lemons, make a lemonade. Or something like that.

Then, would it be too much of me to ask, if I'd choose for this to be a second chance rather than a coincidence? A second chance to make it right and hopefully get my best friend back.

So, as much as it pained me to make small talk, I knew I have to take the first step if I wanted to make it work. "So... how have you been?" I started. "For the past ten years?"

Alex glanced at me, perplexed that I was starting conversation. "I'm okay, Adi." She looked back at the road. "You don't have to force yourself to do small talk. *We* both know how much you hated that."

The reference on still knowing my quirks tugged a little on my heart. "Well, what if I changed already and love small talk?" I tried to tease her to ease the tension, but it seemingly backfired when I saw a dark look passing over her face.

"You're right," Alex agreed stiffly. "I might not know this version of you anymore."

I realized my mistake too late. "No, that's not what I meant, Lexie." Her childhood nick name slipping out of my tongue. "I..." I have no words. I didn't know how to recover from this.

Timing as my foe, Alex stopped in front of the apartment, not giving me the chance to explain myself further.

Alex unlocked the door and turned towards me to say goodbye, but I spoke first, "Do you mind going in?"

Alex froze midway. She glanced at me with an intriguing look. "What for?"

I was stunned to silence. *Yeah, what for?* However, I recovered quickly as much when I answered, "I just want to talk to you. Ten years has passed, and I really wanted to catch up." I could see the hesitation on her face. "I don't want monetary compensation for the incident. This is my term. Just go inside for a bit so we can talk, yeah?" A last-ditch effort.

Alex's reaction was ice cold. No acknowledgment when I mentioned our history nor when I showed intent to reconcile our friendship.

"You're dating my best friend," Alex reiterated. "Trust me, *I* don't want to be in the middle of *this* relationship," she finished as her lips tightened in a straight line.

Heaven only knows how I was going to handle this situation between the three of us.

"We're not dating." I finally said with a pained grimace in my face. "Did you even see her ogling the hostess earlier? How would you call that *us* dating?" I timidly admitted out loud as I looked down at my shoes. The embarrassment was just too much. "Besides, I'm still trying to figure out this side of myself anyway."

This was met with a tense silence as the two of us sat a foot away from each other. I could feel the weight of Alex's stare at the top of my head, could feel the weight of the ten years that had passed between us.

I was expecting to be rejected, understanding where Alex would come from; but Alex surprisingly got out of the car and had started walking towards the apartment, hopefully a non-verbal agreement that she was willing to talk. I had my hopes up, thinking that maybe she was back in my life for a reason—for a resolution to what happened before between us.

Finally, I contemplated to myself. *Maybe things will look up from now on.*

I followed Alex and was stunned when she stopped walking abruptly that I almost bumped into her back. I was about to ask why when Alex whispered, *"Careful,"* sounding more of a threat than a caution. "You can't go around hurting people just because you still can't figure your shit out."

And that hit me right in the fucking chest.

Chapter Eight

I LED the way to Nico's apartment, buying myself some time to prepare before I sit down with Alex. Nico was still out with work friends for a dinner date, giving me the space to have this conversation. And I knew he wouldn't mind having Alex visiting, realizing that he already knew Alex was back in town even before I saw her.

Left out, again.

We settled down by the kitchen island, feeling like this was a more appropriate setting than the couch—a formal conversation. I wasn't oblivious to the heavy air that was surrounding us, suffocating me at least. This was not how I imagined this possible reconciliation would go. I did not even consider if Alex wanted to reconcile with me.

"I'm here, so let's talk," Alex said in a very business-like voice as if this was a transactional discussion that she merely needed to go through.

I paused and looked at Alex. *Really looked at her.* She was sitting in the kitchen island, legs and arms crossed—a non-verbal cue that she was not as accepting as I hoped she would be; her face stoic. No emotions evident on her face to give me even the tiniest clue as to what was going on in her head.

Did I really want to do this? Was I ready to face this reality check?

I was given a second chance to save what was once our relationship—*I owe it to myself and Alex to at least try, or if worse comes to worst, a closure that we both needed.*

"Let me grab us something to drink first? Do you want any coffee? Tea? Pop?" I was clearly stalling.

"Just water please," Alex said quietly.

"So, how are you? What have you been up to lately?" I tentatively asked while grabbing the cups and filling them up. A few seconds have passed that was met by silence. The thought of just giving up and letting Alex go crossed my mind, not wanting to keep her in the apartment unwillingly.

I was about to let her off the hook when I heard her sigh and answered, "I'm doing good. Work pretty much takes up my time." Alex waited for a few moments before following up. "How about you, Adi? How have you been in the past ten years?"

A sense of relief passed through my body that she was willing to give this conversation a try. But the feeling of anxiety about the can of worms this was going to open, was starting to claw its way up in my stomach.

I offered the glass of water to Alex.

"I have been doing good… I guess," I hesitated for a minute before adding, "A lot of changes happened in my life recently—thus, the partying at the club. It was supposed to be a night to get everything off in my head and just *enjoy*."

Enjoyed was a relative term. I internally cringed at the memory of the incident with Damien.

"And by the way, thanks again for backing me up. I might've been locked in a basement somewhere where no rays of sunlight could enter if both of you and Eli hadn't come to the rescue." A humorless joked about my misfortune, hoping to cut down the tension.

"Wine," Alex said out of nowhere. The confusion might have been plain obvious on my face that Alex clarified. "Wine. Do you have some wine? I need to have at least a glass if you want to have this conversation."

Oh. Maybe, it's not just me that was having a hard time with this conversation. Liquid courage?

I stood up and went to the fridge. "Red okay for you?" Alex nodded. I proceeded to grab the opened bottle from the fridge and two wine glasses. Alex carefully reached out for it and started swirling the liquid in her glass.

Alex was looking down on her drink when she finally asked,

"So tell me, Adi. What do you really want to talk about?" then took a gulp of wine.

Here we go.

I took a swig from my glass as well and waited for a few seconds before I raised my gaze to meet Alex's scrutinizing stare. "I… I wanted to apologize for what happened ten years ago."

I held her stare to see any kind of reaction, but she remained indifferent and silent. No response if my apology was accepted or denied. Nonetheless, I was not going to let this chance go, to clear things up between us. Worst case scenario was, we won't stay in contact and not see each other ever again. At least, I could close an old chapter and finally move on from my life.

"I know you might probably don't want to hear this and you might not care," I continued. "But I do. I've tried searching for a way to reconnect with you after we graduated high school, but I couldn't find you. It's as if you disappeared. *Literally.*" I took a drink again from my glass, the alcohol helping me find the guts to spill it all out.

Maybe I was the one who needed the liquid courage after all.

Alex remained silent with a contemplating look on her face. I suppose that she was letting me have my moment to let it all out – so I took it. "I wanted to apologize. Even months after we drifted apart. I wanted my best friend back in my life. I wanted *you*, back."

I poured myself another quarter of wine, offered to pour another to Alex's which she accepted. She stayed quiet, taking sips of her drink, merely waiting for me to continue.

"I even asked Nico if he was in contact with you, but he said no as well. You disappeared. You just disappeared." I could feel the alcohol slowly warming up my body. "Then, I took that as a sign that you didn't want us or *me* to talk to you anymore. So, I gave up. I gave up *Lexie* because you didn't want to be found."

Alex finished her second glass and gestured for the wine bottle for a refill. I thought that she was going to stay silent, but Alex answered quietly, "I didn't. I didn't want to talk to you because you clearly made your stand when shit went down." Alex was looking at her wine glass. "You clearly showed me, and everyone at the school for that matter, that you didn't want to be involved with me in any sort of way anymore." Alex finished and looked at me, holding my gaze, daring me to deny it.

"I was scared, Lexie…" I admitted. "You knew that. You knew how my parents were. You knew how it was going to be if I took your side during that time."

It seemed that Alex was starting to feel the effects of the wine as well. The emotions were now showing on her face, and the way she spoke was more uninhibited—no more restraint.

"*You think I wasn't?*" Alex asked just above a whisper. "You could have made any excuse, Adi. I was willing to bear the grunt of the punishment, or whatever judgment if you stayed by my side…"

I have no words to say. It was a ten-year old wound that had healed and scarred, but we have started scratching the surface – and now it was bleeding again.

"We were kids, Lexie." I was on the brink of tears; my voice starting to quiver. "We were kids, and I was scared."

Alex might have noticed the change in my voice as she shook her head as if wanting to ground some clarity into her. "This is going nowhere, Adi. I did not come here to point fingers as to who was to blame when we drifted apart. Shit happens and it's unfortunate that our relationship did not survive that." Alex stood up as if to indicate that this conversation was done. "Though not together, we are here. We survived and we get to move on with our lives. So, live it. We don't need to go back to the past and hope for the best that we could relieve what we had before. People change. *We* changed, Adi." A tone of finality in her voice.

My breath hitched as I realized that this was probably the last time that we're going to have this conversation.

Alex tried walking towards the door, but the alcohol seemed to have finally caught up with her system, causing her to wobble a little bit. I made a run to catch her but hesitated and stopped a few meters back. I couldn't handle any more rejections for tonight.

"Stay for a while and rest," I offered. Alex started shaking her head to decline but I cut her off. "You are tipsy, and you are planning to drive. I don't feel comfortable letting you go considering you can't even walk straight." I grabbed her by the forearm and led her in the living room. The physical touch making me yearn more of what we had possibly lost. "I won't bother you. Just take a nap and you can go once you're sober." I sat her down at the couch and forced her to lie down.

"Please don't be stubborn, *Lexie*. Take this as a repayment for saving my life last Friday." I took a blanket from the ottoman by the wall and threw it on top of Lexie, tucking her in like a child. "I'm saving your life by not letting you drive. You still don't hold your liquor well, Lexie. *That didn't change.*"

I did not give Alex an opportunity to decline and had started walking towards the washroom. I drew a bath, hoping to ease the buzz that has started creeping in my head already. I didn't admit nor tried to show any sign of my tipsiness, to make sure that she wouldn't use the argument that my confession was just drunk talking, but I was tipsy. The alcohol from earlier not helping in this situation.

But it was the liquid courage I needed to talk to Alex.

The liquid courage that resulted in too many good memories during our younger years.

The liquid courage that eventually resulted in the ruin of what Alex and I had.

"NO, NO. I'LL BE THERE." I was greeted by the sounds of keys jingling and light footsteps on my wood flooring as I stepped out from the bath. "…within an hour "

I took a quick glimpse at the clock ten PM. Alex napped for an hour, and she might've missed the opening time for her club. I didn't realize that I've been soaking for that long. The cold water should have been a good indication, but my thoughts were running all over the place, knowing that Alex was merely a few feet away from me, yet I could feel the distance growing between us as the clock ticked second by second. Maybe this situation was unsalvageable. And I was only holding on to a hope that a familiar face could save me from all the chaos that I have been lately.

I gathered up my thoughts and walked up to Alex, to at least say goodbye. I don't want her to feel that she should be sneaking out as if this was a forbidden tryst. *Or maybe it was.* I realized that I didn't even know if Alex was in a relationship.

We just talked. I convinced my guilt-ridden subconscious.

And before I could spiral down to the rabbit hole of punishing myself for assuming that I have the right to ask if she was in a relationship, I called out to Alex. "Are you going? Are you feeling better?" I should at least see if she was okay and good to drive before letting her go. I assured myself that it was the appropriate thing to do.

Alex looked up from fixing her shoes, as if a deer caught in headlights. "I didn't want to disturb you." She stood up and started walking towards the door. "I have to go to the club to help Scar out."

Scar. "Oh, she's my general manager at the club." Alex might have seen the question on my face. I stepped around to open the door for her but before I could unlock the door, a loud bang echoed on the other side.

"ADI!" A male voice shouted. Alex glanced at me, a dark expression already on her face. I knew that voice. I would recognize it from anywhere. I could feel my body stiffen, breaths starting to shorten, nausea starting to set in.

"ADI! OPEN THE FUCKING DOOR!" The man kept on banging at the door.

I looked at the door, then at Alex, then back at the door; my heart hammering inside my chest, the cold sweat starting to drip on my back. I was frozen, not knowing what to do.

I thought I had escaped this. I unconsciously took a step back, my body wired to run away from this. *I thought he was behind bars. How did he find me?*

And before I could answer, Alex held the knob and slowly turned to open the door.

"Don't." I grabbed her arm to stop her from letting Damien in. "He's gonna hurt you." My warning as weak as my bravado.

Alex turned towards me and held my stare, eyes lidded with an emotion I couldn't describe. I have never seen her like this, even from before. She pulled down my hand and held it with hers.

"He can try."

Chapter Nine

TWO WEEKS AGO

"MOM," I started. "Listen to what I'm saying."

I went to my parents' house to discuss my current engagement with Damien. He was the son of a family who had recently became close to us, and my parents had agreed to allow Damien to court me since we were both single and nearing our thirties already. It was a sound plan in my parents' head, regardless of if I was on board with it or not.

I could barely call Damien an acquaintance when we first started 'dating.' I only saw him during get-togethers and that was not saying much as I was not really interested in mingling with others. I would rather burrow my face in a book at a corner where no one would disturb me. However, Damien was the complete opposite. He drew the crowd to himself and was mostly surrounded by enthused listeners and laughter from whatever he was saying. My mom was a sucker for him.

I couldn't blame them though. Objectively speaking, Damien fit the mold of a high maintenance man. Standing over six feet, with broad shoulders and a toned physique visible under his well-fitted suit, he easily towered over nearly everyone in the room. Yet rather than intimidating people with his imposing stature, he compensated it with his charm and inviting smile.

Such a pick-me-guy. I always thought to herself whenever I see women across the room giggling over him.

So, imagine my surprise when Damien pitched the idea of setting up the engagement between us during one dinner a year ago at the Palace in the Sky.

"*Since both of you are single and not dating anybody,*" My mom set the tone of the discussion like a business proposal rather than a decision that will alter both of our lives forever. "*I don't see any problems with agreeing to this proposal, don't you think, 'Mare?*" Her look at Damien's mom full of hope and possibility.

I was halfway through drinking water when the bomb was dropped. I choked on my drink for a good fifteen seconds, surrounded by total silence around the table. My mom gave me a disapproving look and Damien continued with a small, endearing smile on his face.

"*I have talked to your parents, Adi, and they had agreed. We have been family friends for years and it will be a dream come true for our parents if we marry each other. Imagine the grandchildren and holidays both our families will have together.*"

I looked around the table. It was as if I was the only one who found this idea absurd. I turned to eye my dad's reaction to see if he could be my savior in this absurdity, but to my dismay, I found him smiling encouragingly at me.

And on cue, my mom said, "*I agree with this plan.*" My mouth almost dropped to the floor. I was astounded. How could these people decide for me when it was my life that would be changed forever? For fucks sake, we haven't even gone to one date and we were now talking about marriage and grandchildren?

"*Since my only unica hija here, doesn't even put the effort in trying to find someone to marry, I did it for her.*" She looked at the people around the table proudly, as if looking for validation of her efforts.

"*What do you do for work, Adi?*" Damien asked, not giving me a chance to even offer my decision to the arrangement.

"*I work in HR for Rogue.*" My mind was still reeling from this absurdity.

"*That's good then.*" Damien clasped his hands, grinning. He turned to look at my mom. "*Mrs. Castillo, you don't have to worry about her anymore,*" He assured my mom. "*She can still work for now, but once we have kids, I'd rather have her stay at home and take care of the household. I will provide for everything. She'll be well taken care for.*"

My mom looked at Damien as if he was a miracle sent from heaven. She had that triumphant expression that she finally got what she wanted… again.

"*Oh, my, how lucky we are!*" My mom clapped her hands with excitement then turned to me, "*You see? I know a good one when I see one. And just like me and your dad, he's gonna take care of you while you take care of him and his house. This arrangement will be perfect!"*

I stayed silent during the exchange, knowing that confronting my mom right there and then will not be the best idea because it will ruin the perfect family façade that she had worked so hard to maintain. I kept my head down, looking at my almost full plate, appetite gone.

"So, it's set then!" My mom stood up and turned towards Damien's parents. "Sandra, we can let them date for maybe a month then we can start discussing the engagement. Adi's twenty-seven already and we need our grandchildren soon!"

Both of our moms squealed with excitement while my dad looked at me now, with concern.

That evening ended without even a word from me on how I felt about this arrangement. I tried talking to her out of it, but she wouldn't budge.

My mom has been a big believer and advocate of traditions, and that reflected on how I was molded growing up. She taught time and time again that children should always honor their parents, and even though it wasn't implied, the fine prints more likely included following parent's decision regardless of their children's opinion or feelings. I never had a voice against her. And even if I took the ounce of courage to explain my side, she would take it as a disrespect because I was talking back. That was how it was for me. The debt of gratitude should be repaid in all forms and views, since they were the one who gave life and supported me growing up—and the included saying yes to dating a man I barely know, for their happiness and dreams of having grandchildren. Arranged marriage has not been a part of our customs but she took it into her own hands to make sure that I would be following a path that she wanted herself.

Mothers know best. And that dinner was a flex of the power my mom had over me.

But now, it was different.

I finally woke up and decided that I get to decide what I wanted to do in my life. I would take back the control that I had given up to my mom for a very long time.

"Mom, *listen to me.*" I reiterated as my mom chose to ignore me with her crocheting for the last few minutes. My mom waved a hand as if telling me to just continue.

I sighed and rolled my shoulders. I was already preparing for the worst.

"I'm breaking the engagement off."

Chapter Ten

ALEX OPENED the door, and I was ready to face the worst. We were greeted by a red-faced, seething Damien. By instinct, my body curled inward defensively as if I wanted to disappear and just hide. I know what happens when Damien was in this mood.

I know all too well.

"You took your fucking time!" Damien yelled at our faces. "Why haven't you replied to my messages?!"

I did not answer right away. I wanted to be brave and show this person that he could not control me anymore.

I wanted to be brave.

I needed to be brave.

But I knew deep in my being that I was terrified beyond my wits, hoping that this would just end. I was an impostor, and all this courage was just a facade.

"Do you know this person, Adi?" A quiet voice on my side.

Out of the fear and dread, I almost forgot that Alex was still there. And that reminder had awoken something inside me – a sense of shame and embarrassment that Alex was witnessing a part of my life that I wanted to leave behind and forget, *again.*

But more importantly, fear—I needed to protect Alex from Damien.

I tried taking a step towards my ex-fiancé to possibly deescalate the situation and hopefully not end up with anyone getting hurt. Knowing Damien, a few more nudges would likely result to a fist fight most especially if he realized that this was the same person who sent him behind bars.

I had to get Alex out of here.

I was determined to bear the grunt of whatever repercussion this confrontation would have, but not her.

Not Alex. Not anymore.

Before I could take that step, a hand held me to my spot. I glanced down and saw Alex still holding my wrist and I could feel she was slowly pulling me behind her back.

Protecting me instead.

I stole a glance and tried getting Alex's attention to show her that I could handle this, but she was looking straight ahead at Damien, rather formidably.

"I am her fiancé!" he shouted at Alex, puffing his chest out, trying to make himself bigger and more intimidating.

Alex blatantly dismissed Damien's claim. "Last time I heard, you were an ex already."

Damien's eyes widened and his nose flared with anger as he stepped forward. "We are not breaking off this engagement! Unless I decide to!"

"Adi," Alex called my attention. I looked at her and was shocked to see how menacing she appeared. She stared down at Damien, exuding her dominance despite him being a tad taller than her. "Is this guy welcomed on your property?" she asked.

I didn't realize that my body was shaking, and tears had started filling in my eyes. The fear that Damien had ingrained on me was still intact, and the control it has was still overpowering my sense of rationality. The only thing that was keeping me grounded was the person beside me, knowing deep inside that she would protect me. So, I meekly shook my head, and I knew that answer would throw Damien off. He wouldn't just back down.

"This is not even her property, stupid bitch!" The condescension, always his weapon.

"Yes," Alex confirmed without breaking her stare. "But she is a welcomed guest of the owner of this property. And I am, too. I couldn't say the same for you." The sarcasm dripping in her tone.

"Who is this person?!" Damien's rage even fueled with the mockery. He looked at Alex then at me, then back to Alex, as if trying to connect the dots. "Wait…" A realization dawning to him.

"You're that woman who sent me to jail!" I could see the wrath in his eyes as he balled his knuckles. "Are you fucking this woman?! Is this why you broke up with me?!"

With Alex's protected stance in front of me, it was no wonder he came to that conclusion. Instead of denying the claim, Alex discreetly reached out to grab my hand again, as if to reassure me that it was going to be okay.

"*Sir*," the word was supposed to convey respect, but the way Alex said it made it sound as a threat. "Adi clearly said that you are not welcome in this property."

" –The fuck I'm not!" Damien interrupted. "Just wait when I tell your parents about this! They will take my side for sure! Getting it on with a woman! What were you thinking?!" he said in a triumphant tone, face smug as if that would be enough to have me back.

Well, getting my parents to side with him is a win for him, for sure. I thought cheerlessly. *But that's not news.*

"What? Is she so good with her fingers that you forgot that you have a fiancé?" he sneered "Was my dick not enough for you that you have to look for someone who can wear whatever size you want?" I could feel Alex's hand grasping mine tighter and tighter. "Or did she eat that cunt of yours so well that, that tongue made you lose your senses and decided to go against your parents?" Damien was laughing so maniacally to himself, so convinced that his comebacks were that good.

"*Sir,*" patience running out on Alex tone. "I am not done talking." The dominance clear and unwavering in her voice, enough for Damien to shut his mouth. "If you do not vacate this property, we *will* call the cops on you." Damien seemed not taking the threat seriously and was about to run his mouth again, but Alex did not give him the opportunity to interject. "And I will happily inform them about the incident in *my* club last Friday. Two strikes would be enough to put you back in jail, no?"

Damien's eyes bulged, as if a deer caught in headlights. "And once we have Adi's statements to prove what a worthless scumbag you are, we could probably build a case to put behind bars for a longer time."

His face was calculating, planning his next moves and

surprisingly, he stepped back in resignation. I was hopeful that this would be the last interaction that they will have, but knowing Damien, he would not simply give up and would always want to have the last words.

"I will be back." His words a bit feral. "And next time, you won't be able to say no to me anymore." He slowly stalked away from us and disappeared out of the driveway.

It took a few seconds before I released a breath I didn't know I was holding. Alex freed my wrist, turned to me and asked, "Are you okay?"

I wasn't in the right head space to digest all of these just yet.

Alex closed and locked the door and led me back to the kitchen. No words were spoken. A silent understanding that I needed time to recover before she could start asking questions. She handed me a glass of water and a glass of wine on the other. *A choice.*

Without blinking, I grabbed the glass of wine and had drowned it within seconds, trying to push down the anxiety that was clawing inside of me. I set down the glass and finally looked at Alex, who was leaning against the kitchen counter, waiting for me to calm down.

"I'm sorry you had to witness that," I started. "And you didn't have to defend me from him. I could've tried handling it on my own." Impostor, that I was.

"I'm glad I was here." I couldn't read Alex's expression. "I don't know him, but guys with disposition like that are mostly bad news. How did you end up with that person?"

"Parents…" I answered with just above a whisper. Alex body went rigid.

How could my parents leave their daughter to marry that kind of person? I have always asked myself.

No, I called myself out. *Shut it off. You got out.*

"Would you feel safe if you stay here?" The question pulling me back to reality. I did not want to burden Alex anymore, but I knew it was not a good idea to be alone after that confrontation. I knew Damien. I knew how far he could go to make sure he got what he wanted

So, I shook my head.

"That's okay," Alex reassured me. She pushed herself away from the kitchen counter and had started walking towards the living room. "Go on and grab some clothes for a couple of days. We'll call Eli when we're on the road and figure it out."

I stood up and peeked at Alex.

The past few days have been crazy to say the least. A week from breaking free, almost getting kidnapped, meeting my best friend again, my ex-fiancé behind the almost kidnapping... but I was glad that out of all of this shit storm, Lexie was back... *somehow*.

Before deciding against it, I took the few steps towards where she was standing and hugged her from behind. Alex's body stiffened like a statue, surprised with the physical contact.

After a few silent seconds, Alex's body relaxed, and she turned to face me. I did not let go and had buried my face in her chest, pulling her closer. Alex started rubbing my back for comfort.

"It's okay. You're safe," Alex reassured me repeatedly. I couldn't contain the emotions in my chest anymore and finally stopped pretending that all was okay. I let the stream of tears down.

After a few minutes of ugly crying, the embarrassing realization of how I was probably smearing snot in her shirt made me laugh humorlessly. "What's so funny?" Alex asked quietly. I felt her warm breath close to my ears and when I decided to glance up, my eyes widened with surprise, seeing the distance of her face from mine. *Or the lack thereof.* But Alex's expression stayed the same; a subtle hint of humor playing on her eyes after seeing how flustered I was.

I tried pulling my senses back. "Thank you," I segued. "For protecting me."

Alex did not respond but had brought her hands up to my cheek to wipe off my tears. It was my turn to stay still as a statue, my heart beating crazy inside my chest. I've never expected this act of intimacy in a million years after our fall out.

Alex might have noticed the change in my demeanor and had taken this as a sign to stop. She dropped her hands to the side.

"I'm sorry," Alex started, "I didn't mean to..."

Alex never got to finish the sentence as I grabbed her face and pulled it down on mine.

And Alex kissed me back.

Chapter Eleven

WAS THIS *truly happening?* I tried to scramble my thoughts into a coherent one before I got fully pulled into Alex's whirlpool. However, my attempts were futile. My body felt like it was going to combust at any given moment, Alex's kisses the fuel to ignite the spark that has long died inside me—us, merely a blur of clashing lips and tongues, both hungry for each other.

I felt her hand gripped my hips on both sides, pulling me even closer as if the distance was far too much for our bodies—the pressure, proof on how much she was restraining herself.

But I wanted more.

Yet as soon as it started, she pulled herself away from me, straightening out my clothes that had ridden up.

I would lie if I said that I wasn't disappointed.

"You're not thinking straight," Alex said as she started grabbing her things. "And I don't want to be another part of your experiment that will be discarded when you don't need it anymore." She straightened up and headed for the door. "Grab your bag, I'll wait for you by the door."

And out of humiliation from the rejection—*again*, I turned around and started stuffing my bag with my things that I could reach, not caring if they were what I needed or not—just something to hide my face as tears had started falling from my eyes again.

Alex walked away with her phone on her ear, and the last thing I heard was Eli's name as she shut the door.

As soon as I heard the door clicked, I ran to the bathroom and splashed cold water in my face. *What are you doing?* I stared at the mirror. *Why would you kiss her in this circumstance?*

I wanted to reason out that it was from the adrenaline from the incident earlier with Damien, or the relief that passed through me when Alex was able to remove him from Nico's place. But I knew it was something deeper—something that I have been pushing down for the longest time. And the only thing that was keeping me away from letting it come out fully was the courage to accept that this was what I wanted. And if being honest with Alex was the first step to go, then may it make or break whatever the universe has given us right now.

With a new sense of determination, I stepped out of the washroom and stalked towards where Alex was standing. She turned around with her phone still on her ears, and before she could say anything, I pulled her face into mine, the momentum pushing her against the door. I let my lips and tongue convey my desire, and all the unspoken words that I have failed to tell her when we were young.

Her hands stayed still for a few seconds, unaware of what was unraveling in front of her. I was losing it—my rationale, my sense of judgement, and my care. *I wanted this*, and I wanted her to understand that. And slowly, as if finally regaining her senses, she inched her hands up in my waist, the subtle touch on my skin sent waves to my core.

No one was stopping, and I was scared to let go. *Again.* I wrapped my arms around her neck and tried tugging her closer, as if it was not enough. She smirked as she understood what I was trying to do. She pulled away for a second, giving me a chance to look at her face. And something clicked inside me. Finally grasping the depth of what I had lost ten years ago, I couldn't hide any longer from the unknown emotions that I had been suppressing ever since I lost her.

What if I mess it up again? I pushed the thought as I grabbed her face once more and pulled it towards me. And she answered each kiss with intensity, her hands gripping my ass tighter as I locked my legs around her waist, my hips involuntarily grounding itself against her body. Everything was heat and lust. And I was about to erupt. Not only from the physicality of it all, but also the collapse of all the bars I have imprisoned myself with.

Was there always a part of me that wanted this before?

I finally slowed down, trying to savor each and every second. Our tongues danced against each other, as if they had known one another for a long time. A new yet familiar emotion. A warm and intense feeling was coiling in my groin. A call to release my inhibitions.

You are not the young girl ten years ago, Adi. I reminded myself. *You have the freedom to choose.*

I pulled her towards the couch and as soon as she was sat, I climbed on top of her—reticence all thrown out the window.

I was ready to give all of myself to Alex. *Finally.*

Alex started moving her kisses away from my lips to the base of my neck and up to the small delicate spot just under my ear, earning a low, sensual moan as I threw my head back to give her more access.

I felt in control and out of control simultaneously. I didn't even notice that I had started grabbing Alex's soft hair, pulling her closer, *asking for more.*

Alex took a quick second and stole a glance at my face, an unreadable expression on her face. I soften my grip on her hair, a gesture to ask if she was okay. She closed her eyes and let out a huge sigh. The moment Alex opened her eyes, I knew this was a different Alex—filled with thirst and craving, unapologetic of what was about to come.

"Do you want this?" Alex asked in a very low voice, almost a growl. She let her hands splayed at my lower back, unmoving until I say yes to her. It stabbed me in my heart knowing where this was coming from.

I slid both my hands to the sides of her neck and pushed her upper body to lean back on the couch. I slowly lowered my face and peppered her neck with kisses, gently nipping the lobes of her ear, resulting to a sharp intake of breath. "Yes, Alex," I whispered against bare skin. "Yes," I whispered again when I really wanted to tell her was, *I'm sorry.*

I pulled myself back, shooting a glance at her. She looked at me under her lashes, her eyes glazed with a stupor of desire. The unabashed portrayal of her need gave me the courage to take things further.

Without breaking eye contact, I started undoing the buttons of my shirt, painfully slow one after the other. The tension in me was building up, and I was feeling more powerful than I ever have.

As the last button was undone, it revealed just a peak of my perky breasts, giving away that I was not wearing anything underneath.

An invitation. A consent.

Alex pulled me closer, breathing in my bared naked skin in front of her. She dragged her mouth in between my breasts, her warm breaths making my body shiver all over, intensifying the arousal that has been building inside me ever since I tasted her lips.

I was getting impatient, and Alex was just taking her sweet time.

The cunning smile in Alex's face was a proof that knew she was pushing my limits. She explored my breast with kisses, leaving kiss marks across. I have never wanted hickeys on my body as far as I could remember, but this felt different. The night was hers to take and my body hers to claim. I didn't mind getting marked if it was her way of telling me I was hers.

My body was tense and wanted release. The pool of wetness in between my legs was a tangible proof. Alex ran her tongue along one of my nipples, finally giving me what I had been anticipating. The way my body was quivering, I knew I was at her mercy, too. I ground my hips against her, my body almost having a mind of its own. It knew what it wanted, and it wasn't afraid to ask for it.

Alex slid her fingers in on my waistband, feeling the skin underneath. Every touch was a direct attack in between my thighs, the throbbing sensation of wanting a release becoming too unbearable at this point.

"*Please…*" A whisper. A plea.

"Please what, Adi?" Alex asked against my lips.

"*Touch me.*" Finally admitting it out loud in front of Alex was something I never thought I would be able to do.

Alex started pulling down the only thing that stopping her from getting full access to my bare body when she stopped midway. Both of our heads whipped at the direction of the table as her phone started ringing.

The alert fell on deaf ears as I continued to remove my shorts, not wanting to stop whatever was happening right now.

But her phone just *Wouldn't. Stop. Ringing.* The annoyance from being pussy-blocked had started to dampen the mood.

Alex let out a huge sigh and looked at me. "I'm sorry." I felt I was more disappointed than she was. "Let me answer this just real quick." She picked up her phone and checked who was calling. And the name on the screen was a cold bucket of ice poured down my back: *Eli.*

I stepped away from her and pulled up my almost-removed shorts and quickly snatched my button-down, the realization of what I had done already gripping my stomach, making me want to throw up.

I was seriously considering asking Eli to be in a friends-with-benefits arrangement just a few days ago and here I was, baring myself naked to another person.

That was different. My inner voice called out. *It was a means to an end.* And as much as that was true, I knew I fucked up. Yet again.

I stole a glance at Alex, sitting in my couch, hair tousled, and lips almost swollen from our kissing. She looked breathtakingly beautiful as always. I touched my lips, knowing that I pretty much looked the same.

As I stepped closer to offer Alex a glass of water, she clicked her phone to speaker, letting me hear Eli's voice on the other line.

"Yo! Adi!" Eli greeted with such enthusiasm that it made the remorse even worse. "Are you down to go out and grab some drinks?"

"Hi, Eli!" I answered as I tried to steal a glance at Alex. "I'm at Nico's apartment. You want to go out right now to grab drinks? Where?"

"*Tala*, of course!" Eli retorted with a chuckle. "Since Alex is still with you, she can drive you here." No one answered, nor reacted from what she had just confirmed. "Speaking of which—Alex, why are you still there? It has been hours since we were done from the restaurant?"

I glanced up at Alex, afraid to see what her expression would be. I don't know if Alex knew something happened between me

81

and Eli, given that they're best friends. And if she does, she has not shown any indication of it... just yet.

"We were *talking*. We were about to call you to meet up." Alex did not meet my eyes.

"Yeah, why are you *still* there?" Eli pushed. Alex finally met my stare, urging the other to give an explanation, but no one answered. After a few awkward seconds, Eli just continued, hopefully unassuming. "Anyway, always my impeccable timing, eh? Okay. I'll see you at *Tala* then. In an hour? I'm quite far from the city."

"Okay," Alex confirmed and ended the call.

I grimaced as Alex turned towards me. She narrowed her eyes and asked, "What is it?"

I started to wring my hands, my eyes trained towards the floor. I did not know how to tell Alex or if I should tell Alex. She leaned forward on the kitchen island, both arms caging my body in between. The closeness of Alex's proximity and the faint smell of her perfume, a mixture of cardamom and mimosa, triggered my inclinations to go back to what we were doing, but I knew it would just add to all the wrongs I had committed against Alex—and this was supposed to be my retribution era. To myself and to the people I loved.

I grabbed Alex's face in between my face and was only supposed to give her a peck. But as soon as our lips touched, her arm wrapped around me and pulled me closer, her head dipping to deepen the kiss. And I gave in. As easy as that.

"We have an hour before we need to be there," Alex whispered against my skin. "I can drive us in half an hour." I knew what she was implying. *And I want it, too.*

It took all of my strength to give her a little push for her to stop.

Not ready for the consequences I was about to face, I just went for the jab. "Eli kissed me last week, when she dropped me off here after the hospital," I started. Alex drew back a few inches and cocked her head to one side, her face asking where this statement was going. "Amanda told me to explore. To understand what I want. She told me to, and I quote, 'hoe it out until you figure out what you want' so I did. And it just so happened that Eli was the first person who showed interest in me. You looked at me as if I was a stranger and I thought you would never give me the time of day again. If I knew..." Realizing the what ifs made me want to cry even more. "And I'm sorry I didn't tell you, but I got so lost in the moment. And I've missed you so much. And I needed to forget what just happened with my ex. And I did as soon as I kissed you. So, I let my body take over without thinking of the consequences."

"Just like before," Alex whispered more to herself, her face stoic.

That felt like arrows shot through my heart. She was right. Just like before.

"I needed to forget. I needed to. Because I would breakdown and shatter if I let it all get to me. I thought I was free, but the shackles kept on coming for me, trying to drag me back to the shit state I was in." I was grasping at straws to try and make her understand me. Yet I knew there was no recourse to what I have done, before and now. "But meeting you tonight and kissing you—it felt like the universe was giving me a second chance with you; to let me make it up to you. Seeing you again made me feel that it was all coming back together. Seeing you filled a void that I didn't know existed and that it made me feel whole again somehow."

Alex stared at me. I hadn't noticed that she took a step back to create some space between the two of us. I knew that she was drawing back from the connection we had moments ago. And I didn't have anyone to blame but myself.

"*Adi...*" Hearing Alex call my name broke something inside me. "*I understand.*"

This was not the response I was expecting. Mad should be on top of the list. Disgusted too, maybe a top contender.

"I understand that you have been in a bad situation that was out of your control," Alex continued. "But now you are free. And you have control on how you're going to live your life. You said I make you feel whole. You can't depend on other people on making you whole, Adi. You have to heal and process all that shit from your past so it wouldn't have power over you anymore." Alex walked closer again, holding on to my shoulders. I could feel the tears just flowing freely from my eyes, my suppressed emotions finally spilling. "Focus on yourself first, Adi. And the rest will follow."

I rested my head against Alex's chest in defeat. "I'm sorry," I whispered.

"Sorry for what?"

"For kissing you and your best friend." I wanted to drip this response with sarcasm, but I did not have the energy anymore.

"Add that on your list, too. Figure out your shit with Eli. I don't want to get in between whatever you have with her," Alex answered, the detachment and coldness already seeping back in her demeanor. "And to clear it up, *I don't like you like that anymore.* I'm sorry if you misinterpreted this as that. I just wanted to help you forget what happened."

I didn't know I could feel heartbreak for something that didn't even happen.

"This will be the last time I will be kissing you, Adi." She leaned down and give me a quick peck on the lips. "We don't want you making *mistakes* again, do we?"

Chapter Twelve

"SCAR..." **BEFORE** Alex could finish her sentence, the scarlet-haired bartender had already put down a glass of beer in front of her. She crossed her arms and glared at Alex for a couple of minutes before realizing that I was existing within their six-meter radius.

The bartender's eyes darted from Alex to me and back to Alex with a questioning look, as if trying to confirm what my relationship with Alex was. And after a few awkward seconds, she sighed with a disappointed look at her face and stomped away to cater to the other customers at the bar.

I was not oblivious to the fact that she might be the girlfriend, and the guilt was eating me alive.

Alex gave me a small lingering tap at my shoulder, trying to reassure me that she got the situation handled. She walked off and went behind the bar to approach Scar, and I could do nothing but just to stare at her retreating back.

The two women were only a few feet away from me, but I cannot hear a single thing they were discussing over the loud music from the dance floor. Alex was shaking her head, her face looking distraught.

The bartender turned her head to stare at me, not caring that I was looking straight at her as well. *This is it. This is where the girlfriend comes back to slap me in the face.* I was bracing for the worse.

To my surprise, she just turned her attention back to Alex, sighed and smiled sadly at her.

Looks like they made up. A thought that was supposed to be a relief but somehow, made me feel disappointed. *Adalia Reia Castillo!* I had to reprimand myself as soon as I realized what I was feeling. *You were not raised to be a home wrecker! Get a hold of yourself!*

But that doesn't take away the pang of pain and longing that reverberated through me as I saw Alex wrapped her arms around the bartender and gave her a kiss on the cheek. I forced myself to look away, unwilling to participate in this self-torture anymore.

I grabbed the untouched beer that was supposedly for Alex and took a gulp. *What happened to staying away from alcohol?*

"How's my favorite customer?" a sultry, deep voice asked. I looked up and saw the bartender talking to Eli who had just arrived. She beamed at the person behind the bar. "Still causing trouble with the ladies?" I was surprised to see her obvious flirting with Eli in front of Alex.

"You know I would always have a special spot for you in my heart, Scar. Just say yes to me," Eli quipped as she dramatically asked for Scar's hand and kissed it so lightly.

The bartender, Scar, released a heartfelt laughter and swatted Eli's hand away from her.

"Behave," Scar reprimanded. "We're in front of guests." And with that, Scar finally decided to acknowledge my existence.

"Is this person bothering you?" Scar jested. "Just tell me if she's too much. This woman needs some spanking one of these days."

Eli laughed loudly at that, joking that the only spanking she wanted was from Scar.

They continued to chatter about how the opening went without Alex, ensuing continuous death glares from Scar to Alex, who was now sitting beside Eli. I looked at the scene as if I was gazing through a window, just observing from afar; an invisible separation between me and the group who seemed so familiar with each other. I was clearly the outsider in this group.

A stab of envy pierced through my chest.

The three were engrossed in their playful banter which gave me a chance to finally soak Scar's presence in. Looking at the bartender, I wouldn't be surprised if all the women *and* men were lining up to get her number and shoot their shot. Despite the club being pretty dim, the under-cabinet lights that lit the booth were emitting a soft glow that was accentuating everything about her.

Scar's lips, painted in bright red lipstick, in itself, was enough to lure someone and make them dream of kissing her. Accentuated by those chestnut brown eyes that scrunched at the corners whenever she laughed, and her long, wavy hair, tussled, making her look effortlessly alluring. She was dressed very plainly with a black, vintage, loose crop top which revealed just a peek of a toned stomach, and a high-waisted jean short. Yet the way she carried herself with such confidence and comfort, made her look like she was walking down on her own red carpet, living her best main character life.

Scar was perfect for Alex... or Eli.

And on cue, Eli was up front in my face, waving a hand.

"Hey, Adi," Eli tried catching my attention. "Do you want to go home? You look sleepy as fuck."

I didn't realize that I was staring at Scar so intently and apparently, Eli has been calling out my name a few times already. The group was looking at me with a worried expression.

"No... I'm sorry. I'm okay." I grabbed Eli's hands to stop it from moving in front of my face. "I just zoned out for a bit."

Scar walked towards me. "Do you want a drink? It's on the house sweetie. I got you."

I stared at her. How could I not like this woman? She was gorgeous and she seemed kind. What else could anyone ask for?

"No, I'm good for now." I offered a small smile. "But just a glass of water, I guess."

"What? You're not gonna offer the owner and your best customer drinks on the house?" Eli teased Scar.

She only rolled her eyes and gave me the glass. I was about to reach and grab the glass when the spotlight from the dance floor had shone through the glass and reflected against Scars right forearm, showing a healed, large slash across. I bashfully looked away, but I knew that Scar saw me gawking. I tried to school my expression back to nonchalance, but it was too late. I'd already been caught.

Scar smiled at me. "It's okay. It's a long story. Hence, the nickname, Scar." She extended a hand towards me. "These idiots didn't even introduce us formally. My name is Cleo, but you can call me Scar... or Cleo."

I took her hand and shook it.

"I'm Adi," I answered meekly. I felt unnerved even though she was not doing anything to intimidate me.

"Have you guys known each other for a long time?" The courage to ask finally came up. I felt I needed to do this. And as much as I didn't want to expect the worse, considering what I saw just a while ago, I must know what the connection was of these three.

"We've known Scar for about...." Eli looked at Alex while thinking. "Almost a year now after that incident." No one expounded on what the incident was, but I guess it was safe to assume it was the cause of the healed slash across Scar's forearm. "After that, Alex hired her to help around the club until Alex agreed to make her the manager of the club."

"I basically run everything here," Scar playfully glared at Alex. "I manage the staff, the logistics and just the daily needs for the club to run. Alex handles the admin and paperwork. I don't have patience for that."

The conversation eventually lulled into my queries about how Scar runs the club, while Alex and Eli had a separate conversation over their glass of beer. After an hour of idle conversation with Scar going back and forth talking to me and serving the club goers, Eli finally stood up and announced that we were calling it a night.

"Alex will drop you off at your friend's house. She told me what happened, and we'll try to see first what we can do to help you out temporarily," Eli explained as she stepped closer to me. "I'll be going to Alex's place for now. She said she wanted to speak to me about something." Eli shrugged. "I'll text you later, yeah?"

I nodded and was surprised when Eli kissed me on the cheeks. "I'll see you later, hon."

Both Alex and Eli walked off towards the back of club to the parking lot, leaving Scar and me alone, for the first time this evening.

I had a million questions in my mind as to how Scar's presence played into the lives of these two women. Were they together before? With whom? How long? Why did both of them made out with me then if that was the case? Were they just playing around?

"Spit it out," Scar said point-blankly as she dried the beer glass. I was surprised that she saw right through me.

"How do you know what I was thinking?" I asked in bewilderment.

"Sweetie, your face is screaming everything to me," Scar smiled. "No, there's nothing going on with any of us. The three of us are just very good friends." She put down the glass that she just finished drying. "I have very few good friends, Adi. And I'm very protective of them most especially if they have been treated unfairly in the past." Scar was staring straight into my soul. Did she know my history with Alex? "I want them to be happy. And I would not take it lightly if someone would treat them like that again."

I couldn't determine if there was an undertone to what Scar was saying. Was she saying this in general or was she specifically targeting me?

I sighed and straightened my back, trying to steel my resolve. I would not take this intimidation lightly, too. I was trying to be a better person by asking her relationship with them so I would know what boundaries to set. *I was not raised to be a homewrecker.*

"Since you're a good friend of them," I stared right back at Scar. "You wouldn't mind if I pursued one of them, right?"

Scar gave me a knowing smile, hinting that she was in on a secret that I didn't even know. "No, I wouldn't mind," she answered and signaled me to come closer, as if to share a something that no one else should hear. Scar leaned closer, stopping just merely inches from my ear.

In an amused tone, she whispered, "Which one do you like better, though?"

1

Chapter Thirteen

THE DRIVE to Amanda's place was bearable despite all the things that had happened in the last few hours. Alex remained silent, contemplative at best. She let the soft RnB music play a bit louder, drowning out the suffocating silence that started to creep in.

The familiar driveway to the apartment emerged and the music was cut off as soon as Alex turned off the car. I knew it was my cue to get out, but something was stopping me from doing so. I didn't want this to be the end of my lifeline to win Alex back, most especially after what happened tonight.

"Is something wrong?" Alex asked after a few more seconds of still silence. "I thought you'd feel safer to stay with Amanda. Nico said that he's going to be there, too."

I looked up at Alex. "No, yeah, for sure. I texted her, too."

"Don't worry about Eli," She turned to face the road ahead. "I'll explain everything to her tonight, and I would make sure I won't be the reason why you won't be able to freely date her if you want."

Oh. That was what she was thinking.

Alex opened her door and stepped out of the car. My brain, hardwired to always think of the worst, thought that she had enough of me and wanted to get out of the enclosed space. To my surprise, she walked around the car and opened the door for me.

"Come on." She motioned for me to give her my duffel bag. "I'll walk you to the door."

There were so many things I wanted to say to Alex, but I couldn't figure out what to say first. The emotions in me were all so muddled and disorienting, making it hard for me to articulate anything but silence.

Yet I knew, I was determined not to make the same mistakes again.

We reached the front door and before Alex could knock on the door, I grabbed her hands and enclosed it with mine.

"Uhmm..." I hesitated. "I want to figure whatever this is out first." I gazed down at our hands. "I still have a lot of things I want to talk to you about. But that could wait. Just let me make amends." Alex stared right at me, her emotions hard to read.

Finally, after a few seconds of nothing, she gave me a small smile and gently squeezed my hands. The words that left her lips crushed the hope that had started budding ever since I saw her again.

"You don't have to. You don't have to make up for anything. This is a new version of you, this is a new version of me. We're acquaintances now. We don't need to live according to the past. We can be friends along the way." Without waiting for my response, she dropped my hand and knocked on the door.

The door opened and Nico emerged in his matching PJs. His eyes widened as he took note of my eyes that had started to water. His eyes darted to Alex. "Okay. Should I just magically disappear for a few more minutes? Is this some unfinished conversation that you need to have?"

"No," I called out too quickly as I tried to subtly wipe my tears.

"I was about to go," Alex added. "Thank you again, Nico. Tell Amanda I said hi." She stepped in to give him a one-armed hug. "I'll see you later." She nodded at me and Nico and started walking off.

I knew this was something I couldn't brush off and had to explain to Nico once we were all alone.

"Okay, I know you have questio—" I started as we walked towards the living room.

"Amanda stepped out to grab some grocery for us." Ignoring the question first. "And no, Adi. I don't." Nico stopped me before I could even finish. The flash of hurt in my face could have been obvious that he immediately followed, "Not unless you want to do it right now with Amanda, and share and hear some hard truths, I won't ask any questions." He sighed and stepped around me to plop down at the couch.

I took the opposite side of the couch, facing him. He offered me a glass of wine. "What do you mean *if I'm ready to face some hard truths?*"

"You really want to do this now?" His tone not sarcastic or mocking, but full of genuine concern. "I heard what happened tonight. I thought your ex was done for already?"

I thought so, too. But apparently not.

I gave Nico a rundown of what happened when Damien came for a surprise visit and how Alex protected me from him.

"Wait, why was Alex with you tonight?" he asked after. *Here we go.*

"Is it so bad that I wanted to make amends with her?" As far as I knew, Nico was not aware of what actually happened even though he was there. All he knew was Alex and I had grown apart.

Nico sighed in defeat. "You're my best friend, Adi. Since high school, we were inseparable. I was with you when you took your first taste of underage drinking. I was there when you spent late afternoons for your journalism club. We were together when we graduated. I was with you during your engagement party, as much as I hated the prick. I am here with you right now to support you as you start over, and you know I'm always here for you during the fun and the not-so-fun times." I started tearing up as he held my hands close to his heart. "But don't forget that Alex is my best friend, too. I don't pick sides. I've been Switzerland through and through. I love you both so much, but I don't want to see my other best friend be in such pain *again* that her only way out is to leave. Have you ever considered that I lost ten years with her, too?"

The truth was a slap in my face. I knew what he was implying. The remorse that I had been trying to push down for ten years have found its claws back and had started tearing me apart inch by inch inside. *Did I deserve this second chance with Alex?* The consequences of my inaction were now finally catching up to me and I was left paralyzed with self-loathing. I was lost for words, adrift the guilt and the pain lacing through my body as I cried it out.

Nico wrapped his arms around me and stayed quiet the whole time, giving me the time to let it all out. He wrapped me in a blanket and offered me water as soon as I started calming down from my breakdown.

"These hard truths..." I was trying to squeeze the words in between sobs. "I want to hear these."

Nico looked at me with hesitation. And I would understand. If I was looking at myself right now, I wouldn't want to add insult to the injury, too. But I knew I couldn't hide with false pretenses if I wanted to make things right. And facing the harsh reality to take accountability was one thing I could do that was within my control.

"Please. Tell me."

"You tell me, Adi," Nico answered quietly. "You tell me what happened ten years ago. I heard the rumors, but you or Alex never told me what actually happened. I didn't want to believe it. I didn't know what I saw that night. I knew a kiss happened but nothing that would destroy you and Lexie's friendship. I knew how close you were. A fucking kiss happened when we were kids. As much as it was a dare, yet you continued being friends."

"I got hurt when you started acting like nothing was wrong when Alex started distancing herself whenever we were together. Alex started pushing me away 'cause she told me that you needed me more, more than her. Two of my best friends were not talking to each other anymore and I was left in the dark. Then, she left. Without further explanations." I could feel that Nico had kept this sentiment pushed down for the longest time. "And you asked me once if I have heard from her but after that, no more. It was as if you've forgotten her altogether."

"I'm sorry." I reached out to hug him. "I didn't know I hurt you. I thought by pretending that everything's all right, then everything will be all right. I should have told you."

"You can tell me now." Nico wiped his tear as he pulled away and weakly smiled at me. "Nothing changes, Adi. I'm still here for you."

"I can't take back what happened ten years ago, Nico. But I can try and make it right, now."

Finally facing and accepting this reality that I have no idea what's going on in my life was a punch in my gut. The illusion of control was one of the only things that was keeping my sanity together. I intended to believe that I chose to break up my engagement; that I chose to drink and party last week; chose to accept that kiss from Eli; chose to make out with Alex. But all facade aside, I was out of control. Everything was out of my control. I was letting my emotions get the best of me. And most of the time, it hurt the people around me. And I was done doing that to the people I loved and cared about.

"I think I knew it in myself that I liked Alex before when were in high school, but I was just too afraid to acknowledge the fact that I was attracted to a girl, knowing how conservative my family was. You know how they are." Nico nodded with a sad, knowing smile. "I didn't know who to tell. I know you were there for me and for sure, would help me figure this shit out. But some part of me was so ashamed to admit that I liked my best friend just because she was a girl, too.

"You have to understand, I was raised to believe since I was a little girl that women are only for men, that you have to obey your parents regardless of what you think is right or wrong for you... I admit, I sometimes do things behind their back, but not to this extent. You know the drill with these conservative beliefs."

"Yes, I know. Us queers have one-way tickets to hell." Nico rolled his eyes teasingly.

A sardonic laugh escaped my mouth as I realized the incredulity of it all. "I knew I couldn't ask my mom—that would be a nightmare. Can you imagine the horror?"

Nico gave me a side-eye.

"So, I did one of the most stupid things..." I told him how I went to one of my mom's friends whom I considered a mentor. I thought that given his standing in our community, he would be able to give me a sound, unbiased advice. It took me a lot of courage to step out of my comfort zone and ask for a piece of advice to further understand something I knew, was heavily frowned upon, only to hear the words... *Don't worry. This is just a phase. Maybe because you haven't tried being with a man yet.* He doubled down with reinforcing the belief that women are meant for men only and same sex relationships were unforgivable sins.

And repent.

Repent for who I was.

"Are you fucking kidding me?!" Nico stood up suddenly, anger visible on his face. "How old were you back then? Sixteen? Seventeen? And he told you that shoving a dick inside you was the resolution to your... sexuality?" He paused and after a few seconds, gave me a smile full of irony. "I mean, that's what happened to me. Shoved a dick inside and confirmed that I was gay. Anyway..."

The gag in the middle of this serious conversation was just what I needed to feel a bit better. I busted out crying and laughing at the same time.

"I wish I was," I continued after we settled. I could still remember the self-disgust I felt as the reinforcement that my feelings were abnormal and should come to a stop immediately if I don't want to go to hell. "I was turning eighteen at that time. I didn't understand the implications of what he said to me, but it really made a huge impact on how I dealt with what I was feeling for Alex back then."

"I was so lost and confused. And I realized that I couldn't go to any adults to ask for advice because I would be admonished. They will tell my mom. And that's what happened ten years ago. My mom caught us. She threatened to kick me out and not send me to college. You know how hard I've been working on to get into a good school. So, I swallowed my pride and molded myself to the perfect daughter she ever wanted. Even if that meant that I had to lose one of the most important people in my life and lose my sense of self in the process too."

"I wish I knew, Adi." Nico scooted and pulled me to a side hug. I rested my head on his shoulders. "I wish you talked to me about this. I didn't know you were going through so much."

"I know." I gave his knee a slight tap to gesture that it was okay. "But that still doesn't give me the right to hurt Alex as I did. And hurt you, too. I knew you hated it when I asked you to act like you were straight when we were at home. You always joked about it, convincing me that acting like a straight boy was like cosplaying for you. I didn't even consider how you were feeling at that time and how it would affect you." I grabbed his hand. "I was selfish. I'm so sorry, Nico. You didn't deserve that, too."

Nico stared at me, mix of emotions spiraling in his eyes. And before he could say anything, we heard the front door open.

"Is she here?" Amanda called out.

I yelled a quick hello to make my presence known.

"Good. Because I have food and booze!"

PART II
Ten Years Ago

We were stupid.
We were young.
But age didn't take away the genuineness of our love,
Or the pain of our heart breaks.

We were stupid.
We were young.
But that didn't undermine the sacrifices we made,
All for the sake of love.

We knew *we* could happen.
We knew *we* could end.
We took a chance.
All in the wrong time.

Chapter Fourteen

ADI

IT WAS late afternoon, and classes had ended a more than an hour ago. Everyone's almost gone home. The sun had started to dip, and the early evening chill breezed inside the journalism club room. It was supposed to be empty but two busy bodies were still working through the deadline for their school's newspaper.

"Lexie," I called out to my best friend and journalism co-officer, without looking up from the newspaper layout draft I had in front of me. "Can you shut the windows? The wind will blow out all the papers in my desk."

Without even a word, I heard Lexie step away from her worktable and the squeaking of windows as they were closed. We usually spend afternoons in the journalism club room like this—surrounded by a comfortable silence and the presence of one another. Given that we have been spending our daily lives almost together for the past five years, I didn't want it any other way or with any other person. Lexie coming into my life has been a moment of serendipity.

I stared at the spread of newspaper article cut outs in front of me, trying to figure out the best possible layout with the most possible content for the last edition of the newspaper under our administration.

"Adi, come on. We need to start cleaning up. We can continue this tomorrow. It's 5:30 already," Lexie called out as she approached my worktable.

I glanced up at the clock and realized that we've been stooped at our work areas for at least an hour and a half already. No wonder my back and shoulders hurt.

"We could grab some cake before we go home. I'm craving for something sweet right now. I just got my allowance. I'll buy you your favorite."

"Yes." Thinking of that strawberry shortcake was making my mouth water already. "But can you give my shoulders a squeeze first?" I've always known that Lexie has stronger hands than mine. "My body's so stiff. I feel like I'm Batman."

This earned a chuckle from Lexie as I mimicked a few robot moves. She gave my shoulders tight squeezes, and I could already feel my body relaxing beneath her hands. I can't help but release an audible sigh. I turned to Lexie, "What will I do without you?" And gave her one of my toothy grins.

It was true though. Lexie had been a crutch for the past five years. Being in the student council, I get surrounded with superficial friendships that always drained the social energy out of me. The visibility and responsibility of my position had forced me out of my introverted self, and I needed to function like a social butterfly to establish good connections. Lexie and Nico, the other best friend in our trio, were my retreat after a long day to recharge. It was heaven sent when I discovered Lexie was into photography and I literally pushed her inside Ms. Grace's office to apply for the photojournalist position.

"In this journalism room, buried in papers, suffering alone." Lexie replied without a beat. She rolled her eyes and started picking up the clutter on my worktable. I teasingly grabbed her hand and pulled her down to my eye level. I wrapped my arm around her neck and said, "I know. I'm so lucky I have you in my life."

I could see Lexie's eyes widen with surprise, a reflection of mine as I slowly comprehended what I did. Her body stiffened; her hands stayed frozen on her sides.

Physical touch has always been a love language for me, even with my friends. When I first met Lexie, she would shy away from any physical contact even as simple as me grabbing on her arm as we walk along the hallways. She would always pull away. I noticed, even in moments that I simply needed to wipe something off her face, or fix a stray hair, she would back away. As times passed, she became accustomed to my constant nagging to let me at least link arms with her. Finally relenting, she would offer her arms and that had become a routine for us.

But this was different. Lost in the dynamics of our daily banter, I didn't realize what I did until it was right in front of me. The moment of shock passed by quickly, and I witnessed the change in Lexie's reaction as she smiled mischievously at me.

Out of nowhere, Lexie heaved me up from my seat and pushed my back against the edge of the table, her hands holding me firmly on my hips. My eyes widened as I realized what was happening. An unfamiliar heat, rising from my body to my face.

I've only seen this side of Lexie once. And I still wasn't sure if I liked it or not. It did a lot of things that confused my mind... *and my body.*

It seemed that the time stopped, and everything was in slow motion. I could see Lexie's face drawing in closer and closer until a mere few inches were between our face.

Lexie knew exactly what she was doing—a playful smile spreading across her face.

I was so lost in the intensity of the moment and the emotions that had started hay wiring my brain and body. I dared not move so as not to break whatever this was—my eyes trained on her face, most especially her lips.

"Had enough?" Lexie's breath a warm caress in my skin.

Before Lexie's word sunk in, she stepped away, leaving the cold air rushing in the distance between us. I tried blinking my way back to the reality of what just happened.

"Come on, Adi," Lexie started picking up her bag. "No one's here and they're gonna close the school soon."

My brain was still trying to catch up with the string of events that happened within the past few minutes. *What the fuck was that?*

I started grabbing my things, trying to draw myself back to my homeostasis. *Stop it. It was one kiss that I had dared her to do.* I stopped for a minute and put my hand in my chest, my heart beating so rapidly. *No more repeats.*

But why was I hoping for her to close the distance between our faces?

I turned to look at her. "What was that, Lexie?" I finally asked for the sake of my sanity. She merely shrugged and continued walking towards the door. "Tell me, Lexie. Or we're gonna get locked in here for the whole night."

I was known to be tenacious for a reason, and I could see the debate on her face as she turned around and marched towards me. Personal space has not been an issue between the two of us ever since we crossed the milestone of arm-linking, but Lexie, standing less than a feet away in front of me was getting my body wired up for some reason.

"Let me ask you your question then," Lexie retorted. "What was *that* about?"

I was taken aback, awareness finally sinking in that I had definitely played a hand at the unfolding of events. I didn't answer, and that seemed to irk Lexie more than what I did.

Lexie leaned in, just enough to whisper in my ear, "*Play stupid games, win stupid prizes, Adi.*"

Chapter Fifteen
LEXIE

"OH, GOD, what are you doing?!"

Adi quickly stepped away from my space, hearts almost beating out of our chests with the thought of being caught. To both our relief, it was our best friend, Nico, who was at the door, eyes wide open and mouth agape. "Is this a game of dare again?"

I tried stealing a glance at Adi, gauging her reaction. I knew that we didn't do anything wrong, but being caught in that compromising position was just as bad.

She was staring blankly down at her shoes, eyes wide in shock, and face ghostly pale. It sent a pang of guilt in my heart. I knew I should not have given in to her teasing and just ignored her as usual.

I was sure Nico would not tell anyone, but I needed to verbalize it, for Adi's sake more than mine.

"Nico—" I took a step towards him when Adi suddenly dropped on the floor. I rushed to catch her and was shocked when I felt how cold and clammy her hands were. I could see her breathing's getting faster and faster, her face turning a shade of purple. "She's hyperventilating," I called out to Nico. "Grab a brown bag. Hurry."

I saw Nico in my peripheral, rummaging through the room looking for it. I went back to tending to Adi, instructing her to breath through the nose and exhale through the mouth, just as our health class had taught us.

After a few more minutes of reassuring Adi that it was all okay, her breathing was back to normal, color finally returning to her face. She looked around, trying to see where Nico was, and I assured her that I saw him ran outside to see if there were any faculty members at the school to ask for help.

"Are you okay? What's happening?" I asked, trying to figure out what went wrong. Adi looked up at me, eyebrows furrowed with confusion as well. All I wanted to do was wrap my arms around her, to make sure she felt comfortable and safe; to tell her that I was here and would be here as long as she wanted me around.

But I knew it was impossible.

No hope for her to accept me as I was. We didn't even do anything remotely affectionate, yet the horror in Adi's face when we almost got caught, was enough of a proof that she would never do it again. *No alcohol to make as an excuse.*

At best, I knew how to show little to no emotions, but from the realization that I could never be close to the one person I like and show what I truly felt—the visceral pain of a broken heart had me clutching my stomach, ready to run out.

This was the confirmation I needed. My emotions might have been plain on my face as I saw Adi's reaction of hurt when I started moving away from where she sat. I was about to turn away when I felt her hand grab my arm. I crashed against her body with the force as she pulled me towards her.

"Adi, wha—" I didn't get to finish my question as she tightened her arms around me. This wasn't the usual friendly hugs that she does whenever we say goodbye.

This was needy. Greedy. And I poured all my heart and soul as I pulled her closer to me, too.

I am here for you. How ever you want me to be.

Adi pulled away; her face was painted with pain I do not understand. "What's wrong?" I held her face in between my hands. For the longest time in our friendship, this was the first time I was seeing her like this.

"Lexie," she sobbed. "Don't go. Don't leave me alone"

"I'm here," I wanted to console her feelings, even at the expense of my own. She clutched her heart as she stared straight at me, tears pouring endlessly from her eyes.

"I—"

"It's okay, Adi. Take it easy."

"I… I don't know Lexie. What if someone else saw us?"

Oh.

Adi pulled me again and continued sobbing inconsolably on my shoulder. I could feel her breaking in my arms, whispers of her fear repeated over, and over again.

"It's okay, Adi." I wiped her tears; the reassurance ringing true *for her.* "We'll figure it out. We always do, right?" At least, now I did.

I finally realized where I stood with her. I thought I had a chance—hoped that she also saw me in a different light, in a moment of vulnerability. After she dared me for a kiss, something changed. She started becoming playful, borderline flirtatious, stringing me into a game I didn't know I was playing. Until I was lost in the depths of my emotions for her, consumed by the thoughts of her; not knowing I was addicted, until I was looking forward each day to see that smile. But it was a lifeline cut after seeing the fear and the pain in Adi's face with just the thought of being caught.

"No one saw us, aside from Nico," I told her firmly. "Don't worry, *nothing happened.* You don't have to be scared."

Adi gave me a small smile, a reprieve from all the chaos. A privilege I wish I had.

Adi leaned back and closed her eyes, tears finally calming down. "I don't know what to do. I'm scared," she whispered more to herself than me.

"There's nothing you need to do." I stood up and offered my hand to help her. "We just need to go home before six PM. We don't want to get locked in here."

She looked up and took my hand.

With just a smile as her response, she straightened up while pulling my arm to aid her. Not expecting that she'll give me her full weight, she stumbled back in the chair while I was able to stop myself halfway through crashing into her.

Life was really taunting me—dangling the girl I loved in front of me. A few inches away and yet seemed so unreachable.

I have stayed as her best friend and had been loyal to that role. I have never strayed away from my path, knowing the consequences if ever I decide to cross that line. I would never give Adi the burden of knowing my affection for her, knowing that she may never return it. But this. This was too inviting. The universe has been tempting me too much to just come out with my emotions and be done with it.

I straightened up, not liking the pain this closeness was exuding. I offered my hand again, this time ready for her tug.

"We got this, okay? No one saw. It's just us. We didn't do anything wrong." All I wanted was for me to be her safe space, where she would never feel scared, or insecure, or the need to hide. I've known the feeling of being terrified and I never wanted her to experience that alone. "I got you."

"Lexie," Adi whispered as she gazed straight at me, her expression indiscernible. She held my hand, not making a move. "I don't understand *this*. What should I do?"

This. Despite the screaming red flags, my heart still swelled at the hope this possibility was offering. *Was it the same for her?*

We stared at each other, not enough words to explain the weight of what has just been unraveled.

Adi stood up and stepped closer and without any warning, she grabbed my face and pulled it towards her. And the last thing I remembered was her lips against mine.

No more dares needed.

Chapter Sixteen

ADI

ARE WE *still considered best friends if we kissed even without a dare?* A question I should have probably asked before putting myself in this situation. Yet I did not give myself a moment to ponder as my face unconsciously closed the distance between our faces.

Is this really happening? Our lips finally met. And it felt so nothing less but surreal. *What are we now?*

Best friends.

Young girls exploring.

Lovers?

I have kissed more boys after *that* night, merely out of curiosity or to prove to myself that I didn't prefer her lips on mine even if it was just a dare. But always in secret, hoping that the adults would never discover. It was always sloppy and full of slobber, our teeth crashing, and tongues just shoved inside my mouth. I never found the lure of it and wanting to do it again.

Not until now. *This. Nothing will beat this.*

A warm feeling was unfurling from my body to my face, my stomach all jittery. But I was not sure if I was nervous – or excited, finally experiencing and realizing the magic of kissing *her* felt again. My body felt so wired up, my senses hyper focused on Lexie's lips on mine; her gentle grasp on my hips, as her fingers touch a small part of my skin where my shirt must have ridden up.

I pulled away and gazed up at Lexie, hoping to make sense of the emotions that has been overpowering my rationality. I wanted nothing but to be comforted by the warmth and safety of Lexie's arms yet also run as far as away as I could from her touch.

Her arms wrapped around me, holding on tightly as if she was going to break if she let go. She gazed at me, eyes blazed with different emotions. *Why?* She asked me. A question I kept asking myself as well.

Why did I do it? I knew it deep inside that something was brewing yet I continuously pushed it down, knowing that my life would be ruined if I gave in to it. For the years we have been best friends, Lexie has been a crutch I hold on to whenever things go wrong. She had always offered her hand to help, her mind of wisdom, and her heart of acceptance, that I was more than my achievements, potential, and reputation; that I was just a young woman, still trying to figure her shit out in this world. And that was okay.

She gave me a safe space to just *be*.

But to accept that I found comfort in another woman's arms, much so, a person I introduced to my parents as my best friend, would've been considered a great betrayal to the values and beliefs that my kin had so graciously ingrained on me.

Was there going back from this?

The confusion had put tears in my eyes, my heart being split into two different directions. Lexie was so wrong, yet I knew I wanted her so badly. Though I didn't realize *how* I wanted her, not until now. She was a sin I was not sure I was ready to commit. And just like any sin, she was so enthralling that I gave in as soon as she gave me another peck on the lips, savoring the quiet of this moment, and just letting things be.

"Hmm…" Lexie smiled against my lips. And I couldn't help but smile to myself as well, now that both of our hands were revealed. "This is nice." She tightened her arms around me, burying her face on my shoulder, giddiness radiating off her.

I was about to tease Lexie, when the club room door opened with a bang, both of us expecting Nico to be returning as he has been gone for a while already. Us hugging was not a new sight for Nico. He knew how clingy I was, most especially to the both of them.

"Nico, you didn't have to make a grand entrance like that." I was stifling a laugh. I looked up at Lexie's face, checking if she was in on the joke. But her face was nothing but horrified, all the blood drained to paleness.

"Why?" I turned towards the door and saw what Lexie was looking at and it finally dawned on me why she looked so petrified.

"M-mom?"

We were stunned to silence, and no one moved except for my mom who was storming towards us. I could feel my world suddenly crumble down as I saw how infuriated she was. Mom harshly pulled me away from Lexie's grasp, gripping my arms and shaking me so strongly.

"WHAT ARE YOU DOING ADI?!" Mom was shouting at my face. I kept my head down, not daring to face her wrath. I could feel my body starting to tremble and tears blurring my vision.

"Is this what you're doing instead of studying?" She gestured towards Lexie with full of disgust on her face. "What did you do to my daughter?! She would have never betrayed me like this!"

"Mom!" I tried interjecting. "It's not—" I did not see my mom's hand coming in and wasn't prepared for a slap in the face. I should have felt the pain from falling to the floor, but my mind could not register that my mom just hit me. In the face. *Hard.*

Lexie was stunned. I could see her eyes darting between my mom in front of her, and me on the floor sitting. I knew well in my heart that she was about to run towards me, to put herself in between me and my mom. She has always been like that. Selfless. Protective. But before she could take a step, my mom also grabbed her in the arms and yanked her away, farther from me. I could see the vein in her forehead throbbing, as if threatening to pop any moment her anger unleashes.

"What. Did. You. Do. To. My. Daughter?" Mom's grip tightening with every word.

"I-I-..." And even before Lexie could even start her sentence, my mom's hand found Lexie's cheek, a smacking sound rang across the room.

I was frozen, glued to where I was sitting. I wanted to run to my best friend and protect her. But I couldn't even protect myself from my own mother.

"You are an evil person!" Mom shouted at Lexie. "You corrupted my daughter's mind with sin!"

I could see the hand that was going to hit Lexie's face again for the second time, and all I was able to do was shut my eyes and brace for the impact as if I was the one who was going to get hit.

"Mrs. Castillo, please stop that immediately!" An authoritative voice came from the door. "Assault is a part of our zero-tolerance policy and that includes anyone who is in the school vicinity, not just the students and employees."

We all whipped our heads towards the door and saw our Journalism Adviser with Nico trailing behind her. The tension in the air was enough to cut through my skin.

"You're telling me that you are stopping me from hitting the person who sexually assaulted my daughter?" My mom was seething.

Ms. Grace glanced between me and Lexie, quite surprised with the accusation and a questioning look on her face. "Is this true?" She turned towards me who was cowering at the corner of the room. "Did Lexie sexually assault you?"

I stole a glance at my mom and saw the anger that was simmering underneath her skin.

I glanced at Lexie, a look of hope in her eyes.

I drop my gaze into my hands. *A sin I was not ready to commit.*

And stayed silent.

Chapter Seventeen

LEXIE

NEVER TOUCH *my daughter again.* Five words that rang in my head over and over, and over again. I could never imagine how a five-minute interaction between me and Adi could fracture everything we have built together so quickly.

The night concluded with our Journalism Adviser, Ms. Grace, escorting me to the faculty room to protect me from Adi's mom. The rage and anger in her face was enough to convince the adviser that it was not safe for me to stay in there. Adi, on the other hand, was whisked away from me, as far as her mother could.

Ms. Grace was looking at me with concern, repeatedly asking if I was okay. She was holding me up as my body finally gave in from all the stress within the last ten minutes. She sat me over the couch on the faculty room, hesitant to leave me alone. There was nothing I could do but assure her that I would be fine. A few minutes alone to gather my thoughts was the one thing I needed. Ms. Grace stepped out, but not after looking back at me for a minute with eyes full of worry.

"Now, tell me what happened." She handed me a cup of water and hot tea—*to calm the nerves,* she said. Ten seconds of silence passed. No one spoke. I focused my senses on the stale smell of the faculty room, the quiet buzzing of the heating unit, and the warmth of the cup I was holding. I knew in my gut that everything would change after this night. And saying it loud would make it feel more real.

"I have worked with the both of you for the past three years," the journalism adviser started. "And I've seen how you grew into these amazing young women who regard themselves with respect and good moral character, most especially that you are a part of the leadership team of this school."

I had expected this sermon already. I knew that all this talk would eventually lead to us being in the wrong just because we want to express our affections to each other.

"I cannot say that I am not disappointed with the both of you." *Here it goes.* "Sexual acts within the school vicinity are a violation of the code of conduct from our school handbook. But *if* what happened was non-consensual, this will not only violate the school policies, but legal actions could be taken..."

Ms. Grace let the last sentence hang, hoping I would continue to explain and clarify if the incident was indeed a sexual assault. The realization of the repercussions of this evening has finally slammed into my reality.

Adi did not outright deny that I forced myself unto her.

And that leaves a lot up for interpretation.

"No... I," my voice breaking. "I promise I didn't force myself to her. I—We got carried away, Ms. Grace."

The adviser was looking at me with sympathy in her eyes.

"Okay. I would need to talk to Adi tomorrow to get her statement regarding the incident. I will send this report to the principal and discuss course of action," Ms. Grace concluded as she started to stand up. "For now, just don't do anything that will worsen this situation." She gave me the look that I knew what she was talking about.

What would happen to me now?

"Wait for me at the front gate. I'll just grab my car. I'll drive you home."

The fifteen-minute ride to drop me off was surrounded with the most excruciating and suffocating air I had ever experienced. My thoughts swirled with wanting to check Adi to make sure she was okay, and to make sure that things were still okay between the two of us. To know that after this ordeal, we can go back to what we used to be.

A pessimist could still hope, right?

"Alexandria," Ms. Grace called out. "There is no judgment in liking the same gender as you. It is who you are as a person and what you do with your life that makes the difference." She turned to look at the road ahead. "Just be appropriate within school grounds. You have a reputation to uphold within the school community."

With a nod, I walked back home.

WEEKS PASSED with stares and whispers surrounding me.

"Did she really do that to Adi?"

"I knew it! I knew she was a lesbian! I can see how she looks at girls!"

"Ugh! I was changing clothes in the shower room with her!"

I did not have the energy to bother looking at who was gossiping about me anymore. The tone of the conversation was all the same—disgust. As if I did not feel disgusted enough with myself already.

"Hey," Nico was a saving grace, as always. "You want to have lunch at the bleachers? Let's get some sun. I packed some kimchi rice for you. I know it's your favorite!"

I gave him a weak smile, appreciating the optimism he has been trying to share with me.

We walked together towards the oval when we saw a familiar figure sitting at one of the benches already. Nico gave me a side-eye, waiting for a go signal if we should proceed. I nodded, hoping that a neutral person would facilitate any kind of conversation between me and Adi.

Two weeks ghosted. Adi clearly showed where she stood.

"Hi, Adi!" Nico tried to sound as cheerily as he could. "Long time, no see? Have you been avoiding me?" He wanted it to sound as a joke, but Adi's body froze with the question. She looked up and saw Nico, then her gaze turned towards me.

Adi stood up and fumbled with her things as she tried to put them in her bag quickly. "Hey, Nico!" she greeted, scrambling. "No, of course not! I was a bit busy with everything since graduation is around the corner. Oh! I remember that I need to consult something with Mr. Vicenzio about the logistics! See you later!"

We weren't able to do anything but stare at Adi's retreating figure. And to our utter surprise, Sam, one of the basketball varsity players, came up to her and wrapped his hand around hers. They continued walking until the hallway crowd swallowed their figures.

"*What. The. Actual. Fuck?*" Nico's reaction, only a fragment of what I was feeling inside. "What did I just see?" He turned his head to me. "Sam and Adi?! Since fucking when did she go for the jock types?"

I shrugged as I felt my insides squirm with dread. I didn't realize that a heartbreak this great was possible as young as eighteen years old.

"She did not talk to you at all after the incident?" Nico asked again. I slumped and released a sigh. "What are you going to do about this?"

"What is there to do, Nico?" I covered my eyes from the sun's glare. "She drew the line. And I will respect that."

Nico straightened his back and crossed his arms. "*Does she know?*" he asked.

Silence.

Ten seconds passed.

Silence.

"*Does she know?*" Nico demanded.

I finally sat up straight, faced Nico and sighed.

"No," I finally answered.

"She was kissing you!" Nico exclaimed. "I thought you already told her. Was that not a confirmation that she liked you back? Or was I imagining things?"

"She was just playing around, Nico," I mumbled. I was going with the story that she told Ms. Grace. "Just like Halloween night, she was only on it out of curiosity."

An experiment that she had conducted at the expense of my emotions—a variable discarded.

"And I was just trying to scare her at first, by making her think that I was going along with it. I was just really gonna scare her," I explained. "So, she would stop doing this to me. But it backfired."

My heart.

My heart was hurting, and I couldn't keep it bottled anymore. I tried to grab my chest, an attempt to make the visceral pain go away. "But she kissed me, Nico. She kissed me."

I haven't cried since that night. But right now, the overwhelming feeling of hurt and betrayal was far too much to push down. So, I cried. Cried in front of my other best friend because I knew he would understand.

Nico scooted closer and wrapped me in his arms. "But if you saw her reaction after," My voice was trembling. "you would see how scared she was. So scared, that she denied whatever happened right away."

Nico continued rubbing circles at my back. "I'm sorry, Lex. What are you going to do about this?"

I broke away from the hug and wiped my tears. "Nothing," I said with conviction. "She thought it was a mistake so that's how we're going to treat it. A *mistake*." Even saying these words were crushing me inside. I could not force this. If she doesn't want it, I won't force it. I will respect that.

I stood up and walked towards the direction of the school gate. Nico followed suit, not even knowing that I was planning to skip afternoon classes.

"Lex," Nico finally said after a few minutes of walking in silence. "*I'm here.*"

Two words.

Two words that had broken everything inside of me. I turned around and pulled Nico against me. Nico tugged me closer, burying his face on my shoulder, repeating the two words over, and over again, knowing that this was the only consolation we could get from this cruel world.

I'm here. All this time I thought I was alone—not realizing that despite being outed against my will and being accused of sexual assault, there were still people at my back who believed my innocence, supported and loved me as I was.

I cried my eyes out for a good five minutes more, and Nico just patiently stood there as my support. I released one final sigh and pulled away. He offered me a sad, knowing smile. He lifted his hands and wiped my tears away.

"Not everyone will understand us, Lex," Nico started, "but that doesn't mean we don't have a place in this world. We can still be happy in our own little ways."

I smiled at my best friend. "How do you do this?" I asked him. "How can you be so brave?"

Nico held my shoulders and squeezed it.

"We don't have a choice, Lex." Nico started walking again. "The world will eat us alive if we cower to its pressure."

I realized that I haven't given much thought as to what Nico had to go through these past years when he came out as queer in our school. I had always seen him as the energetic, joyful, sunshine and rainbows type of friend in our circle, but I didn't realize that as young as he was, he might be carrying something a lot heavier behind that facade.

"I promise to be a better friend," I said out of nowhere.

Nico glanced at me, as if he knew what I meant. He looped his arms around mine as we walked outside the school.

"But you do know we're cutting classes, right?"

He responded with a laugh. "Anywhere with you, Lex. I'm here."

My heart wanted to burst from gratitude. That despite the shit storm that was happening between me and Adi, I still have my other best friend who continued to be my safe haven.

"Don't go emo on me Alexandria," he said jokingly. "No more tears to shed, no more shits to give. The world may fuck us up for choosing to be true to ourselves, but I promise you, we're gonna fuck them right back."

And that was the first time I had seen him with this expression on his face; a promise, a promise that he would not be bullied into anything. And I could only think of one word to describe my best friend: *Brave*.

And I could only wish I have even half an ounce of the courage and grit Nico had.

I wished I was that brave.

Chapter Eighteen

ADI

TWO MORE weeks before graduation and I would finally be free from the grasps of my mom.

After the incident, I was forced to distance myself from Lexie and Nico, for their own good than mine. It was my fault that we were put in this predicament, and I should suffer the consequences of it, not my best friends.

Best friend. Could I even call Lexie *just* my best friend? I knew there was something different when I was with her. And I only thought it was because we were becoming closer. But I had a wake-up call to rethink my emotions when I saw one of our classmates, flirting with her. And I could still remember the distaste of seeing her wrap her arms around Lexie, even just to tease her. The satisfaction of seeing Lexie swat her away was too good too savor.

Only a few people knew that she was bisexual—that she was still trying to figure herself out. And it wasn't ever an issue in our friendship. Nico came out years before Lexie had decided to talk to us about her sexuality. There was one rule though: *Never tell my parents.* As much as it didn't bother me, my parents were a different story. We all knew how conservative my parents were, most especially my mom. And if she figured out that both of my best friends were queer, let's just say that I wouldn't be the only one who would feel her wrath.

Except as a young woman who was confused with what she was feeling for her best friend, it was a dangerous territory to explore. I always convinced myself that whenever I try to link my arms with Lexie, or that I wanted her eyes only on me, that it was a thing that *super close* friends did, no underlying emotions involved aside from being platonic. But deep down I knew that I was fooling myself.

Two weeks before the incident, we did a slumber party at Nico's place. It was the usual movie night with snacks on a weekend. Except this night, Nico snuck some cans of beer from her parents' fridge, *again*.

We were so excited, as any reckless teenager was. When his parents were finally asleep, we took out one can each and started drinking eagerly. As bitter as it was, we were able to finish the two cans each after a dare that whoever finished last, would be the one responsible to clean everything from our slumber party.

The effects of alcohol easily made its way into my system as I stumbled to the washroom to pee. Lexie, as the ever-reliable friend, assisted me until I was safely in the washroom. She was about to leave when I grabbed her arm and beg her to stay with me. I could feel my inhibitions were starting to lower, feeling more courageous and honest with what I was feeling.

I knew that kiss from Halloween did a number on me, despite the denial that I had been convincing myself.

"Stay," I held Lexie by her arm. "I want you here."

She looked at me, confused at what I was saying. But she stayed and turned around as I started to lower my PJs to take a leak.

"What am I?" Lexie tried laughing it out. "Your assistant? Do you want me to wipe you, my master?"

She stayed facing away, giving me the privacy that I didn't want.

"I like the sound of that," I teased.

I walked towards her back and started trailing down my hands until I reached her hand and grasped it tightly. She turned around in surprise, not expecting me to be less than a feet away. Without a word, I wrapped her around my arms, tightening my hug as I buried my head on her shoulder.

Lexie didn't move for a few seconds, until she wrapped her arms around me too and started drawing circles at my back. "Are you drunk?" she asked with a chuckle.

"I should only be the one who can hug you like this," I told her as I untangled myself, gave her a peck on the cheek, and walked out of the washroom.

We didn't talk about that night after, but I knew something changed between us. It was the same safety and security I felt whenever I was with the group, but whenever it was just the two of us, a charged energy was always surrounding us. But no one made a move. No one disturbed the peace of what we have at that time.

The confusion and chaos inside me were undeniable. I was going against everything that I was taught, and I knew I had to talk to someone I could trust, to unravel whatever this was. Mom was not a choice obviously; dad was always working, and he might tell mom. So, I decided to talk to one of the people I look up to, hoping the trust I was giving this man would not be misplaced.

And that backfired, worse than I thought it would. That was the reason mom came barging in like that at school. That man told my mom, worried that I was being misled by Lexie. That she was leading me into a path of sin and vile.

I kept repeating that night that Lexie did not sexually assault me; that I was the one who made the move. But it was useless, my mom made up her mind that I was brainwashed into thinking I liked girls; that I was a victim. But I knew deep in my heart that she was wrong—that I chose this because that was what I was feeling during that time. And no matter what I said to explain or defend Lexie, it all fell on deaf ears.

And when I needed my dad to at least be the one person to listen to reason, he wasn't anywhere to be found—always working, prioritizing putting food on the table. *'I'm a little tired from work, princess. Let's go to your favorite park this weekend?'* He'd pat my head endearingly, giving me hope that maybe he would listen to me and be on my side. Yet that weekend never came.

I need you more than I need the food on the table, dad.

I explained to Ms. Grace what happened, trying to deescalate the complaint my mom was submitting to the school. I clarified that we were just playing around and got carried away. I didn't mention what really happened, knowing that if I did, it would reveal Lexie's sexuality to the public, and I knew she wasn't ready for that. It was the only consolation I could give out of this mess. And to make it more believable, I even convinced Sam to date me, even just for show—to prove to my parents and the adults around me that I was straight.

And to finally put the nail in the coffin, I bargained with my mom that I would never talk to Lexie again, just to stop her from filing a formal complaint to the school board about Lexie and a request to expel her. She didn't deserve that.

So, I kept my end of the bargain.

To keep her safe, even from myself.

PART III

Alex

Something shattered inside me.

This wasn't supposed to happen.

She felt different.

She felt similar.

Nostalgic.

An evocative representation of how it was supposed to be.

How could she have turned her back on this?

How could she have turned her back on me?

Chapter Nineteen

THE TRAFFIC in Vancouver gave me some buffer to settle my emotions and gather my thoughts. The past week has turned into a circus that I wasn't ready to participate in. After all these years of trying to distance myself from the past, it came barreling out of nowhere towards me like a ten-wheeler truck.

Adi.

I made a promise to myself that once I set foot back here in British Columbia, I would be the cold, stoic, detached woman who was molded by the lessons from the past, if I ever got the chance to meet her again; I promised myself that I would never be vulnerable again, most especially in front of her. But seeing her helpless and in danger last week from that motherfucker who was dragging her *in my club*, I knew something broke inside of me and all I could think about was how to save her because I was not going to fail her again.

I failed to protect Adi from her mom ten years ago—I was a helpless child, navigating the trenches of my unexplored emotions and sexuality caught in a moment of vulnerability and confrontation. But now, I was a grown ass woman who would not let anyone cross her anymore. This was a retribution that I had to pay from my lacking from ten years ago.

I could never forget how terrified Adi was, the moment Mrs. Castillo had hit her in the face, right in front of me. It had haunted me for the last decade. Over and over again, the scene playing endlessly on my mind. The guilt and helplessness I felt became a motivation that pushed me to become the woman I hope I was today, strong and independent. And doing all of these for Adi was to placate the remorse that had been eating me for the last ten years. And now, I had the chance to make it even and let it all go. But that didn't mean I want her back.

Or do I?

A decision has been made, given the events that happened this night. Adi was somehow still the young woman that I left ten years ago—still confused and unsure what she wanted in life, not the wants dictated by society, not by her family—just her wants and needs. And flinging herself to me in a moment of weakness was a repeat of ten years ago. And I wouldn't be caught in that net again.

I could feel the resolve steeling inside me, knowing that the priority would be Adi's safety and after that, no more.

So, first things, first: *Eli*

Eli has been a best friend more than an ex-girlfriend. Our relationship was so short-lived, but I got to know how the woman operated. As different as we were, I found comfort in her carefree outlook in life, and the adrenaline boost from her shenanigans; a break I needed from time to time, away from the numbers and business meetings. But tonight, tonight was different. As much as I loved Eli as a dear friend, I knew it from the three years we have spent together, aside from the parties she couldn't get enough of, one of her weaknesses were meek girls. And I know that was how she saw Adi: a meek girl, ready for an awakening. And judging by what Adi said, Eli had already made her first move.

And Adi made hers as well.

I COULD hear the faint noise of the TV when I opened the door to my apartment, followed by a familiar laugh from the couch.

"I see you've made yourself at home." My voice lacking the usual energy whenever I talked to Eli. I dropped my keys and removed my shoes as I enter the foyer. I went straight to the kitchen to grab myself a glass of wine, *again*. The memories of my lips, exploring Adi's body earlier this evening had me almost spilling the red liquid.

That couldn't happen anymore. I shook my head for clarity. I had to remind myself that it was the main reason why Eli was in my home as well.

"Ohhh," Eli cooed as she got off the couch. "You said you wanted to talk to me, I didn't realize that it'll require us getting drunk." She walked towards the kitchen to grab herself a glass while I went to sit on the couch and turned the volume of the TV down. Eli strode towards the other end of the couch and flopped down enthusiastically.

"I've never seen you this serious before, Alex," Eli said as she sipped her wine. "And that's saying something, knowing how serious you are every single day," she continued teasing. "Would it hurt to smile when you see me?" Eli guffawed as I rolled my eyes in response. "See? Proving my point."

"Seriously, Eli. You know what we need to talk about." An open-ended statement, letting Eli interpret it as she wanted.

"Adi, you mean?" Eli didn't even bat an eye before answering. "Her safety and all that shit from her ex?" She leaned back, relaxing into the couch as she turned her eye to the almost muted TV. A flash of anger had started to escape my composure, seeing how unserious she was.

"Yes and no." Eli turned towards me, confusion on her face. "Yes, we are talking about her safety, but not only that."

This caught Eli's attention and recognition finally dawned on her. "Wait, did she tell you that I kissed her that morning?"

My silence was all the answer she needed. Eli looked agitated. "Come on, Alex. Didn't we have this conversation before?"

We did. After breaking up, we have agreed not to talk about the people we slept with or got involved if we decided to continue as friends. And it was not a problem for me. After Eli, I have not gotten into anything remotely intimate with anyone. But not Eli. It was a hard pill to swallow, but she admitted that I wasn't her type. My coldness and bluntness urged her to pursue me only as a challenge. And I relented because I knew I have *needs* too, but I wasn't the type to sleep around, so I stuck with her. The decision slapped me back in the face when I realized how much of a player Eli was, and I had no one to blame but myself. Ironically, as fucked up as our situation was, something came good out of it; a friend who helped me, in her own way, be more comfortable with who I was.

"This is different, Eli." I doubled down. "I knew her personally. And if you're not planning to be serious with her, stop stringing her along."

Eli scooted closer with a discerning look on her face. "What is this about, Alex? I fucked people you know before, but you haven't given me shit about it." She held my gaze. "Not until now. And to think it was just a fucking kiss."

The perfect question. *Why?* Why was I giving a fuck if Eli was getting involved with Adi.

"You know her situation. I've just told you what her ex-fiancé did to her." Eli just stared at me, waiting to further my explanation. "And stringing her along when she's still healing from her past may break her even more."

It was a pathetic excuse though there was some truth to it. I mostly cared about Adi's well-being and safety. Once everything was sorted out with Eli and she was safe, I would take my hands off and continue as before.

It was my retribution from ten years ago.

After that, I was done.

"Besides…" Eli stood up and started casually walking around the living room while sipping on her wine. "If that was her first time being kissed by a woman, who else to teach her better, right? She seemed a very willing student from what I've seen."

The surge of anger from before had returned ten folds. I stalked to where Eli was standing and grabbed her shirt, fist already balled and was merely waiting for the swing. And instead of looking shocked or frightened from the outburst, she was looking at me tauntingly, as if urging me to go through with the plan. Her nonchalance confounded me, throwing me off balance.

"Go on," Eli sneered. "Punch me, Alex. Beat the shit out of me until you feel better for yourself."

I let go of Eli's shirt and stepped back to take deep breaths and calm myself. I have never been a violent person, and this persona was a new territory for me as well. I've never felt much anger to the point that I wanted to hit someone else.

"Finally got your head together?" Eli seemed so unbothered how out of character my actions were. I nodded and took my seat back. Closing my eyes and leaning my head back, I released a sigh.

"I'm sorry."

The apology went unnoticed.

"What if I choose to pursue her? Will you intervene, Alex?" I propped my head up and looked at Eli. She held my gaze as she continued, "What if I win her over, and she becomes my girlfriend, will you have a say in it?"

No. No, I won't. If Eli straightened her ways and chose to pursue Adi, I would not have a say in it. I knew it would be the best outcome from what I had planned. As soon as I ensured her safety and she's in good hands, I would step away. My self-imposed debt would be paid.

I had promised myself for the past decade that I would not make the same mistakes again—and that mistake included Adi. She said she wanted to make amends, and the best I could offer is friendship, nothing more. What happened hours ago was a mistake on my part; a weakness that I easily gave in. No more of that. No more replays.

Eli placed her wine glass on the coffee table and stood up, distracting my musing. "You really are stubborn." She sighed and started grabbing her coat.

"Eli," I finally called out to her. "No, I wouldn't get involved if you choose to pursue her. Just be good to her and keep her safe."

Eli stared at me for a few seconds before taking the steps towards the door.

"Seriously, Alex," Eli opened the door and started stepping out. "When will you start being honest with yourself?"

Chapter Twenty

FIVE DAYS have passed since my conversation with Eli. I had not heard from her, neither from Adi. *Not that I was waiting for it.* And as far as what Scar had shared, Adi had been staying with Amanda for the past week while Eli has been picking her up here and there to drop her off at work. *It was the better outcome than I have wished for.* Eli has a habit of not being seen with the same woman more than twice and given what Scar told me, it seemed that Eli was really straightening her act out for Adi.

It was the best-case scenario. *So, why am I feeling like shit?*

Closing the lid of the rabbit hole that was constantly taunting me for the past weeks, I stepped out of my office and was greeted with the sound of *Club Tala* in full house. Before I could even sit on my usual, a glass of wine was already waiting for me. Scar gave me a wink as she tended to the customers. The seat was towards the end of the long bar, giving me a good visual of the customers at the bar and people at the dance floor, too. A stained-glass separated the two sections, muting a bit of the sounds, allowing the people at the bar to make conversations without shouting at anyone's ear.

I couldn't believe it has almost been more than three weeks when I first saw Adi again in this very club. *My club.* At first, I didn't know how to proceed, seeing the person who had broken my heart as young as I was. Yet I know I have to thank her for that. Without her betrayal, I wouldn't be in this place in life.

As much as I hated myself for it, I knew I had to cut contact with Nico as well when I left Vancouver. For the reason that if I didn't, I knew I would keep tabs, always wondering what she was doing, how she was, or who she was with. And that was torture in itself.

Nico, as the gracious and understanding friend he always was, accepted my reason without forcing me to explain myself. He knew that moving to a different province for university was merely a justification to get away and I was not even sure if he knew the full reason why.

Before I left, I simply told him that Adi would need him more than I did, and I would contact him once I was ready. I lost ten years with Adi but the grief of losing my other best friend was something I carried, too. So, as soon as I went back to British Columbia, he was the first person I asked to meet. And it has become a weekly thing to catch up and make up for lost time. He had always asked if he should tell Adi that I was back and I always answered, *not yet*. But after asking for the millionth time, I finally said yes, a few weeks ago. He was ecstatic and was so excited to bring Adi. However, he made it clear that it didn't mean I had to meet her; only if I was ready to talk again.

Nico knew how that the incident ten years ago had scarred and made me feel so uncomfortable, even in my own skin. And thinking that I was going to see the person who left me all alone, when I was willing to give her my all, *even outing me*—it was as if the scared young woman was back, trembling and scared of her own identity.

I took a gulp of my wine. *You are not that person anymore. It's a wonder how I had to remind you this affirmation more often these past few weeks.* I scolded myself internally.

"Lex!" Nico was waving his hands as he walked towards our usual seats. "Sorry, I got caught in the rush hour traffic. Or Friday night traffic. This place is packed!" He gave me a peck on the cheek and a crushing hug.

We stared at the dance floor together while he was waiting for Scar to fix his drink, a comfortable silence lingering between us.

This was what I liked with Nico—there were no pressures, no expectations, even when we were back in high school. He was always there to support me, even if I knew I haven't been good enough to him. And I promised myself to change that.

"So…" Nico started. "How are you? I haven't been able to catch up with you after the incident." We cancelled our supposed meet up last week, given the circumstance that we were in. "I didn't know Damien would go to the lengths of taking her, even in public, just to get her to come back home."

The flashback of seeing Adi being dragged by a stranger flashed in my mind again and I sensed a tinge of rage and panic that I felt on that night. It was good that we were able to report the incident on that night. At least a record of the incident existed if ever shit hits the fan again.

Yet the unspoken question hung in air. "I didn't know she was engaged. You didn't tell me?"

Nico's gaze visibly softened. It was as if he was already expecting the question when he mentioned Damien's name.

"I wasn't sure if you wanted to hear it," Nico started. "When I asked if you wanted to meet Adi, and you said no, I assumed that you were not ready to hear anything about her yet." Nico has a point—and was prioritizing my well-being again.

"You're right," I finally said.

"As much as I want to tell you about Damien, I'd rather you ask her. It's her story to tell." The disdain in his face was too obvious even if he tried to hide it. "But just ready yourself with whatever you will hear."

Was it that bad? My thoughts went back to the confrontation I had with Adi's ex-fiancé last week. Seeing his aggressiveness and how Adi was inadvertently protecting herself, it might be worse than bad. "Is she okay now?"

Nico shared that it was a good distraction that Adi was going back to work already, and Eli has been picking her up at work. He tried making it sound as nonchalantly as he could, but I knew he let the last sentence hang for a few seconds before continuing, "She had started settling in Amanda's living room which is becoming a problem because her sex life is the one suffering." He laughed.

"You know, Eli offered," Nico continued as he took the last sip of his beer. "Adi said she will think about it. But she asked, or more likely forced Eli to stop picking her up from work. She said Eli no longer mentioned the offer to stay at her place, but he still insisted on picking her up from work"

This was surprising. I thought that after the conversation with Eli and knowing Adi had already consented to being intimate with her, *at least what Eli had smugly implied* that the relationship would

139

progress.

"You know, she's still trying to figure herself out." Nico had a contemplative look on his face. "You know how her mom was, and that continued until recently. She only allowed Adi to move out with the premise that she was going to try and actively date to find a man to marry. And living with her parents was not a good impression in western date culture. It was all bullshit, but her mom relented after long conversations of having grandchildren soon."

How ignorant I was, to assume that it would get easier for Adi once she was old enough.

"She had a few boyfriends here and there," Nico continued. "But nothing too serious, not until Damien. She got out of her place and moved in with him in a matter of months." A dark reaction crossed his face. "Believe it or not, within the ten years from the time you left, Adi had never mentioned that there was a possibility that she was queer. Not until last week, after meeting Eli…" He stared at me. "After meeting you, *again*."

I felt a tug in my heart and an emotion I was so familiar with: *Hope*. Yet I intended to crush it down before it even rooted.

I gave Nico a knowing look.

"I'm done, Nico." I gulped the last bits of my wine. "I am never going back to that." A flare of resentment that I haven't allowed my younger self to feel, spurred in my gut.

"Did she tell you?" Nico gave me a curious look. "Why people stopped talking to me? Why our classmates said I was disgusting?"

He shook his head. "I heard rumors. And only knew that you were outed."

"Her mom told Ms. Grace that I sexually assaulted her." The memory was as clear as a day. "And she didn't deny it. She stayed quiet, Nico. It didn't even matter that she was the one who kissed me first. She stayed quiet."

And her silence was my ruin.

Nico looked torn apart with the revelation. "Why didn't you tell me, Lexie? I knew the rumors about you being gay had spread like wildfire at school, but I didn't know that they were telling that stuff because they thought you did… *that*." He stood up and wrapped his arms around me tightly. "I should've known. We could've cleared it all out."

No. I am done. "No, Nico." I stepped away from his grasp. "It was how it's supposed to be. She finally made me see where she stood. And that was what I needed to be able to move away."

He gave me an understanding nod.

I knew out of all the people, Nico was the one who would understand me the most. "And see? I have learned. And *Club Tala* might've not existed if it wasn't for that incident."

"But are you okay now? Knowing that she's within your circle, possibly dating your best friend?"

"I am not the same person as before, Nico." I gave Nico a self-assured grin. "She told me that she was going to make it up to me. For whatever happened. But I'm not really expecting anything. She can do what she wants, and I'll do what I want. Besides," I nudged him playfully. "You're my favorite best friend now."

"I'll hold you to that!"

I would be forever grateful for having Nico as my best friend. He knew this was a topic that still haunted me, so he didn't push it anymore. The laughter died down and the conversation about Adi was left at that.

Nico left for the dance floor while I asked for Scar for another glass of wine. "Rough night, boss?" she asked as she handed me the glass.

I shook my head. "Just trying to remove the stick up my ass and hopefully have some fun tonight." Scar chuckled. "Do you mind? I've finished up the sales sheet from the past quarter. We could talk about it on Monday. We might need to hire more people if my numbers are correct."

Scar gave me a go signal to not be an employer for the night. "I'll be at the VIP section. Please send me a bottle."

The VIP section was situated on the second floor, tucked away in the darker corners of the club, for patrons that wanted a more secluded experience. Not that it was meant for indecency but for people who did not want to, or not ready to be seen just yet. But it gave me the view of the whole dance floor while being hidden by the shadows.

A sense of fulfillment purred inside of me, knowing that I have built this from the ground up with the mission that it'll be a safe space for queer people to be just themselves. I looked around and I could see different types of people, all beautiful in their little outfits, dancing to the DJ's music, as if an entire entity of their own.

I was lost in my thoughts, just people watching while sipping the red liquid in my glass, until a silhouette of a woman blocked my view. I redirected my gaze to her, trying to figure out if I knew her.

"Summer," I finally called out. "To what do I owe the pleasure of your company?" The formality, a mockery of our love-hate relationship.

"I was wondering why the owner of this very lively club," Summer stepped into the booth, settling a few feet away from me. "…was melancholic and all alone in a VIP booth."

"I'm not alone," I clarified. She teased by gesturing at the empty space beside me. "My best friend is on the dance floor… doing gods know what."

She chuckled.

"Then, you wouldn't mind if I join you while waiting for him to return, right?" Summer has been upfront with her attraction to me, and I've always thwarted her attempts. But instead of stopping, she said it made her want me more.

A repeat of Eli was what I always thought. She mostly stayed respectful of my decision, and this dynamic had started an inside joke between us.

"If I said no, would you stay away?" The coldness in my voice, a pun.

"No, it'll make me want to stay more." For some reason, this made me laugh.

"Oh, you find me funny now, Alex? That's progress." She smiled sweetly.

Summer stayed in the booth but kept her distance. Both of us now, watching the people dance. I sneaked a glance at her, the lights playing on her face. If I was going to be honest, people would probably jump at the chance to be with Summer. She was the perfect fit for the conventional beauty standard this society has imposed. Dark, wavy mane reaching just the top of her lower back, her tight little black dress accentuating all the right parts and her bare back tempting me to run my fingers along her spine just to see how she would arch her back and ask for more.

I've always thought that her asking me out was some part of a joke, but maybe tonight was the night I could try and see.

"Are you objectifying me?" I didn't realize that she had caught me staring. "Finally liking what you see, Alex?" she teased with a coy smile.

I do like what I see. What was stopping me from taking it when it was offered to me in a silver platter?

Adi? I gave a middle finger as an answer to my inner voice. I had to remind myself what I had told Nico a while ago. Adi was free to do whatever or *whoever* she wanted, and I, the same. If she wanted to be with Eli, I wasn't going to stop that, so why would the thought of her stop me from doing what I wanted, too. Right?

Chapter Twenty-One

THE AIR in the booth was filled with a teasing tension, ready to pounce if one gave in. I turned my body towards her, inviting her in. "What if I said yes, Summer? What would you do?"

I could play this game. I thought to myself.

I don't have to abide by anyone's rule but mine.

Go on, convince yourself, until you actually believe that. If my inner monologue had a physical body, my fist would have a buddy to play with.

The mental battle with my inner monologue was squashed when Summer scooted closer, reaching over and running her hand along the open buttons of my shirt, right down at the middle of my chest. Before she continued lowering her touch, I grabbed her hand, and pulled it closer to my face, smelling the scent of vanilla off her skin.

No one's stopping you. I told myself. *Go on and play.* The permission I had to give myself to reinforce the wall that has started to crumble ever since Adi came back into my life.

"Sweet," I whispered across her skin. *I know how to play this game well.* I looked at her face, her mouth slightly opened, as if entranced. She closed the remaining gap, the distance barely existing between our thighs.

I dipped my face closer, moving her hair away and letting my lips linger on the nook of her shoulders. "Hmm… seems sweeter here." I could feel her body giving in to my touch, her head thrown to the side, as if to give me more access.

I turned her face towards mine, and I repeated my question against her lips, *"What would you do, Summer?"*

Summer smiled seductively and grabbed both sides of my neck. "I'll make you forget." She held my gaze and continued, "why you were even sad in the first place."

Before I could even react to what she had said, Summer crashed her lips against mine, making me put aside the emotion her statement had stirred. She forced my lips open, hungry for what I could give. And I let her. I let her devour me, like a person who was starved to death. I lifted her to my lap, making her little black dress scoot higher up her thigh. She smiled arrogantly, knowing I could see her lace underwear.

"You can take that off if you'd be good to me tonight," she purred.

I grabbed her hips tightly, pressing it again my groin. "Oh, my little hussy, you're wrong." I traced my lips on her collarbones, hovering on the ample cleavage her little black dress offered. "By the end of the night, you will be begging me to take everything off." I sucked a little mark, leaving it for everyone to see. "Are you sure you want that?"

Summer looked at me from under her lashes, the warmth of lust radiating off her skin. "And if I said *no*, Alex? Would you leave a beautiful woman to fend for herself?"

An icy feeling snuck in my gut, making me want to throw Summer from my lap, and make a run for it. *Not this again.*

Summer saw the change in my face and immediately tried taking back what she said. "I'm just playing, Alex." She grabbed my face to look at her. "I went to this booth willingly to shoot my shot, *as always*." She traced her lips slowly across mine, sucking my lower lip before continuing. "I wasn't expecting anything to happen. And this…" She coaxed my mouth open, giving me a deep sensual kiss. "is more than I could ask for."

Summer guided my hand, tracing her body. From her shoulders to her breasts, to the curve of her hips until she stopped on her inner thigh. "If it wasn't clear enough for you," she inched my hands closer to her core. "Yes, I want this to happen." She threw her head back as I caressed her inner thigh, the pool of wetness starting to seep into my pants. I looked around to see if anyone had paid attention to what was happening, but we were blanketed by the darkness as the disco lights playing were now focused on the dance floor.

I touched her core lightly, feeling the throbbing clit against the lace. "Tell me again," I commanded as I gently caressed her center.

Summer was so lost in the moment, her eyes unseeing but with lust. I grabbed her lower back and pulled her closer, her clit pushing harder against my hands. The movement startled her, her eyes clearing for just a moment.

"Tell. Me. Again." I reiterated against her lips.

"Yes," she whimpered. "I want this."

I lifted Summer up from my lap, the action confusing her as she woke up from her daze. I started walking away.

"Alex!" she tried shouting above the loud music. When she was finally able to catch up, I was already walking across the dance floor, the quickest way to the office.

Summer grabbed my hand and turned me around. "What the fuck, Alex! You're gonna leave me like this?" The dancing bodies pushed us against each other; her whole body pressed against mine.

I lowered my head until my mouth was dangerously close to her ears. My hands, barely hovering above her ass. "I didn't say I would." My warm breath giving her chills. "You wouldn't want me to fuck you when there are people around." I moved away to look at her face.

Summer, as stubborn and strong headed as she was, gave me a challenging look. I raised my eyebrows at her. "Or do you?"

She smiled knowingly, pulling me closer so now her lips are at my ears. "I'd like you to fuck me out of my wits in front of whoever's making you this miserable. So, she can see what's she's actually missing."

Oh. The feeling of proving that I was no longer affected by Adi had me grabbing Summer's hands, dragging her towards my office. I have never been the one to mix business with pleasure but something about Summer's taunting made me cross that boundary. It was as if she was triggering a side of me that wanted to rebel against the idea that someone has the power to make me say no to whatever she was offering. And that didn't sit well with me.

I have needs, too.

I walked towards the couch and sat, leaving Summer in the middle of the room. "Well, do you want to continue, or are you just gonna stand there?"

She smirked at me as an answer.

She stalked towards the couch, slowly lifting her black dress over her head. I raised my eyebrow as I saw what was underneath, or the lack thereof. "No bra tonight?"

She answered with a smirk as she climbed on my lap, grabbed my hands and guided it to caress her naked body. I could feel her body starting to shiver as I ran my lips across the center of her chest; her fingers tangled in my hair, pulling me closer.

I drifted my mouth towards one of her breasts, while my other had started descending to the wetness that was asking to be satiated. Slowly and softly, my fingers traced her hips to her thighs, goosebumps rising at the almost-touch. My fingers lingered to her inner thigh, rubbing circles, accidentally touching her core here and there, but not fully giving her the satisfaction of it just yet.

I sucked the flesh of her breast, leaving the existing mark darker than it already was; that will surely not fade for a few days. And I knew she liked it, the wetness in between her thighs, a testament to it.

Summer pulled my hair to force me to look up to her. "I'm getting impatient, Alex."

I merely answered with an innocent smile.

I started rubbing her clit against the lace, giving more friction, her hips automatically grinding against my hand. A loud moan escaped Summer's lips, but I wasn't worried. The volume of the music would drown all the noises from this room. Her hips started grinding faster, racing towards the peak that was starting to build. I could feel her body almost buckling when I removed my hands.

Summer's gasps echoed across the room. She looked at me with an almost annoyed look. "What the fuck, Alex! I was almost there."

"I know. We've not started yet, though." I removed her from my lap, walked towards my desk, and started removing the clutter. Once I was done, I stole a glance at Summer, pouting like a child on the verge of throwing a tantrum.

"Come," I beckoned. "Come here and bend over."

Summer's eyes widened with curious excitement. And like a good girl, she bent over, her ass up in the air, everything for me to see. I started stroking her ass, skirting towards the lace of her panties.

I pressed my fingers against her clit and started rubbing it in circles. I could see her fingernails digging into the desk, and grinding against my hands, slowly but surely, buckling into the pinnacle of her release. And before she could recover, I thrusted two fingers and started the rhythm for another peak.

"Fuck!" Summer gasped.

I grabbed her long, black hair, as I plunged deeper and deeper until Summer was writhing on top of my desk, unable to move and high with the ecstasy of her orgasm. The feeling of power thrummed in my veins as I slowly pulled my fingers out, the evidence of her orgasm dripping in my hands.

I went on the other side of my table to sit on my office chair, giving me a view of Summer's post-coital face. She was drenched in sweat, her eyes laced with bliss, still trembling. "Look at you," I showed her my fingers. "So needy. We didn't even come to remove everything you're wearing." I smiled innocently as I tucked her hair behind her ears. I took out hand wipes and was about to start cleaning my hands when she grabbed my hand and slowly sucked the fingers that was just inside her.

I was startled. An uncurling feeling started to bloom on my groin as the feeling of suction and her tongue playing with my fingers call to a need that I haven't satiated in a while.

Summer smiled knowing what she was doing.

Deliberately slow, she laid on her back and started caressing her body until her hand reaches the space between her thighs. And I couldn't lie, this view? I wouldn't mind seeing this again.

It was the distraction I needed.

She started building the rhythm, finally pulling my face on hers as she worked on her release. Her moans against my lips were a taunt to my need. If this wouldn't stop, I might need to go home early and string along this woman who was deliciously naked on top of my table.

But I knew Scar would not approve. *And of course, she wouldn't either.* I pushed down the thought and the face that had appeared in my mind, dampening the arousal that had almost made me make an impulsive decision.

I was still a professional after all, and this was a place of business. So as soon as Summer finished, I pulled myself away and started cleaning hands up.

Summer was still splayed on top of my table, a half naked mess and still weak to stand. "Do you need help?" I motioned her to come over to my side, so I could clean her up. She obediently strode and stood in front of me.

"Remove your panties, so we can clean you up properly."

Summer removed her lace underwear and handed it to me. "Take it as a souvenir." She smirked playfully. "For being the gentlewoman that you are, helping me with the post-clean up. You are a rare breed." She chuckled.

I started wiping her vaginal area, removing the wetness that has started running down her legs. A shudder ran across her body as I wiped her clit clean. It was obvious that she was trying to stand up as steady as she could, fighting the urge to fold as the rhythmic movement kept her tethered to her peak.

"One more?" I asked innocently. Summer opened her eyes and looked at me, as if caught doing something naughty. "Greedy much." I chuckled before I rubbed her clit again, her hands gripping my hair as a shaky breath escaped her lips. Her body trembled for another orgasm, her knees almost giving up on her.

"Fuck. Fuck. Alex!"

I caught her just by her pits, her whole-body weight giving in to me. When I realized she couldn't even stand, I picked her up and carried her over to the couch.

"The stereotypes were right. The quiet ones are always the best." She smiled weakly. "I don't think I've ever cum as much in a quickie."

I laugh quietly in response, not believing a single word the woman said. "I just know what I want, and how I want to do it." I gave her another set of wipes to clean herself up and handed over her black dress. "Going commando for the rest of the night?"

Summer grinned mischievously before shimmying down her black dress. I walked over to the locker at the corner of my office, pulling out new pants.

"You're ready for this kind of night, huh?" Summer teased as she fixed her hair and make-up. I didn't answer. I didn't tell her that it was for nights that I needed to sleep at the office because as what Scar had told me, *a workaholic boss.*

I was waiting by the door as she finished fixing herself up, trying to look less disheveled from sex. "Is there a chance we can have a yes, for a second time?" I only smiled at her before opening the door. "And maybe I can repay the good services I received tonight?"

"Ale—," I stopped midway from stepping out of the office.

Adi was standing outside my office, hands raised, ready to knock. We were silent for a few seconds, just staring at each other.

"*Oooh, is that her?*" Summer innocently asked while holding on to my arm. I almost forgot she was with me and what we have done just a few minutes ago.

"Hi, I'm Summer. Nice to meet you." She extended a hand towards Adi.

Adi reluctantly took it. "I'm Adi." I could see Adi's eyes darting from the arms that were clutching mine, and the kiss mark that was visible on Summer's chest.

And as if Summer didn't know how to read a room, *or maybe she does so well,* she turned and pulled me down to her height, then gave me the most explicit make out session. "Tonight was fun. Let's do that again, soon." She smiled knowingly at me, as if we were in on a secret that I don't even know.

Summer then gave a small *oh, sorry about that,* acknowledging Adi's presence, before sauntering into dance floor, not a care in the world. Adi was just standing in front of me, looking awkward and confused.

"Adi," I cleared my throat. "You were looking for me?" I could see in my peripheral that Scar was watching the events unfold. I knew she'll give me a lecture later after seeing a woman with after-sex-glow coming out of my office.

"Uh…" Adi seemed lost for words. "I wanted to talk to you…

151

but it seemed like you're busy."

"What do you want to talk about?" I was curious. We didn't have anything to discuss anymore. Knowing Eli's taking care of her, I could just ask for any updates from the friend group. *Not that I needed to.*

"I didn't know you had a girlfriend." I didn't. But I didn't bother correcting her either. Let her think whatever she wanted.

I stayed quiet, using the awkward silence to urge her to continue.

"I... I wanted to talk to you about something, but it doesn't matter anymore."

She started to walk away, her reaction leaving a bitter taste in my mouth. I ran after her, grabbing her by the arms to stop her. "Adi! Wait!"

"What?" Hurt was painted across her face. *Hurt? Why the fuck is she acting like this?*

"What?" I asked her back. My temper flaring. "You came to my office, saw me with a woman and acted like you were upset or something. I should be asking *you* the questions."

Adi looked at me as if I just stabbed her in the heart. Her emotions laced with pain and her voice quivered as she tried to speak. "You should've told me."

"Told you what?" My patience was running thin.

"That you were seeing someone else." She seemed genuinely hurt. "Or at least sleeping with someone else."

I didn't realize that this was the straw that would be breaking the camel's back.

"Yeah, like when you told me you kissed my best friend before climbing on top of my lap and removing your clothes?" Adi looked like I slapped her, but that didn't stop the emotion that made its way to my mouth, from enduring the impact of *that* one single accident, for years. "Or the fact that you know you wanted me to fuck you and deny it the second someone else knows?"

Her eyes widened, tears threatening to burst.

This was it. The snap that I was trying to prevent for the longest time. And like every build up, I couldn't stop it anymore.

"You're mad that I fucked her? Why? At least she didn't deny me even when there were people around. Can you say the same? Or are you still the coward that you are? Hiding behind your perfect mask, afraid to go against the current, even at the expense of losing yourself." I took a step closer, towering over her shaking body. I knew that I should stop, but the dam had burst and there was no stopping the emotions that had built up for the ten years that haunted me over and over again. "You tell me you've changed but tell me, do you still quiver at the thought of being seen with a woman? Do you still stay silent, even if it meant ruining other people's lives?"

"I'm not!" Her voice shook, but she didn't back down or walk away; her insolence a reminder of what I loved about her before.

The realization of my thoughts had me letting out a sardonic laugh, feeling pathetic that I was reminiscing a moment in my life where I wasn't even accepted as who I was.

"Okay then, I dare you, Adalia." I took another step, mere inches separating us from each other. "Kiss me."

She looked up at me from under her lashes, and the fool that I was, thought that she was finally going to do it. A smile almost reached my lips when she stole her glance away and looked at the floor.

"Please, don't do this Alex." A whisper of plea. "This is unfair."

My temper flared again. *Unfair? Who was she to tell me that this is unfair?*

"You know what's unfair?" I grabbed her chin to make her look at me straight in the eyes—for her to understand the depths of the scars that I have to carry just to heal and be able to move on. "Turning your back on me when I needed you the most."

I released her face and started walking away, stopping the urge to spare her even a single glance. And even before I could reach the office, I felt a hand grabbed my arm, halting me in my tracks. I looked at the owner and saw Scar's disappointed look.

"You are such a piece of shit, Alexandria"

As if I didn't already know.

Chapter Twenty-Two

I KNEW I fucked up. Scar didn't need to reiterate that.

"Was that really necessary?" Scar closed the door behind her then turned towards me.

"Shouldn't you be manning the bar?" I ignored the question. I'd rather not have this conversation now, when all of my thoughts were still in a disarray. I couldn't shake the feeling of guilt as I remember Adi's face, almost crying.

Scar huffed and plopped at the couch. "The night's dying down, and Rey's up on the counter. It's part of his training." She made a disgusting voice and abruptly stood up. "Ugh. Please don't let me know what I just sat on."

I put my head in my hands, trying to get a hold of myself and the emotions that were swirling inside of me. Everything was at war. I wanted to run to Adi and assure her that Summer was nothing, but the logical part of me was putting her foot down that I could do what, or *whoever* I want.

Why would I even need to explain myself to her when she was with Eli?

"I know she had hurt you before," Scar pried my hands out of my face. "And you promised yourself that you would never put yourself in the same position again." She walked around the table to put her hands on my shoulders. "But that doesn't mean you have to be a piece of shit about it. You told me she's going through a lot right now. Will it hurt you to be kinder?"

A flicker of the anger that I had suppressed long before, had started clawing itself out to the surface. I thought that I had gotten over it—healed over it. Yet as soon as Adi came back in my life, the wounds have started bleeding again.

"Tell me, Scar." I stood up and started pacing. "Did she show me the same kindness when she abandoned me before? When the school started talking about us, me? When her mom had spread rumors that I sexually assaulted her daughter?"

Scar looked at me with pity in her eyes.

"Not once, did I hear her stand up for me, or clarify the situation. I had to go to school, every fucking day, as a pariah." I haven't cried since the day we saw Adi held hands with Sam. I promised myself that I would not cry for anyone again anymore but now, I could feel the tears brimming in my eyes, ready to spill. "Nico was gods sent. If it wasn't for him, I don't know how I could've survived until graduation."

Scar enveloped me in a tight hug. The only kindness she could offer me right now. "Hey," she whispered softly. "You always told me that if it wasn't for that incident, you wouldn't be the person you are today, and you wouldn't have what you have today." She smiled at me affectionately, trying to comfort the sadness that was starting to take over. "At least, you have me now." And gave me a wink.

I chuckled. The most unlikely friendship almost, always, were the best.

I let go of her and started fixing myself. "I am grateful for what I have right now, Scar." I ran my fingers through my hair, the exasperation still visceral. "But that doesn't take away the pain that I suffered. And that doesn't give her the right to rub it in my face and act hurt, as if she wasn't the one who left me alone when I offered my heart to her."

Scar shook her head with an amused smile on her face. "Yes, boss. You were young and stupid." She reached out a hand to me. "But you've learned. And now you're here."

I smiled back at her as I grabbed her hand and made our way towards the door.

"Still stubborn, though."

I smacked her arm. "Just like you?"

She merely shook her head. "Still. Very. Stubborn."

DAYS HAVE passed since the night with Summer, and I drowned myself with work and meetings with potential business partners in an attempt to venture to another business on top of *Club Tala*. It was the perfect distraction I needed to stop myself from overthinking and spiraling over the incident with Adi.

It has been days, and I still have not heard from her, nor Eli. *Again, not that I was waiting for it.*

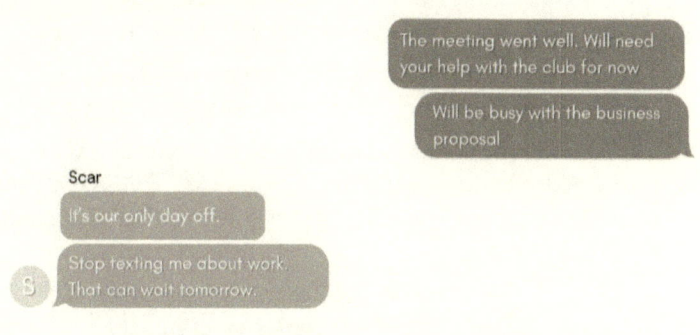

The meeting went well. Will need your help with the club for now

Will be busy with the business proposal

Scar

It's our only day off.

Stop texting me about work. That can wait tomorrow.

I dropped my keys at the foyer and plopped into my couch. I grabbed my phone to shoot a quick text to Scar.

A few seconds passed with the three dots on my screen. My phone beeped again.

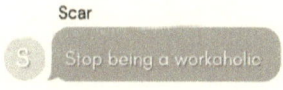

Scar

Stop being a workaholic

A chuckle escaped my lips. I really found the most unexpected friendship with Scar. She always kept me grounded when I start to get overwhelmed with work, and taking over until I could recover. She always told me that she wouldn't be here if it wasn't for me and she would never forget her life debt, but I think it was the other way around. We met each other when we both needed to be saved.

But Scar's right. We only get a day out of the week, might as well make use of it.

I looked around the apartment to check if there was anything I needed to do. My bedroom was mostly untouched, given that I rarely sleep on it, but my office was the other way around. Papers were strewn all over, notes on the wall and books scattered all over. I grabbed a trash bag and started tidying up. I have just started arranging my books when the doorbell rang.

Huh? I looked at my watch. *Two in the afternoon. I wasn't expecting anyone to come over. I didn't order anything either.*

I walked over to the door and peeked at the peep hole. *Huh.* I opened the door.

"Eli, what are you doing here?"

"What a way to welcome me," Eli said with indifference. "No hi or hello?" She stepped inside, not waiting for the invitation.

"Well, I didn't know you were coming over." I closed the door and followed her to my living room. "So, color me surprised."

Eli looked at me, frustration evident on her face. "When are you gonna pull your head out of your ass, Alex?" *Excuse me?* "This has been going on for too long. Your stubbornness is not cute anymore."

I was at a loss for words. The audacity of this person to come into my house, to just call me stubborn. Not even explaining what she was talking about.

Oh, I think you know. My inner voice whispers. *You use your ignorance as a shield from the chaos this torment has been inflicting on your 'well-protected' inner peace.*

Fuck you. Not you, too.

"Okay, tell me then." I sighed. "Tell me what I am being stubborn about, that you have to come all the way, in my own house, just to call me names."

Eli ran a hand through her already-messy hair. She plopped down on the couch and looked at me with a seriousness that I have not seen before. "Adi."

I knew Eli was going to say it, but I never expected that her name alone would start a crack in the façade that I have been wearing.

"Why?" *Did she come over here, just to brag about her girlfriend?*

"Haven't I told you that I wouldn't intervene? Haven't I told you to just keep her safe? And you're free to do whatever you want?" I stalked closer to her. "I kept my end of the deal. You never heard me speak about your relationship again, so why are you here?"

I tried hiding the contempt in my voice, masking the havoc that had kept me up for the past few days. Adi had hurt me, more than anyone in my life. She made me feel disgusted of myself, second-guessing myself and my actions ten years ago. At one point, I even questioned myself if I really forced myself to her, her mom's words ringing on my ears, haunting me until the only thing I could do was run away. The feeling of safety and comfort was stripped away from me, even from my own skin and mind.

Was this another rerun to remind me?

Eli sighed and pulled me down to sit with her on the couch. "You know that I love you, right?" She grabbed one of my hands and started rubbing circles with her thumb. "I've never seen you so miserable, Alex. In fact, I've never seen two people so miserable."

I was caught by surprise. "What do you mean?"

"Just talk to her, man," she said while shaking her head. As if she has lost sleep, solving this problem.

"You are telling me," I snatched my hand away and tried maintaining the calm in my voice. "That *your girlfriend* is miserable, because I am not talking to her?"

Eli was about to nod but then scrunched her eyebrows, as if confused. "Huh? What do you mean girlfriend?"

My patience was running thin, and I didn't need anyone rubbing it in my face that my best friend was now dating my first love. And in my house. This was more than I could tolerate

"Did you come here to rub it in my face then," I reiterated. "That you're now dating Adi?"

Eli ran a hand across her face. "Man, do you hear what you are saying?" She stood up and started pacing. "Damn, Alex. I have known you to be the smart one. But why are you insisting on being so stupid right now?"

So, we're continuing with the name calling. Eli might have seen the reaction in my face. She quickly added. "Do I need to spell it out to you? I. Am. Not. Dating. Adi, Alex."

I was stunned. Out of all the things, I wasn't prepared to hear this from Eli's mouth. I was ready to accept a reality that they were together.

"What do you mean you're not?" I stared at her, the impatience winning over. "I was told that you even offered her your place. You were picking her up and dropping her off at work. So, tell me, isn't that you, dating her?"

An unexpected smug grin flashed across Eli's face. *A very punch-able face right now.* "So, you are keeping tabs, huh?"

I couldn't answer. I stalked towards the kitchen and grabbed a bottle of water. The flashes of emotions with this confrontation were starting to drain me. Eli followed me, quietly grabbing a can of pop from the fridge as well.

I stared at her, deadpan as if asking, '*Really?*'.

"What?" she asked while opening the can of pop. "I know you still love me even though I can see that you really want to punch me in the face right now." her innocent smile adding to the urge.

Silence ensued for a couple of minutes Both of us, standing by the kitchen bar, staring at the drink in our hands.

"You know why I did those things?" Eli broke the silence. I glanced up at her. "Because I realized that you're going to be this stubborn. You almost flew at the man who attempted to take her, stood up against her ex-fiancé that was at least a foot taller than you, and you were ready to fire the security guy, who didn't tackle the ex-fiancé right away even though you knew he can't at that time. All these, to ensure that Adi was safe from the people who wanted to hurt her," she continued. "Then out of nowhere, you just handed her to me as if she didn't mean anything to you. Saying '*Just be good to her, Eli.*'" The mockery didn't go unnoticed.

"So, while you were figuring your shit out..." Eli took a gulp of her drink, as if trying a dramatic reveal to her grand plans. "I tried keeping tabs on her and keeping her safe, if in any case the ex comes back again."

"Yeah, right," I rebutted. "How are you going to convince me that you're just taking care of her for me, after you already had kissed her? Is that a part that you should take care, too?"

Eli snorted. "Oh, Alex. Let me get this straight—you want to be the one handling that for her?" *Fuck.* I was caught in her trap. She walked towards me, stopping just a feet away. She brought up her hand to run it through my hair. "Oh, my sweet, Alex. I know you can take care of her not only with kisses but also... other things. Between the two of us, you are more... eccentric with your taste in sex." She flashed a knowing smile. "That's why we never worked, right? You weren't able to fully have me submit to your... taste."

I stayed silent, not giving Eli the satisfaction of admitting that I thought about it. How Adi would look in bed, drenched in sweat, trembling from what I would do to her.

I shook my head to clear my train of thoughts. *Not a good path to continue.* I returned my gaze to Eli, irritated that she was already staring at me with a knowing look. She knew what I was thinking.

"Alex," Eli pulled me back from my thoughts. "You didn't tell me it was *her* when we rescued her at the club. Yes, I'll admit, it was weird how frantic you were when you saw what was happening, and the only thing I thought about that was, you were afraid that the incident might result to closing the club down." Her words were kindly spoken. I could feel the sincerity of it. "She didn't know that you were the owner of the club, too. You can't blame her, me, or both of us, if we didn't know what we were dealing with." She grabbed my hand across the table.

"I'll admit. You know my taste and she fit it to the tee—well, aside from the hair." I gave her a knowing look, remembering that I called her out on this. "And if she wasn't your woman, I would've made my move. But after Scar telling me that she was the woman you were talking to us about, how could I pursue her? How could you forget? You come first. I love you first. And I would not do or *try* not to do anything that would hurt you."

How could I also forget that Eli was my best friend first, and that her intentions might not have been to hurt me. Yet I shunned her right away, without even knowing her side of the story. I operated based on the assumption that I had.

"I was able to confirm it with Scar when I told her about our conversation; How your whole personality has changed ever since that incident. When she told me that it was *her*, the one you've told me who broke your heart years ago, I knew. I definitely knew that you're still not over her."

I had to stop myself from letting the truth crush my heart. Eli's right. I knew, but I chose not to tell them. And I couldn't blame them. I brought this down to myself. *They don't know what they don't know.* I knew, and I chose to keep it to myself and pushed them away. It was an attempt to keep my heart guarded yet it all resulted in me hurting the people I care about.

"You want to know how she feels about you?" Eli asked. "I've offered my place to her, many, many times and she always says she'll think about it. I think she just didn't say no directly to avoid being rude."

I remembered when Scar shared this to me, humorlessly laughing at Eli's frustration with convincing Adi to move in with her temporarily. "Text her. Text her you have an extra room that she can stay for now while she's looking for a new place."

I looked at Eli. "I don't have an extra room." She laughed.

"Dude, you have two rooms in your apartment. A massive, barely slept in master's bedroom and an office. I think you can squeeze her in here or something."

Eli stood up and gave me a quick peck on the cheek. "I have to be somewhere in an hour." Then, gave me a quick forehead kiss. "I love you, but stop being stubborn. Text her. This might be the universe giving you a chance or something." She offered me a kind smile. "You know I don't believe in this fate bullshit, but if it does exist, it's definitely this."

Eli started walking away but stopped before she stepped outside the door. She turned back to me and said with a sad smile. "Second chances don't always come around."

Eli knew what it was to lose someone and never have the chance to make it right. This was her way of telling me not to make the same mistake.

And it left me with an emotion that I promised to crush:

Hope.

Chapter Twenty-Three

> I didn't know you moved out already. Eli told me you were looking for a place to stay temporarily.

> I have a spare bedroom. You can stay here until you find a place.

> Nico told me that Amanda's sex life is suffering already. lol

FIVE. TEN. Fifteen. Twenty. Twenty-five

Thirty minutes have passed before the three dots appeared on my screen. Not me, just waiting for a reply that I may not even receive.

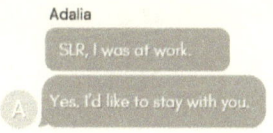

Adalia

> SLR, I was at work.

> Yes. I'd like to stay with you.

A sense of uneasiness had started creeping in, the reality of the inevitable confrontation setting in. Would she ever forgive me for the all the words I flung to her that night? This was either going to make us or break us. What did I just do?

Oh, I am fucked.

PART IV

Adi

Chapter Twenty-Four

LET ME *know when I can pick you up.*

My mind had been scattered since this afternoon, constantly glancing at the response Alex sent. I have given up the hope that she would agree to reconcile, given the last conversation we had. *'Yeah, like when you told me you kissed my best friend before climbing on top of my lap and removing your clothes?'* She wasn't wrong, though. I did do that. And she had every right not to talk to me anymore. I started peeling myself away from Eli, thinking that removing myself from Alex's circle, was one way to atone.

My fingers were hovering on top of the screen, not knowing what to say. I said yes to Alex in a whim, not even thinking about the possible recourse of that answer. It was an olive branch extended to me when I thought I was completely falling off, and this might be chance to finally set things right. Alex was right. I needed to be accountable to whatever was going on in me, and it was not right for the people around me to suffer the effects of my past.

Okay, Adi. I released a huge sigh. *Welcome to your mature era.*

I typed a quick response, threw the phone in my bag, and concentrated on the work that I had in front of me.

> You can pick me up tonight from Amanda's.

THE AFTERNOON rush in the office distracted me from grabbing my phone to check if Alex has responded. By five PM, my upper back was hurting, and my brain had almost melted. As much as being in human resource drained the soul out of me, I loved what I was doing, and it made me feel competent. *At least in one aspect in my life.* That was why my heart completely shattered when I thought I was going to leave the workforce once I marry Damien. I would have been the perfect housewife my ex-fiancé and my mom had molded. *Or so they wished.*

"Still not going?" Germaine, my co-worker was gathering his things. "That beautiful specimen of a friend of yours, going to pick you up again?" Of course, he was talking about Eli. As queer as Germaine was, he always reiterated that he could still appreciate a woman's beauty, most especially if that woman was as handsome as Eli.

"I don't know." I started picking up my stuff as well. "She never tells me if she's going to pick me up or not. She just… appears."

Eli's actions have bewildered me for the past few weeks. She had been showing up at my work to pick me up and drop me off, not really explaining what her true intentions were.

When Eli offered me her place, she clarified that she was not interested in me romantically anymore. *Okay, ouch.* But she explained that she was doing this just to make sure that I was safe from my ex.

That, I get.

But to extend this effort for someone she was not interested in, was confusing as hell.

After that night at the club when I saw that woman with Alex, I knew what I needed to do. I started texting Eli that my co-workers and I were going to eat after work, and I would just take a taxi to get to Amanda's. She was against it at first, but she eventually gave up and had not picked me up for the past few days.

I reminded myself that I could deal with my own problems, and it was not right to inconvenience their circle any further. They have done much already.

"Do you mind if I walk with you again to the Skytrain?" I asked Germaine as we entered the elevator.

He nodded, since it was becoming a routine for the both of us: grabbing boba at the store before the train station, and sitting inside for at least fifteen minutes, just to decompress and let out the mindless complains we had about work.

We were talking if we could instead go to the new coffee place one block away from the train station when we beeped our IDs to exit the building. As the glass door opened, I stopped halfway, causing Germaine to bump into my back. He had started complaining loudly since his phone dropped to the floor with a loud clang. "Adi! You don't just stop walking half —"

"Alex," I whispered.

"Alex?!" Germaine asked in annoyance while picking up and dusting away his phone. "Who the fuck is Alex?"

"Adi," Alex greeted back. She looked breathtaking, even without a smile on her face. Unlike the few times I saw her, today she was wearing a more casual outfit. A green short-sleeved button-down shirt, denim pants, and black sneakers. Her hair perfectly messy as if it was styled to show an *I-don't-care-how-I-look-but-I-know-I-look-good-anyway* style. She straightened up from leaning against the wall and had started walking towards me.

Why she was here, I had no idea.

"Eli spoke to me and said that you told her not to pick you up anymore." Alex stopped six feet away from me. A good distance… if I have a communicable disease. "Is there a particular reason why?"

"I don't need a babysitter," I didn't know where the petulant attitude was coming from, but Alex's unexpected presence made me feel a bit on edge. "I told you before and I am telling you now, I can take care of myself, even from him." A dark look crossed her face, but it was immediately gone as she schooled her expression neutral.

"But I…" I completely forgot that Germaine was with me. He

stepped to the side, now completely in view of Alex. "May need a babysitter. Are you available?" He extended his hand to Alex with a flirtatious smile on his face. "I'm Germaine, Adi's co-worker."

"Alex." She shook his hand. "Adi's... friend."

"*Where are you pulling these gorgeous women from, Adi?*" Germaine not-so-discreetly whispered in my ear.

I gave him a scolding look as a response.

I returned my gaze to Alex, a questioning look as to why she was here, in front of my office. *Waiting for me.*

"I thought I could just pick you up since you're moving in tonight anyway. It'll be faster and would give us more time to arrange your stuff."

"You are moving in with her?" Germaine did not bother being discreet anymore.

Stop it. I mouthed to him. There was no reason to make this any more awkward.

"Not unless you have any plans right now." Alex offered as she glanced to Germaine, giving me a way out. Her presence was unexpected, and my heart and brain could not catch up right now. I would need more time to prepare myself mentally before I move in with her tonight.

"We actually do. We were thinking of grabbing coffee," I said in a careful voice. A few hours to solidify a plan, with the help of Nico and Amanda of course, on how I would tackle moving in with Alex, was what I needed. "And it might take an hour or two, before we actually head home." I looked at Germaine, hoping he would get what I was trying to imply. "I'm sorry if you wasted your time going here. I can just have Nico or Amanda drop me off at your place with my stuff, if you have other things to do."

Alex looked at me intriguingly. She was about to open her mouth to answer, when Germaine butted in. "Buuuut, you can come with us since you're already here. I would like to know more about you, gorgeous." He winked. He actually winked at her, and it surprisingly made Alex smile.

My eyes widened as I turned to Germaine. *Traitor.*

"Sure." Alex was surprised with the offer. "If that's okay with

Adi. I don't want to impose."

Germaine would suffer the consequence of putting me on the spot next week. He's lucky he has the weekend to enjoy his unbothered life.

"Sure." I was left with no choice. "Come with us then." Germaine laughed, knowing what he has done.

We started walking towards the coffee shop, silence ensuing at first. It was a good thing that a lot of people were bustling around, all in a rush to get home.

"So…" Germaine mirrored Alex's pace. "You and Adi been friends for a long time? Since she's moving in with you and all that."

My eyes widened at the question, a usual small talk starter, but for Alex and me, this simple question was loaded with a lot of unanswered questions.

I waited for her response. A peak into her perspective in what would hopefully become a symbiotic relationship. "Yeah, we were best friends in high school," she answered nonchalantly. Germaine glanced at her, waiting to continue. "I moved away to a different province for university. Unfortunately, we fell off. We didn't talk until recently."

"And now she's moving in with you…" Germaine left the sentence hanging.

Alex just smiled, leaving it at that. They continued chattering, Germaine mostly asking Alex personal questions.

Timing, now as a friend, we reached our destination and was greeted with the waft of brewing coffee smell and the scent of freshly baked pastries. Alex insisted on paying for our drinks, saying it was the least she could do since she intruded on our post-work coffee date.

"You didn't say you were friends with the owner of *Club Tala*," Germaine giggled like a fifteen-year-old girl. "Didn't you know?"

"Know what?"

"A lot of single, queer women go to that club, hoping to shoot their shot with her." He gave me a knowing look. "And the other two women she mostly talks with." I knew that the circle of women was attractive, but I didn't realize that people really do come to the club just for them. At the most, I thought it might be presumptuous to think that women were literally lining up just to see them. "They mostly keep to themselves, and almost always keep a good distance with people who have *other* intentions other than being friendly. Now, women are more interested, given the mysterious and their hard-to-get aura."

Keep their distance, huh? I almost laughed at the comment. *Tell that to the woman who doesn't seem to have a concept of distance, given how she was clinging to Alex like a leech.* I was surprised and had to stop myself from this train of thought. Who Alex slept with was none of my business. *As she had reminded me.*

And speaking of the devil, "Here you go," Alex came with three drinks on her tray, and three slices of cake. She handed our drinks. "I got you a chocolate cake, Germaine. I didn't know what you like." Then without saying any word, she handed me a strawberry shortcake. She sat down beside Germaine, and started their conversation again, as if long-time friends.

I stared at the cake before me. Strawberry shortcake. *Alex remembered.*

There was a tug in my heart, a warm feeling begging to come out. And I promised myself I was going into this arrangement, pushing down this very emotion to not complicate things anymore.

Possibility.

Chapter Twenty-Five

IT DIDN'T take much time grabbing my things from Amanda's place. I have been rotating the clothes that I was able to fit in one suitcase, which was not technically an issue as my closet was mostly composed of different clothes in black. In a matter of thirty minutes, I had all my things packed and ready to go.

Alex offered to help me however, I requested—*no, more like pleaded*, for her to stay in the car and just wait up. I needed time to ready myself for this step that I was going to take with Alex. And I was hoping that Nico and Amanda would be home by the time we arrived, wanting to get some advice and words of wisdom before I go and face this challenge. Unfortunately, after a quick call to let me know that they'd be home late, the courage that had me responding to Alex that I could move in tonight, quickly melted into a puddle.

After procrastinating for a few more minutes, just biding my time before I go out and sit on that passenger seat again, I heard a knock on the door. I looked at the peep hole and saw Alex on her phone.

I quickly grabbed my bag and opened the door.

"Hey!" I greeted rather hastily. Alex looked at my duffel bag and one suitcase, confused that it was the only thing I was carrying. "I had my things moved into a storage facility while I was staying here."

"I thought I'd come and check if you need help carrying anything," Alex said. "Do you need more time?"

There was an underlying implication, as if she understood that I was stalling. And she was still giving me the way out. I shook my head and started closing the door.

I've had her waiting long enough.

The car ride was quiet. Alex did not force any conversation, aside from asking when I would want to pass by the storage facility to pick up the rest of my stuff, and if we needed a bigger car to fit it all in. I waived it off and told her that I would be fine with my suitcase. I wasn't planning on staying at Alex's place for a long time. I really was looking for a place to move in for a good price, and as circumstances permitted, Alex offering me her place was a way for me to try and reconcile our friendship, too.

Two birds with one stone. It was a punch to the moon, trying to take advantage of this situation and hoping for a good outcome. And I owe it to Alex to give it another chance—a chance to retribute. Whatever the outcome was, I would leave it at that, knowing that at least I have tried again.

I was completely out of my element. I had never been confrontational and always seemed to submit to the whims of the people around me. Growing up with a mom like mine had taken its toll on me and I knew it would take years of untangling to heal from the ingrained beliefs that I have been bombarded with since I was a child. Breaking off the engagement with Damien was a huge step for me, but I was pushed to my limits. The decision to confront my mom was almost a life and death situation. However difficult, I left my mom's place with a huge weight off my shoulder, the feeling of liberty making me high.

The memory of my mom's seething face had me smiling to myself.

"Care to share what's funny?" I was pulled from my reverie and caught Alex looking at me with a curious look.

"I was just reminded of a core memory." I left the sentence at that, hoping that Alex would not ask me for more. A conversation with my mom as the topic was not a good way to start. Luckily, timing as a friend again, she stopped the car and parked in front of a condominium. I looked around the area as I waited for Alex to lead the way.

It was definitely a nicer and quieter area of Port Coquitlam. It was only eight in the evening, yet I couldn't see anyone or any car outside the roads anymore. *Club Tala* was at least an hour away on a good day from Alex's place. It was a wonder why she hadn't moved closer to the city.

Alex beckoned for me to follow her inside and had started explaining the logistics of my stay. She said she only have one key fob for the main door, and she would need to ask the property manager if she could request for one more for my access. And for the meantime, we could share the key fob, given that our work hours were different.

Before I could answer, the elevator stopped at the fourth floor. Alex led the way to apartment four-one-seven, and had opened the door to what I could consider the total opposite of my previous place—a well-kept apartment. The walls were painted a darker shade of green, a compliment to the deep, orange-patterned carpet and the cream sectional couch in the middle of the room, not facing the television directly, but the large windows overlooking the lake by the park. Different plants were displayed in various area of the space, and eclectic artworks hung on the wall. Portraits and landscape photographs hung the wall, and I wondered if Alex took those herself. I have always known that she had innate talent for it.

Everything felt so intentionally relaxing, even the hues of the lighting, already pulling me into a lull.

I was still standing in the middle of the living room when I heard my name being called from the hallway. Alex was standing in front of one of the three doors in the hallway.

"This is your room." Alex motioned for me to come inside. "Let me know if you need anything else. I wasn't sure if I missed anything." I didn't understand what she was trying to imply, and it seemed that she saw it in my face, too. She continued explaining, "It was my office before, so I didn't have anything bedroom related here aside from the lamp, I guess. I got the bed and the dressers and the beddings. If you need anything else, just let me know."

Alex left me to settle in and arrange my stuff. I stood by the bed and looked around. She was right. I had the basics here: A white dresser, and a bed that my back will be thankful for. No offense to Amanda's couch, but my back had suffered for the past weeks I have stayed there. I plopped down into the bed and groaned as my body sunk into the softness of the mattress.

"This is it," I whispered to myself as I stared into the ceiling. I was staying in Alex's house for a few days or maybe weeks. And this time, I would put in the effort to repay the kindness she had shown me for the entire time we knew each other; that despite what happened before, she had chosen to show me compassion in a time of need.

Reconciled friendship—that would be the goal. I reminded myself over and over again, trying to convince a part of me that there was nothing more that I should be asking for. Yet I also knew that there would be a part of me that would be fighting with tooth and nail to come out and ask for more; that despite knowing there was a high probability that I would only be getting hurt in the end, a part of me would still want to try.

And this circumstance was a perfect opportunity to shoot my shot. I grabbed my phone and tapped on my messages.

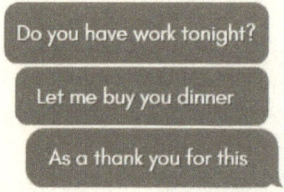

I hit send and threw my phone at the other side of the bed, scared of the inevitable rejection. A few minutes have passed, before I felt my phone vibrating. I sighed and tapped on the new message notification.

Lexie
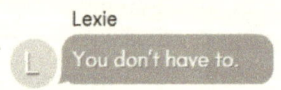

Three dots appeared, showing that Alex was still typing.

A pang of disappointment washed over me. I put my phone facedown at my side, already preparing for a night of defeat. Until I felt my phone vibrated again.

Lexie
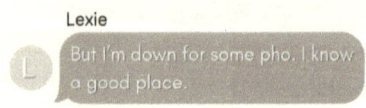

The three dots appeared on my screen again, the anticipation making me giddy for some reason.

Lexie

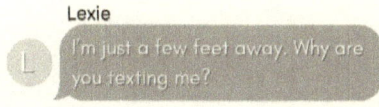

I'm just a few feet away. Why are you texting me?

A smile formed on my face.

Day one.

Chapter Twenty-Six

IT WAS nearing November, and the weather has starting to have some chills in it. Alex and I were standing by the elevator, waiting for it to reach our floor. She was only wearing a sweater while I opted for a toque when she mentioned that we were just going to walk since the *pho* place was nearby. I didn't really do well with the cold and in a matter of minutes, I knew I would start having snot running down my face. Not a really good way to present myself. I hugged myself as we started walking towards the restaurant.

The walk was as quiet as it could get, with the gusts of cold air here and there, and by the time we arrived at the *pho* place, I have covered half of my face with the scarf. The warmth of the mom-and-pop store was a welcoming embrace, and the scent of soup had my stomach grumbling. As Alex mentioned it was a table for two, we were led to a table where I needed to face her directly.

I knew that I had been the one to ask her out for dinner, but it totally flew out of my mind that this would entail facing each other and *actually* talk to one another. We have not had a conversation that ended up on good terms ever since we have seen each other again. And what were the odds that this would result differently?

Alex browsed the menu, unaffected with the lack of distance between us. But this view, was not bad—*not bad at all*. I could see her face scrunched up as she tried to read the tiny description of the food choices, her chocolate, brown eyes bright under the LED light of the restaurant.

"Have you decided on what you're gonna get?" Alex asked with a smile, not removing her eyes from the menu.

I was caught. She knew I was staring.

I could feel my face warm up, my ears were probably red by

now. I forced my gaze to the menu, trying to browse as fast as I could for something to order.

"Yes," I answered as nonchalant as I could. "I'll get number two. You?"

Instead of answering, Alex waved her hand to the old man serving the customers.

"Alex!" The older man tapped her at the back affectionately. "You haven't been here for so long!"

"Danny." Alex returned the vibrant smile back to the man. "I've been busy for the past weeks. But I'm back. I missed your food so much. Is Auntie here?"

They continued to chatter as if old friends and it was disorienting to see this side of Alex. From the time that I have met her again, she has this wall surrounding her whenever she talks to people outside her circle. But this warm and affectionate Alex was a sight to behold. I could hear from her voice that she genuinely liked this old man.

"Oh, I almost forgot. Danny, let me introduce you to my friend, Adi." I extended my hand. "She will be staying with me for a while, so you might be seeing her around often too, after she tastes your delicious cuisine."

Danny tapped Alex's back again, laughing as he did it. Again, another unusual change. I remember vividly that Lexie had a hard time with physical touch. And it took me at least two years from when our friendship started, that she let me grab her arm when we were walking.

It was so immature of younger me to push that boundary of hers. I shook my head at this memory.

"What's wrong?" Alex asked. I didn't notice that our orders have been placed, and Danny had walked away already.

"Nothing," I denied.

She looked at me, a tinge of disappointment shadowing her eyes. But she didn't push for it and left my answer at that.

I felt conflicted. It was only day one of this cordial relationship and I felt like it was just right to leave the serious conversations at a later time. Yet on the other hand, I promised to be honest to Alex if I have ever been given a chance to mend this.

And here it was, served on a silver platter but I was still holding back.

"You know what," I said as I braced my resolve. "I'll be honest with you."

Alex looked up from her phone, a curious expression on her face.

"I just remembered the time when we were in high school," I started. "I remembered that it took a long time for you to let me at least link my arm with you when we were walking. And seeing how you were open to the old man patting you was a big change from before."

Alex looked contemplative. After a few seconds of silence, she put her phone in her pocket and looked at me straight in the eyes before answering, "I didn't let you, because I knew I liked you already early on," she dropped *that* bomb as if it was nothing. "I didn't want to take advantage that we were friends, and I was trying to move on from my infatuation. You were very open to us that your love language was physical touch. And I knew that if I let you in, closer than that, I wouldn't be able to stop myself and move on from what I was feeling for you."

Oh. I didn't know that. She was already moving on even before she admitted she liked me. *Come to think of it, this was the first and only time she had admitted her feelings for me before.*

"Alex, I—" but before I could finish, Danny arrived with our steaming hot food.

I almost forgot the conversation we were having as the bowls were placed in front of us, the waft of the broth making my mouth water already.

"We'll talk about it after we eat," Alex said as she was mixing her soup. "We need this conversation out of the way anyway."

I nodded. She was right. I'd rather have this conversation out of the way, so we could move on and hopefully, start afresh. We have a lot to unpack, uncover words that were unsaid, and emotions that we didn't have a chance to express.

But for now, at least for a few more hours, that could wait.

I dug in, trying to stop myself from moaning from the richness of the broth and the tenderness of the slices of steak. We continued eating in silence for a few minutes, before Alex's phone started ringing. From what I could hear, it was probably Scar, calling from work. She motioned that she would be stepping out for a bit to finish the call.

Ten minutes have passed before Alex walked back, her nose and ears were all red from the chill outside. "I'm sorry," she said as she sat back down. "Scar called about work. I wasn't supposed to be on day off this evening, but she forced me to, even though it was a Friday night." She continued eating her now, room temperature soup. I felt guilty, knowing instead of working and helping Scar out, she's here, right in front of me. Having a conversation I knew she would rather avoid.

"Don't worry," It was as if Alex knew what I was thinking. "I had Eli come in to help Scar manage the club tonight."

The mention of Eli's name had me remembering the stupid mistake that I did after the incident at the club. If only I knew how the next days would play out, I wouldn't have let Eli kiss me, knowing it would complicate *us* more.

"Also," I hesitated but decided to continue. "About Eli…"

"Let's talk about it after we eat," Alex dismissed it again. "But I am curious about on thing. Can you tell me about your ex-fiancé?"

Damien? I wonder why Alex was curious about my relationship with him.

Alex explained that she was trying to investigate if the incident at *Club Tala* was a one-time thing or if he was a general risk for drunk women. She wanted to get good evidence to have him banned not only from *Club Tala* but hopefully from other clubs as well.

The unfortunate tale of how me and Damien were arranged to date and get married had me reliving the worst times of my relationship with him. "We started dating after that dinner, and at first, he was accommodating and was a gentleman. Sometimes, he was quite misogynistic with women aside from me, but I tried to attribute it to how the patriarchal structure of traditional family has been set up and the 'red pill content' that has been trending in social media." I added finger air quotes to emphasize how absurd I thought it was. "I didn't know how deep he was in, until two months after and our families decided it was enough to get engaged."

I could remember the conversation I had with Damien after the engagement party. My mom forced me to take him home and care for him since we were soon to be wed, even though I wanted to stay with them for the night. So, there I was, the ever-good girl who was dragging an almost six-foot tall man, who was slurring his words and couldn't even walk straight. As soon as I closed the door, he began grabbing my body and forcing his lips on mine, that I couldn't even breathe. I asked him to stop so many times, yet it fell on deaf ears.

He continued groping my body, pulling me deeper in his apartment, his grip on my arms hurting. I pushed him away and said no, then everything seemed to move in slow motion. Damien stumbled back, and rage crossed his face as he stalked towards me and slapped me in the face.

That was the first time I understood how that relationship was going to be. Damien shouted at me, with his face as red as a tomato with spit flying. He reminded me that I was *his* woman. That I would do the things he wanted me to do.

"…And as soon as we were married, that I couldn't say no to him anymore." I finished my tale.

Alex wasn't looking at me. She had her eyes glued on the Vietnamese coffee, her hand gripping the cup tighter than usual.

"I was a fool. I didn't run away after that night. I thought I'd give him a chance again after he apologized the next day. He said it was the alcohol." I knew I was stupid at best to give him another chance. He showed me love and affection after—the perfect fiancé for me. He assured me that he would change; that he loved me more than anything else. And it was his overwhelming love for me that he wanted to know me deeper than my skin. So, I gave in. I gave him my body since I desperately wanted to be loved. "It has become a cycle by then. An issue would come up, he would tell me it's my fault and when I try to argue with him, the least I would receive was a slap on my face for answering back."

The worst I could remember was when after a week of vacationing together, he started undressing me despite doing *it* almost every day. I told him no, that my privates were hurting already. Yet instead of understanding that it was from the number times of us having sex during vacation, he accused me of cheating and having sex with other men when he was not with me during the trip, that's why I didn't want to do it anymore. "I cried the entire time he was shoving his dick inside of me until he finished. He didn't say sorry nor acknowledge that what he accused me was a way to manipulate me in to having sex with him. I knew I was weak, but that evening served as a wake-up call for me. I knew I had to get out. So, I tried stalling the wedding planning and stuff, no matter how much our moms were pushing us."

Alex remained quiet. "I said I wanted to have the wedding by October so we could take advantage of the fall colors. But that gave me time to plan things around, so I could get out as soon as I possibly could."

"And see," I tried putting a cheer in my voice. I hated the pity in Alex's eyes. "I'm here! I survived."

Alex peered at me, with an indistinguishable expression. And before I could ask, Danny came over to check on us. We left the *pho* place without paying a single cent, Danny sending us out saying at that it was on him this time, given that he missed Alex too.

We started the freezing trek back to the house. It was unexpected when Alex started with her question again, thinking that she wasn't that invested in my life story. "How long have you broken up with him when you went to the club?"

"It was a week before." I smiled proudly to myself. "I went to my mom to say that I was breaking off the engagement. You should have seen the look on her face when I left her house after declaring that I was done with Damien."

Alex smiled at me encouragingly.

"After that, I texted Damien to meet at a coffee place. No matter what an asshole he was, I thought that breaking up with him personally was the best thing to do. It was a stupid decision. I thought that by meeting up in a public place, he would stay calm and not make a ruckus. As soon as I told him that we were done, he pulled me out of the coffee place and towards an alley. He threw punches mostly in my thighs, saying that he couldn't leave a mark that was visible with clothes on. He told me that it would stop me from wearing slutty dresses or shorts as well."

Alex stopped walking. Her face visibly upset from what I said. "Eli said that you were trying to review the videos if there was an altercation before you stopped him from taking me." I stopped walking as well and faced Alex. "No, that was from the day we broke up." I smiled sadly at her, the sorrow of my ordeal was washing through me again. "No one knew, not even Nico and Amanda. I kept it to myself at first because I really was willing to give it a shot. I was twenty-eight and single, and this was a man my mother wanted me to marry." I shook my head, disappointed at myself from agreeing to this even from the start. "I tried convincing myself that maybe this would work, you know? I never had any good relationship with men, and I always thought there was something wrong with me. And this man was served to me on a silver platter, with good credentials and a charming face. "He was perfect on paper. It was supposed to be something special, that I shouldn't ask for more."

I chuckled at my sad little life, knowing that I had let this happen to me. "Even though I was unhappy that he wanted me to be a stay-at-home wife, I thought I could eventually change his mind." I stopped by the park bench, inhaling the crispy, night air, hoping that as I exhale, all of my woes would be carried along with it as I start this new phase of my life. "And by the time it was over, I still hadn't told Nico and Amanda. I was too ashamed that I had let this happen to me. And I've read multiple stories about reporting domestic abuse."

I closed my eyes, almost crying as I hear Damien's voice in my head. *Why are you crying? Don't be too sensitive! That shit didn't hurt! It's not even bleeding!* And my heart ached, from realizing that I had stayed in that relationship because it was something the people around me wanted, not mine.

"Why the arranged marriage, though?" Alex asked. "I know it's a custom in other cultures but not with yours, right?"

Alex was right. It wasn't. "My mom wanted me to get married. I didn't have long term relationships. She believed she could fix that for me." I sighed. It was as simple as that for her. She believed something was wrong with me and she could fix me—to be the perfect daughter. *"Mother knows best,"* I finished with merely above a whisper.

We continued walking silently, letting the aftereffects of my tragic little story die down. And as Alex closed the door of the apartment, the warmth and comfort of my temporary home, she said, "I'm sorry."

I stopped walking and faced her. "It was an unfortunate phase of my life." She walked towards where I was, a few feet away from each other.

"But I am here, Alex." My lips pulled into a grin at the realization that I was more embarrassed that Alex was pitying me. The absurdity that I had went through that and survived, ashamed that I knew that I deserved better, yet I allowed *them* to do that to me.

"Starting over. But *alive*."

And I had to give myself credit for that.

Chapter Twenty-Seven

THE NEXT day passed by with Alex mostly giving me distance to get used to the space that she has given me in the meantime. Aside from showing me where the washroom was, she mostly pointed out that I could use and eat whatever she had at home.

I took inventory of my pack, trying to identify if I need to do my groceries for toiletries and possibly buy some snacks and produce to contribute to Alex's expense. And if I was trying to win her trust and friendship over, I should probably start exerting my effort to gain some points. The plan slowly took place in my mind as I took note of the date. *Perfect timing.*

I grabbed my wallet and my list and started heading out. As I stepped out of my room, I was greeted by a freshly woken Alex, just coming out of her room. Instinctively, I looked at my watch to check the time: 11:30 AM.

"Busy night?" I spun around to close my door, hoping that Alex could not see my blushing face as she was walking around with only boxer briefs and a loose, cropped shirt on. A peak of her toned stomach, showing.

When I turned back around, Alex was rubbing her eyes trying to remove sleep from her eyes. I saw when the clarity finally set in, that she was standing in front of another person, almost half naked.

Without answering, she stepped back in her room, leaving me bewildered, but grinning stupidly to myself.

An embarrassed Alex. It was fun to see a crack in her persona. Chuckling, I started walking out when she stepped out from her room in sweats and a hoodie.

"Hey," Alex called out. "Going somewhere?" The question felt familiar, and it was as if rain had dampened the giddiness that I was just feeling, my blood running cold from the question.

"Why?" The question came out harsher that I intended. *I didn't know I had to tell her when I was going out.* This thought gave me a visceral reaction, and I could feel that I was starting to become defensive. A rush of anger and fear, realizing that I had to be monitored and to report every move yet again, came through me that I almost lashed out. "Do I need to tell you when or where I'm going out?"

Alex looked at me confused. "No…" She reached out to her back pocket and started walking towards me. "I have the key fob. You won't be able to get back in if you don't have this." She dropped the key in my hand.

I am such an asshole. I closed my eyes and sighed out loud. *It's not him.*

"Are you okay?" Alex stepped back, giving me a wide berth.

"I'm sorry." I looked at her in the eyes, hoping that I could take back what I said. But there were no excuses, so I tried to explain. "There are some triggers that I am still trying to heal from. And I'm sorry if I lashed out on you out of nowhere."

Alex gave me an understanding nod. "Do you want to talk about it?"

I smiled. Typical Alex. Always ready to help even at the expense of her own peace. "I don't want to poop on your mood when you just woke up." I sat and started putting my shoes on. "Thanks for the fob, I'll just grab some stuff at the grocery. Do you want anything?"

Alex glanced at her watch, giving it a contemplative look. "Do you mind if I join you? I was planning to grab coffee, and I have to buy some supplies, too. We can do brunch before we go to the store."

"Uh… Okay, sure."

Alex said to just wait for five minutes for her to get ready.

I walked back to the kitchen to grab a glass of water. It was surprising to see her very accommodating and open to spending time together. It was a good thing for me, but I couldn't help but

188

wonder what turned the tides from the time we saw each other at the club.

Maybe Alex was really secured with her relationship with her new girlfriend, that being friends with me was no longer an issue.

Why would it be an issue? My inner self taunted me. *It's not as if you were her ex, or anything other than a friend.* As much as I wanted to punch my inner monologue, it was right. Why would Alex even consider that it would be awkward to be friends again? I was the one who threw myself on her lap in a moment of weakness. I was the one who kissed her way back when we were young.

Come to think of it, I was always the one making the first move, yet the first to bail out as well.

The realization was enough for me to smack myself in the forehead. A loud thud echoed at the kitchen upon impact.

"Isn't that too early for the day?" Alex stepped out in the same clothes but now, with her hair on a half bun and no more lingering sleepiness on her face. She gave me a friendly smile—a nostalgic smile that we used to share. I answered with the same toothy smile. No words needed to ruin the moment.

We walked side by side towards the lobby. "Do you mind if we grab coffee first?" Alex asked as she walked towards the door. "It's only a block away from here. Then, we'll come back and get the car."

I nodded. I was planning to take the bus anyway.

Even though it was almost noon, the fall weather was still quite chill. It was the perfect weather to walk around. Since Alex's place was near a park, we could see people running, walking with coffee in their hands, and parents pulling trolleys where their children were sitting with their toys. The ray of sunlight hitting my face was enough to lift my mood.

"So… do you have work tonight?" A question to temp-check when I could enact my plan to possibly swoon this person. I couldn't see Alex's eyes behind the sunglasses, but she was smiling.

"Yes, Scar would kill me if I missed another weekend opening."

The instant guilt ate me up as I remember her missing Friday night to pick me from work. I instinctively followed up with an

189

automatic sorry, an apology that Alex immediately waived off.

"You don't have to apologize for that," she reassured me. "Scar practically begged me to take that day off. And I chose to offer to pick you up. You didn't impose."

"Sorry…" Alex gave me a reprimanding look for apologizing for no reason, again. "Force of habit…" I sheepishly answered.

We were greeted with the smell of coffee beans and an industrial looking interior as we entered the coffee shop. A lot of people were already sat down with the pastry and drinks, talking with friends or up in their laptops. I was busy looking around the store when I felt a tap on my arm.

"Do you want anything? Coffee? Pastry?" Alex offered. I nodded, thinking back that I have not eaten anything aside from that glass of water. I walked off to find a seat near a window, hoping to bask in the sunlight while we were waiting. After a few minutes, Alex arrived with our drinks in mugs, and pastries on plates; *for here?*

I thought we were just going to grab coffee and do errands. "We're staying?" I asked Alex as she gave me my mug and the food.

She didn't answer right away until she settled in at her seat, with her cup on her hand.

"You said you wanted to talk about some stuff that we may both find as… sensitive. And I figured that a coffee place will be a neutral ground for you to feel safe," Alex explained.

She remembered. My heart swelled with emotions. *She considered.*

"We'll be living together for a bit and as much as what happened before, I want to be at least… amicable."

"Amicable…" I rolled the word on my tongue, a taste of irony and bitterness from the initial feeling I had. "That would be a great start," I added.

Lies! My inner voice shouted. I squished it in, letting the disappointment wash out even before it reflected in my face. *You said that you only expect friendship, and nothing more,* I reminded myself. Yet I have to be honest with myself, looking at Alex sitting right in front of me, and only hoping for friendship when I knew I wanted more, was a stab in the heart. Who was I fooling?

Okay. I ground myself. *We could only hope for the best but expect the worst.*

"So, ten years ago… I'm sorry."

Alex smiled as she sipped her coffee. "Don't apologize just yet," she added right away. "Let's finish the stories first to see if we really need to apologize."

"Okay, fair." My lips unconsciously pulled up on the side, answering the smile she was giving me. "Let me start again. So, ten years ago… I think I knew that I liked you. But I fooled myself into believing that what I was feeling was normal for two best friends growing closer to each other."

She continued sipping her coffee, letting me tell my story uninterrupted. "After the slumber party at Nico, remember that?" She nodded. "I was so confused with what I was feeling, that I asked for guidance from Uncle Richard. Remember him?" Again, she nodded without interrupting me.

"I reached out to him to talk about what I was feeling for you, hoping that I could trust him since he was part of the leadership people in our community." I could still feel the betrayal in my core. "He told me that what I was feeling was a sin, that I was just curious. That if I experience being with a man, it would change my mind."

I tried to gauge Alex's reaction, and I could see that she's gripping her mug tighter than necessary. The veins in her hand slowly becoming visible with the restraint that she was showing. Still, no words nor comment from her.

"I'll make this short." I gave her a barely-there smile. "He told my mom the day she caught us, that's why she came to the school barging in like that. And impeccable timing, I was actually kissing you when she saw us." And I was finally ready to face the consequences of my actions.

"I distanced myself away from you because that was my punishment…" I trailed off. "And the only way I could save you from my mom. I'm sorry I didn't get to explain it to you, but I was waiting after graduation, when I have a bit more freedom from my mom's talons."

Alex looked at me, a bit of uncertainty evident on her face. "What do you mean you distanced yourself *for me*?" I told her the details of the bargain that I had with my mom. I didn't want to lose her, most especially during the time that I was trying to figure out what I was feeling for her. Yet that was the price I was willing to pay for my mom not to ruin Alex's life—for something that I did.

"I even got Sam to play as my boyfriend in exchange for two weeks worth of my allowance. Just to make sure that my mom was your off your back."

I paused for a minute. Letting all it finally sink in; letting the air in so I could finally breathe freely, as the weight of bearing this secret was lifted from my shoulders. I took a sip of coffee, the taste of bitterness, an open welcome to the moment we were in.

Alex remained silent, staring outside the window, her hands still wrapped around her cup. "So… that's that." My attempt to deviate from the growing quietness between us. "I tried reaching out after graduation to explain… but you were already gone." I left the last sentence hanging, hoping she would fill the gaps.

"I moved to a different province to run away," Alex said out of nowhere. "'Cause your mom threatened me to disappear, or she will report me to the school and the cops. We were eighteen at that time. And since you never denied that I sexually assaulted you, I was so scared that I was going to jail."

A simmer of anger had started to boil in my stomach. I didn't know my mom would go this far, to control me and to protect her image. "I did though," I refuted. "When she brought me home that night, I explained to her over, and over, and over again that I was the one who made the first move. But she never believed me and convinced me that I was the victim; that I was brainwashed." I knew that it was all bullshit but at that time, all the power was in her hands; my present and my future could've easily been ruined if she chose to.

"I'm sorry." I held Alex's gaze. "I know I could not change the past, and the pain and hurt that I caused you. But I'm here to make amends. To at least be… *amicable*." I heavily emphasized the word with finger quotations.

Alex smirked. "Fair enough, fair enough." She held her hand out. "Truce."

"Truce," I repeated. I grabbed her hand and shook on it. "For now."

Chapter Twenty-Eight

THE FEELING of letting go of the burden that we have kept from each other for the longest time, was a necessity I didn't realize. I felt light and a tad happier now that Alex and I had agreed to a truce as we worked on our relationship to at least be friends, again. And before my inner voice could start contradicting the conviction I had for this goal, I stomped it out to the farthest part of my mind and tried to enjoy the moment of peace. Though we mostly remained silent the rest of the time, the quiet was now comfortable, to say the least.

It was on the way back to the apartment after we had done groceries, that I decided to finally ask the question that was clawing inside me. "Alex," I started. "Is your girlfriend okay with me staying with you for a while?"

Alex glanced at me, confused. "Girlfriend?" Then slowly, realization started dawning on her face. She knew who I was talking about. "Oh... Summer?"

I nodded. I knew her name was Summer. Who could have forgotten that name when I was so upset that she technically pulled down Alex's face against hers, just to make a show. Right in front of me.

I waited for Alex's response though her stillness was weighing heavier and heavier, solidifying my belief that Summer was indeed with her. I was about to let the question go, when she answered quietly, "No, she's not my girlfriend."

My follow-up question was obvious. And Alex did not wait for me to ask it before adding, "That was a one-time thing." She was looking at the road with her brows crunched up as if upset. "Just a means to an end."

"I didn't mean to speculate," I added too quickly, afraid that she was annoyed that I was asking about it. "I'm sorry."

Alex stole a glance at me before returning her eyes on to the road. "You don't have to apologize, Adi. Stop apologizing." She smiled. "I was more upset that I did it, more than anything." She left it at that.

Once we returned to the apartment, I had started putting the groceries away while Alex walked towards her room to answer a call. I was almost done when she returned. "Adi, what time do you work tomorrow?"

I turned around and saw that she was already in her robes, ready to take a shower. "Since this is quite farther from downtown, I would need to leave by seven in the morning." I actually haven't thought about my transit plans for work. "I need to check the bus schedule down here to make sure. Why?"

Alex looked at the wall clock, as if trying to calculate my travel time. "I'll be home by six in the morning. I could drop you off at work or at the train station so you can save some time."

I stared at her, surprised by this. *Why is she going out of her way to accommodate me, again?* I couldn't help but feel hope swell in my heart.

Before I could reveal my inner desire in my expression, I said a quick thank you and returned to putting away the things we bought. As soon as I heard the washroom door closed, I flopped down at the floor and put my face in the middle of my hands.

The change in Alex's demeanor was like a whiplash. From the cold and stoic person that I met almost two months ago, she was now back to her usual self when I knew her back in high school.

It was not helping my feeble heart not to expect more than friendship out of this.

Once I was done with the groceries, I locked myself in my temporary room, trying to ground myself into the reality of the situation. I was here to try and make it up to Alex. The most that I could ask for was our reconciled friendship but with how she was treating me, I might not be able to stop myself and expect more. And I would not want that to possibly take her away from me again.

How do I stop myself from hoping for more? So, I did the most logical thing that I could think of. I grabbed my phone and Facetimed Nico and Amanda. Within a few rings, both answered and surprisingly already in their pajamas at five in the afternoon.

"Wow!" I almost clapped. "I am so surprised that both of you are already in your bed, preparing to sleep at a weekend night. No dates?" Nico flipped me off while Amanda showed me the can in her hand and slowly panned the camera to a woman next to her.

"I just answered to say hi," Amanda was grinning from ear to ear. "I have company, and I am *busy*." We both gave her the side eye. "Goodbye, loves, let's meet up soon!" And her video was gone.

"Wow, at least one out of us three is getting laid tonight," Nico commented sarcastically as he grabbed his tea. "With you gone, Amanda's sex life has been reignited."

And in turn, I flipped my middle finger at the screen which was met by a snort.

"Nico, I need help." I flopped down the bed.

"Okay, spill the tea." Nico nodded.

"Alex's getting weird." That was met with widened eyes. Curious. So, I continued. "She was so cold to me when we first met. You know how that was but now, it's different." I told him how I was taken by surprise this morning when she offered to go with me to do errands, and how she made sure that I feel safe when we were about to have a difficult conversation. I couldn't help myself but feel my heart flutter from these things, as little as they were.

Nico put his cup of tea down. "Adi," I could hear the tone of wisdom in his voice. "Let me ask you. What do you plan to do with this situation with Alex?"

"Reconciled friendship," I tried saying in a firm voice. "That's my goal, Nico. Nothing more."

Lies! Shut up, inner voice.

"Adi," now reprimanding. "Are you sure about that? What happened to your promise of being honest?"

"Are you calling me a liar?" I mockingly said as if I was offended by the implication.

Nico just gave me the look.

"Okay, okay." Maybe it was really time to be honest with myself. "I told you I liked Alex. Keyword: *Liked*. Past tense. When

195

we met again, I promised myself that I would make it up to her for what happened before. And I was contented with being just a part of her life again, and her in mine. Even just as friends. Not even best friends." I sighed. The dam that I was trying to stop from exploding was here, ravaging and overtaking the rationale part of my brain. "And I am still holding onto that, that even as just friends, I will be happy. But now that I am living with her, I don't think that I could stop myself anymore from hoping that we could be more."

I knew deep inside even when I was young that I wanted me and Alex to be more than friends. But I was too afraid to admit that to myself since I had no control and no power over my life. Yet I have been given this opportunity, *again*. And now, I have the avenue to decide for myself.

"I don't want to hurt her again, Nico," I confessed. "Now that she's finally here, I'm afraid that if I fucked up again, I would lose her. And there wouldn't be a third chance anymore."

Nico was contemplative. After a few seconds of silence, he finally asked. "Adi, let me be the devil's advocate. How sure are you that you like women?"

I had to take a minute for the question to finally sink in. Growing up, the idea of liking women has been a taboo thus, I've been hiding it at the farthest corner of my mind as I could. The last time I let the thought lingered, I lost my best friend. After that incident, I had put in the best effort to forget that emotion and concentrate on my studies and had started dating men. And one after the other, the relationship ended in a matter of months, not until Damien.

My eyes had finally been opened to the possibility of dating women that fateful morning with Eli. But it wasn't until I kissed Alex again that my heart felt the resolute that I wanted to be with a woman—not just any woman, but *her*, that my rationale was probably compromised, *or finally free from the beliefs that have been stopping me to accept this side of myself*. And my hidden desires took that chance to come out and play.

Well-played, subconscious. I thought to myself with an ironic smile. *Well-played.*

"Like you, I don't want to lose Alex again," Nico continued. "But also, I don't want to invalidate the notion that you like women.

I just want you to be sure. I know your dating history and I don't want this decision to be out of the idea that you like women just because you hate men."

A spark of anger flared in me, but I knew that Nico was coming from a good place.

"Don't be mad, Adi." My emotions were always a display in my face. "At the end of the day, the decision will always be yours. Just consider these questions."

The conversation might have not ended how I liked it to end, but what Nico said was right. I could not go around declaring my affections, if I was not even sure that this was what I really wanted. And I was at a disadvantage, having Eli and Alex as my only experience with women. If you could even call that an experience.

I tried to remember what Amanda said to me as well right after I got discharged. *Hoe it out until I figured out what I want?* I almost smacked myself in the forehead. *No, not that one!* Something about being up front with the expectations so both parties understand what to assume in the relationship. *Yep, that one.*

I sat up and released a sigh. I could feel the resolve steeling inside of me as I decide on what I want to do with this conundrum. I grabbed my phone and clicked on my message thread with Alex.

When's your next off?

I walked out of my room as soon I threw the phone on my bed, to grab a glass of water and prepare for bed and to stop myself from checking my screen every minute to see if she has replied. By the time I went to bed, my phone was radio silent, the message still unread. I put it away face down.

Maybe it was better this way.

I JUST finished showering when Alex came home the next

morning. She went straight to the kitchen and started brewing coffee. The waft of caffeine in the air had awoken me from my stupor, excited for the warm drink in this chilly morning.

By seven AM, I was already done and prepared to go to work. Alex was on her phone by the kitchen island, nursing her almost done cup on her other hand. She looked up at as I started making my coffee as well.

"Ready to go?" she asked.

My heart hurt a little, realizing that she had not responded to my text, yet she was on her phone ever since she came home. Though I know I could not impose, I couldn't shake the feeling of disappointment early this morning.

"You really don't have to drop me off, Alex," I tried convincing her. "I saw the bus schedule and if I leave now, I will have time to even grab breakfast."

I could see Alex contemplating, then she finally sighed. She walked towards me and handed the key fob. "If you say so, Adi."

I offered her a smile then started walking away and before she closed the door to her room, she peeked and called out. "Adi! I forgot to reply to your message. We were so busy last night. My next day off will be tomorrow evening."

She didn't even ask why I was asking but had sent me off with a wave of goodbye before retreating to her bedroom.

I couldn't deny, I felt a sting of disappointment when Alex agreed to just let me go.

You got what you wanted, you said no, and she respected that. I rolled my eyes. No need to rub it in my face.

The commute to work gave me a chance to plan out what I wanted to do on Alex's day off. I could request to adjust my schedule tomorrow so I could leave earlier at work and prepare dinner for her. I started searching for the instructions on how to cook the produce that I bought yesterday. Alex was curious what the food was for, and I hid under the pretense that I wanted to do meal preparation for my lunch at work. The ever-trusting person that she was, left it at that. This plan couldn't be timed more perfectly than this.

I was almost at my workplace, walking with my headphones

on and enjoying the warmth of the early sunlight, when a hand grabbed me and pulled me towards the side of the path walk. My heart dropped as I looked who it was.

I shouldn't be surprised at this point. *Damien.*

"What are you doing?!" I tried yanking my arm away. "Let go of me!"

Some of the people had started looking at us strangely, and I was praying someone would be brave enough to step in. Damien shushed me, his hand gripping my hand tighter.

"You whore!" he whispered angrily at me. "Have you not been reading my text?! Where did you move?!"

I was struggling, trying to pull my arm away but he was too strong. I could feel my insides churning with the fear of getting hurt again. I looked at Damien and saw pure disgust and rage in his face.

"Give me your new address or you know what will happen next!"

I cringed, my shoulders caving in defensively, bracing myself for the blow. I could feel tears starting to swell in my eyes, the overwhelming panic and horror overpowering the rationale part of my brain.

There's no escaping this. My mind was giving up. *Should I just come with him to make this stop?* I thought I was safe and had escaped this. I completely forgot that Damien was a persistent person, which was why he has been so successful in his career. He would do anything to get what he wanted. *And that included me… and Alex.* The daunting realization hit me; once he figured out that I was with Alex, he might do something dreadful to hurt her too, just for the sake of revenge and taking me away from him.

And I could not allow that, even if the only resolution was to come back to him… for now.

"Give me your phone!" He tried grabbing the phone that was in my pocket. "I will wait for you after your work. You will come with me, and we will go to your mom's house, and you will tell her that the wedding is still on!"

As a last-ditch effort, I tried yanking myself away from his grasp. And before I knew it, I was thrown to the ground, my elbow hitting the pavement; my things strewn on the ground. The people around us started clamoring and reacted to the incident.

Damien ran towards me, face now completely transformed into a concerned fiancé. "Babe, I told you. Stop wearing those heels if you can't walk properly on them. Here." He handed me my bag. "Let me take care of those wounds." Upon hearing that, people started walking away, assuming that I was taken cared of.

My mouth was hanging agape, realizing the extent of how good this man could manipulate the people around us. Seeing the window of opportunity, I grabbed my bag and ran towards the office entrance. After I beeped my access card, I turned back and saw Damien standing in front of the office, staring right into my soul.

And right before I walk away, he mouthed the words with a smile on his lips. *"I'll be waiting."*

Chapter Twenty-Nine

THE WORDS kept repeating over and over in my head as I stumbled through the elevator to our office's floor. I pushed back to the side, hoping to hide the fact that my long sleeve was ripped from where I fell on my elbows and the dirt that was covering my back. As soon as everyone had gotten off from the elevator, I ran to the closest washroom to try and conceal the evidence from this morning's incident. Before I could even enter a cubicle, I heard the door open from behind and a familiar voice echoed across the room.

"Adi!" A cheery voice called out. When I turned, Jade, my co-worker, saw what I mess I was, and her expression changed in an instant as she came running towards me. "What the fuck, Adi! What happened to you?!" She immediately grabbed a paper towel and tried wiping the blood that was dripping from my arms. "Did you get into an accident?!"

Fear and shame were the only emotions I could feel right now. The tears that I have been holding back were now freely falling, leaving a trail of mess in my face. I couldn't hear what Jade was saying but she eventually stepped out in a hurry. The thought of being alone scared me, even knowing that Damien couldn't come up here to take me away. I pulled my knees to my chest, hoping that it would be enough to hold myself together. I have a whole day of work ahead of me. And I knew that once they see me like this, they would fuss over and the past that I have been trying so hard to bury would be outed in the public.

My shame for everyone to know.

I could feel my chest starting to tighten, making it harder to breath. *Breath through the nose and exhale through the mouth.* The vivid memory of young Alex helping me breathe properly a decade ago was a comfort in the midst of this chaos. I followed Lexie's instructions: I put my head between my knees and started regulating my breathing. In a matter of minutes, I could feel my body slump, my breathing now even. I leaned back on the wall, letting the emotions wash off me, so I could get back to work and distract myself from the shitstorm this morning was.

As I stood up, the washroom door opened with a bang, and the fear that Damien might have found a way to get in the office overpowered my reasoning, that I started running to the cubicle and locked myself in. My breathe started to hitch again, my palms began sweating. I pulled up my feet up in the toilet bowl, so he wouldn't see where I was. I covered my mouth to help me keep silent, the raggedness of my breathe might be the one to give me away.

I waited. Waited for the doors to bang open as Damien tried to find and take me away.

"Adi…" I heard a man's voice. And instead of cowering, a rush of relief almost made me faint. I jumped out of the cubicle to run into his arms.

"Shh… shh… It's okay. I'm here." I could feel Nico's hands rubbing my back. "Someone called me from your office and said you were in an accident. I'm glad I'm still the one in your emergency contact." I could feel him sighing against my hair. He held me for minutes, waiting for me to calm down. And after my tears dried out, he held me in arms length to see the damage I have in my body. "See? I told you. Having offices near each other was not a terrible thing after all."

I caught a glimpse of my reflection at the mirror. My hair was in disarray, and my light blue long sleeve shirt was dirtied and crumpled. I turned around to check my back and elbows, and I could clearly see the gashes from where I fell. It wasn't as bad as my injuries before, but this was more evident in the public's eye—one that I couldn't hide.

As Nico cleaned my wounds, I told him what happened. I could see the anger boiling under his skin as he gripped the towel tight, and his lips had started to press in a thin line out of rage.

"We have to report this to your office, Adi. It's a matter of your safety."

I nodded. The anxiety of not knowing when Damien would appear in my life and grab me out of the public eye was far too overwhelming rather than the shame of being in this situation. And a couple of people knowing what I was suffering from, was a good price to pay.

Nico said goodbye as I reassured him that I would be okay as long as I was inside the office. I knew that he wouldn't leave me if it was not the case, but he has more important things to do rather than sit with me and wait for the updates from my manager. So, I sat by my desk at the human resources office, waiting for further instructions. I was excused for the rest of the day, given that I was not in the right mental space to be productive. And by two PM in the afternoon, my manager finally called me in his office.

"Adi," Mr. Grayson started and motioned for me to sit. "I heard what happened and I am so sorry."

I had always liked Mr. Grayson as a manager because he seriously cared for the wellbeing of his employees. He constantly checked on us during hiring and recruiting season, taking into consideration the workload that we undertake and seriously determines staffing requirements. He didn't want his team overworked. Not many companies have those kinds of leaders nowadays. So, I knew his concern was genuine.

"This is unprecedented, but I am willing to offer this to you because I value your skill set and contributions to our team," he started. "You can work from home until it is determined that you are safe to come out to the office. The workload for the initial interviews that will be done through video conferencing will be transferred under your task allocation, and the rest of your workload here in the office will be transitioned to Jade. Please coordinate with Germaine as well if there are pending requisition approvals from our ops team that is needed in paper." He looked at me with pity in his eyes. "I'm sorry you have to go through that. To ensure your safety as well once you go back to the office, we will require you to make a police report and possibly request a restraining order for your ex-fiancé."

This was more than I could ask for but going to the police station and airing out my dirty laundry was something I was not looking forward to.

By four in the afternoon, I have my things from the office packed up, ready to be set up at home. Nico had promised that he will be back to pick me up if in any case that Damien followed through his threat. And I was waiting in the lobby, when a familiar dark-haired woman entered the lobby and was waiting by the front desk.

"Alex," I whispered in disbelief. The relief in seeing her after a day of chaos was tangible, that tears had started brimming my eyes again. I ran and wrapped my arms tightly around her. This time, there was no hesitation before she returned the hug.

"See?" Alex rubbed circles at my back. "You should've let me drop you off."

Despite everything, I managed to smile. I knew it was her way of showing that she cared.

We grabbed my things and went through the back door. To my relief, the plan to go home an hour earlier worked and we didn't see Damien anywhere near the vicinity. And as much as my heart sank, knowing that once I report this to the authorities, judgment would be passed, even from people who did not know anything about me nor my relationship with Damien, I knew I had to do this—*finally do this*.

Alex drove us to the police station and started the report. I could see the frustration in her face when the officers told us that they could not issue a restraining order right now because I had no evidence telling Damien that he was not allowed in my property anymore or not to go to my workplace. As soon as we have that message in writing and Damien decided to violate it, then we could come back, and they would file it.

I couldn't stop myself from the despair that was bubbling up. I thought I had a way out, but Damien was right. They didn't consider my state as something urgent because I wasn't bleeding. *Maybe I was too sensitive. Maybe I made it worse by going to the police. He'll know.* And realizing the possible outcome of that made my heart sink, hope completely out of reach.

We drove in silence until we have reached the apartment, the space surrounded by thick air that was almost too suffocating. Alex remained quiet and stoic as we dropped the boxes of my equipment at the kitchen island. My mind was still reeling from all the events that have happened just in a span of less than twenty-four hours, and despite the sinking feeling that Damien might appear again in front of me to do whatever he wanted to do, I could sense a small glimmer of safety as I stared at Alex.

Reconciled friendship. I have to remind myself as I stared at her arms, imagining how it wrapped around me without any hesitations just a few hours earlier. I could feel my resolve slowly crumbling with the aftereffects of my day, affecting my judgment. All I wanted to do right now was hug her and be at the comfort of her presence.

"Is that yours?" Alex finally broke the stillness of the apartment. "I can hear the phone vibrating but it's not mine."

I straightened up from untangling the cords for my monitor and ran to my bag. I quickly grabbed my phone and as soon as I saw the name at the screen, the cold pit in my stomach had reemerged, probably even deeper than earlier.

I clicked the green phone icon. "Mom," I answered in a low voice. I started walking towards my room, hoping that Alex would not get triggered at the mention of the person who actually drove her away from this city ten years ago. "How are you?"

"*Adi!*" Her cheery greeting was quite disorienting. "*Is it true? Oh, I'm so happy, my dear Adalia!*"

Is what true? Did she finally figure out that I was living with Alex. But that wouldn't make sense since she said she was happy. "Is what true, mom?"

"*Oh, Damien passed by earlier today informing me that the wedding is back on!*" My knees buckled as the message sunk in. "*He told me and your father that you were gonna move back in with him!*"

I was left speechless. Damien knew no end. He would pull the string until I would bend for him. Using my parents as an anchor to trap me where he wanted me to be. And I knew I had to stop this once and for all.

"Mom, can I meet you for dinner and talk about this?"

"*I would love to! Let me know when so we could start the wedding planning!*" The joy in her words could not be denied. "*Oh, I am so proud of you, my dear Adi. My baby girl's finally getting married!*"

I am so proud of you.

Six words that I have been waiting to hear from her. Six words that I have been craving since I was young. And now that I was finally hearing it, I couldn't stop myself from crying, knowing that the cost for these six words was probably my life.

Alex found me slumped at the bedside, my head leaned over to my knees and my tears were just free flowing at this point. Though she knew a bit of my situation, I was still not ready to show her this side of me. I had always pride myself of being an independent woman, moving out, climbing the corporate ladder, not needing any help from anyone. But I knew deep inside that it was a façade that I need to upkeep, for the sake of my sanity and not lose myself in the controlling behavior of my mom. I tried rebelling in my own little ways—going out, drinking, being best friends with queer people, kissing boys in secret when I was young, but at the end of the day, I hid it in shame because I still craved for her approval. And now it was a matter of a lifelong commitment that would probably batter the life out of me, in exchange of her approval and happiness.

I felt strong arms carrying me to my bed, gently lying me down and removing my slippers. I could barely see as my eyes were probably swollen from all the crying I've been doing for gods know how long. I was still deep in my thoughts when I heard footsteps walking out and returning a few minutes after.

"Here," Alex voice was tender. "Drink some water." She gently propped me to sit with a pillow at my back. She didn't ask, nor forced me to tell her what happened. She just sat there as I stared at the glass of water sitting between my hands, with no more tears to shed.

"Are you mad at me?" I gazed up at Alex. There was a brewing emotion behind her eyes that she was trying to force down—even I could see that. Her brows were scrunched up together and her lips were pressed into a thin line, borderline looking angry.

"Why would you think I'd be mad at you?"

Why? Good question. I let out a sarcastic chuckle. I have been forced to think that everything was my fault, and I have to temp-check the mood of the people around me so I could always adjust.

My mom was late to an appointment because she didn't wake up on time? It was my fault because I didn't wake her up before I went to school. The weather starting to darken during an outdoor date with Damien? When I mentioned that it was about to rain, he said that I was too negative and was ruining the walk; when I tried to segue into the other direction, saying that I hope the sun would appear soon, he said that I was giving him false hope; and when the rain finally started spattering and I stated the obvious, he said that I never said anything right and already ruined the date. As flabbergasted as I was, the repeated cycle of blame was ingrained on me that I was saying sorry even if I knew that it wasn't my fault; asking the people around me if they were mad, so I could apologize right away and deescalate the mood.

"It seemed to always be my fault why things get ruined." Saying the words out loud even, solidifying the belief that yes, maybe I was the one who always ruin things. *Look at us.*

Alex eyes softened, as if hearing the confession from my thoughts. There was a tug in my heart, aching for the years that we lost together. We could have been happy, if I wasn't such a coward and came out to her when I knew I liked her before. Damien would not exist in my life, if only I had the courage to accept who I was.

And before I could stop myself, I pulled her into me, trying to convey the apology my heart has been dying to say for the past ten years. I rested my head in the nook of her shoulders, a comfortable silence finally settling between us. She began rubbing circles on my back again, lulling me into a calm that I badly needed.

"I don't pity you, Adi," Alex said, barely a whisper. "You are a strong woman who is trying to survive a horrific experience. And sometimes, it's okay to break down." I could feel her hug tightening. "We're just humans, Adi."

I buried my face deeper into her chest, hearing the steady beat of her heart. It was a stability that I could ground myself for now as I count and count, until I felt my eyes drooping, drowsiness winning me over. I closed my eyes, ready to give in to sleep. Yet before the darkness took over, I felt a gentle kiss on top of my forehead and finally, the door closing with a gentle thud.

I smiled to myself knowing deep in my gut that I was finally safe.

PART V

Alex

Chapter Thirty

THE ANGER inside me simmered like I was about to explode. All I could see was red when I witnessed Adi run towards me as if her life depended on it. It had stirred something inside that even I could not recognize. And to sprinkle salt to the wound, the fear in her eyes when she saw that her mom was calling, made me want to shield her from everything that was haunting her. I knew that I could keep her safe. I just didn't know if I had the right to think that way.

I heeded Eli's advice and tried to give myself a chance to explore these emotions I have for Adi. And asking her to move in with me was a way to figure out what it was, and if the feelings were mutual.

I could still hear Scar's scolding right before Adi moved in with me, *'For gods sake Alex, you are not teenagers. I expect, most especially from you, to think that it's ridiculous for two full-ass-grown women to expect reconciliation when neither of you can even talk properly to each other!'*

And it was true. I had to hear it from Scar to fully realize that both of us were acting like teenagers, expecting to know what the other one wanted without even properly talking. Looking at Adi and finally being with her in one space, triggered different emotions that I didn't know if I liked. There was still this remnant of the resentment that I felt when I was forced to come out to my parents, and our schoolmates making a spectacle of my sexuality when I wasn't even ready to come out as queer yet. I wanted to be indifferent to her, right from the start. That's why it took so long for me to allow Nico to bring Adi to the club. I was too afraid of what I might feel, knowing that I was not sure yet if I had fully forgiven her from before. Yet after hearing her side of the story rattled my resolve, now understanding that it was also a means to an end to protect me from her mom.

I had planned to talk with her tonight, and timing as it was, she asked me when my day off was from work. I already had my reservations for dinner, hopeful that she would get on with the plan even if it was unexpected. Yet when Nico called me before I could close my eyes to sleep, and explained what happened, the blood drained out of my face and all I could think about was how to get to Adi as fast as I possibly could

The reassurance that she was within a few feet away from me and sleeping soundly, was a relief at best. At least, I could keep an eye on her.

I grabbed my phone and dialed Scar's number. It took about six rings before she finally answered. "Alex," there was exasperation in her voice. "What did I tell you about contacting me when it's our day off?" I could hear soft jazz at the background.

"It's not about work." My voice so low, afraid to wake Adi up. Scar seemed to notice the difference in my tone and had started asking what it was about. She continued to listen as I explained what happened to Adi this morning and how it went at the police station. "If you can help me contact the people from the buildings next door, see if they have copies of their CCTVs during that night, I will owe you my life, Scar."

"You don't need to commit to a life debt for me to help you, Alex," she answered. "I'm your friend. And I know how important Adi is to you."

I didn't answer.

Was that what it was?

"U-huh." I could feel Scar's smug look on her face. "Don't be stubborn, boss. Accept it. You still like her. *Byeeeee*." And without any second longer, I heard the click of the call being cut.

And before I could even dwell on what Scar said, I browsed through my contacts and found the other number I was looking for. *Summer*. I clicked the screen and the line started ringing.

"My dear club owner," Summer answered in a sweet voice. "To what do I owe the pleasure?"

ADI WOKE up a few hours later, her eyes still swollen from all the crying she has done. She grabbed a bag of mixed veggies from the freezer and instantly covered her eyes with it. She sat at the kitchen island, staring at me while I worked around the kitchen for dinner.

"Smells delicious." Adi's voice was raspy. "What's the occasion?"

"I borrowed the things you bought yesterday." I turned around to flip the steak. "I'll pay you back or we can go to the store again to buy the replacement." I waited for her response, but she remained silent. Curiosity got the best of me and as I turned around, I felt foolish. No one was sitting at the island, Adi nowhere to be found.

And right on time, I heard a toilet flush, and the door swung open. Adi emerged from the washroom, eyes now fully awake. She gave me a small smile and started walking towards the kitchen

"Here, let me help you." She grabbed the skillet and started running the butter on the steak while it was sizzling. "I was supposed to do this for us, you know? But after everything… I completely forgot about it."

The incident was still fresh, and I was not going to force Adi to relive all the dreadful things that had just happened when she can barely open her eyes from crying a few hours ago. "Let me know when you want to talk about it."

I looked at her over my shoulder, and the pain of the earlier incident was still painted on her face. Her brows were scrunched up as if concentrating on cooking the steak, but I could see the blank stare in her eyes, knowing that her thoughts were all elsewhere.

I grabbed the skillet away and turned off the stove. I didn't need to state the obvious that she was not in the right head space to do tasks that could hurt her along the way. She wrapped her arms around her body, tightening as she tried to push down a sob. From that look, I knew she was doing it for my sake rather than hers. She didn't want to look weak in front of me. And that broke my heart

213

even more.

The crucible that had separated us from the beginning was something I thought I could never forget. But as I looked in Adi's eyes, seeing the agony from all the suffering she had experienced the entirety of her life from the people around her, all I saw was a lost little girl, finally trying to find her way into her true self.

But the past kept coming back for her, pulling her to the life she so desperately wanted to escape.

The final piece of the wall that I have built up finally chipped away as I pulled Adi closer, offering the safety my arms could give, even if only for a minute. She welcomed it completely, finally sobbing in my chest, letting it all out. All I could feel right now was not only the urge to protect her and keep her safe, but also the slow brewing anger for the people who made her this way.

I led Adi towards the couch and sat her down. "Hold on." She didn't let go when I tried walking away. "I'll grab you some water."

I tried stepping away the second time, but before I could fully let go of her hand, she whispered, "Stay… please."

And it took all my restraint not to kiss her at that moment. She looked so broken and all I wanted to do was make her forget; to get lost in the trance of lust, even for just an evening; to make her feel that she was safe above anything else.

I realized it was the reason I relented to Summer's whims that night; it was the reason why I agreed to be with Eli—to forget just even for a little. To forget the intensity of my emotion that I have tried pushing down, convincing myself that I was over it. But now, I realized that the people I agreed to play around with was a subconscious manifestation of my feelings for Adi. I saw bits of fragments of her in them; Summer's long wavy hair the same shade as hers, Eli's presence, a comfort, just like the way I felt before with her.

It has always been her. And that realization shook me to my core. It took me to see Adi breaking down, almost rock bottom, to finally accept that the possibility of still loving her was still ingrained in me; that I would do anything to keep her safe not because to make up for what I lacked ten years ago, but simply because I wanted to keep her safe, no conditions attached.

I never got over her even after ten years has passed; that my anger and resentment were shields that I chose to wear, to fool myself into believing that I was done. I chose to wear it because I was afraid that if I remove the anger in my heart, all I would be left with was my unrequited love. And my younger self cannot fathom how deep was that, so it tried to cope by being resentful and promising myself that I would never fall into the same trap again.

And now brown eyes brimmed with tears, looked at me as if I was a lifeline, her hands holding tightly into mine. *Stay*, she said.

Stay and get hurt again? My inner voice whispered. *Stay and be betrayed again?*

Maybe this time, it's different. I argued. *Maybe this time, she'll stay by my side and won't turn her back on me.* My heart ached, finally letting myself recognize the emotions that I have pushed down for so long: The same little girl that was so scared that her feelings might not be returned was still there, trying to hide and proving herself that she had learned her lesson.

Adi had let go of my hand as she released a long exhale. "I'm sorry, I didn't mean to get so clingy." She started wiping her tears away from her eyes, leaving red marks on her already swollen eyelids. "Come on, let's go finish cooking."

And despite the tears-streaked face, all I could see was a strong woman, standing up after being wounded from a tumble. And my heart swelled of pride for the woman she had become.

Adi stood up and started walking back to the kitchen. *Was it the best time to reveal my hand to her?* I shouldn't add up on the stress that she was already facing. There would be another time to talk about this, but not now.

My heart can wait—what's another day after the ten years I have longed for her.

I followed Adi to the kitchen and looked at the already well-done steak. She had started cleaning up while I started to plate the dinner, a charged silence surrounding us. Without anyone breaking the quiet, we were done preparing and was ready to eat within ten minutes. And by the time Adi put down the skillet after drying, I was pouring red wine on the two glasses in front of me.

I passed the quarter-filled glass to Adi. "You told me that you these were for your meal-prep." I was hoping that small talk would make her feel a bit… normal. "But you also said earlier that you were planning to cook for us…" I left the sentence hanging, a curious smile on my face.

Adi's face scrunched up, trying to remember what she said. And a stunned look crossed her face as she sat down in front of me at the dining table.

"Oh," she started, a hint of hesitation on her voice. "It was to say thank you for letting me stay here. And I want to discuss how much I would need to share for rent and utilities while I'm staying here. Most especially that I will be starting to work from home for now." She gave me a smile that didn't reach her eyes, gloom still tangible in her body.

I motioned to do the sign of the cross and started the prayer before meal before answering her question. A few seconds of silence has passed, a bit longer for Adi as I noticed her squeezing her hands tighter, muttering a personal prayer.

I waited before she was done. "You don't have to. I offered you my place…" The words were hard to push out. "Because you're my *friend.*"

Her reaction was unreadable, a smile crossed her face. She looked up and asked, "*Amicable*, right?"

I nodded, my eyes not leaving her face.

Adi smiled again to herself, disappointment briefly crossing her face. But instead of continuing to talk about these non-verbal cues as adults should, both of us left it at that, despite the million questions that were running in my head. I could already imagine Scar scolding me, with her hands on her waist to complete the vibe.

We continued to eat quietly as cozy lo-fi music played in the background. We were almost done with our wines when Adi stood up and went to the fridge. And before I could ask her what she was about to get, she came in the dining area with a chocolate mousse cake on her hands, candles already lit.

"I was waiting for midnight, but I wanted to be the first one to greet you. The dinner was actually for your birthday." She put the cake in front of me and pulled out her phone. "Happy birthday. Make a wish, Alex." There was still a tinge of sadness in her voice, but I knew she was putting in an effort to be a tad cheerful despite the circumstance.

Adi sat at the other side of the table, phone in her hand, ready to capture the moment. And as I closed my eyes, I knew I had only one wish for tonight.

Clapping ensued as I blew out the candles. "So, care to share what Alexandria had wished for, for her twenty-ninth birthday?" She was still taking a video.

I shook my head, a small smile playing on my lips. "I don't want to jinx it."

She gave a chuckle, teasing and urging me to spill it.

"Come on," she teased. "Make a woman less sad by sharing your wish. I promise I won't snitch."

"You really wanna know?" I asked in a daring voice.

And like the old Adi, she was oblivious to the undertone that was implied. She nodded eagerly like a child being let on a secret. She continued holding the phone directed at me.

I slowly stood up and walked towards where she was sitting. Her eyes widened in surprise, gradually realizing what was happening. I took her phone and put it faced down at the table. I asked her again, "Do you really wanna know?" And this time, she looked at me from under her lashes, finally understanding what I wished for.

I grabbed her chin up and slowly lowered my face closer to hers. I could smell the wine from her breath, the warmth blowing in my face. I could feel her breathing starting to get uneven, the anticipation, a wire coiling in her body.

"You can say no," I whispered. "You can always say no, to me." I lowered my lips close enough, before deciding to move my face to the side and letting the kiss land softly on her cheek.

Not tonight. I have to remind myself.

Adi's mouth was slightly opened, her brows wrinkled in confusion. I gave her a teasing smile.

I straightened up and started grabbing the plates from the table. I knew that if I turned around and saw the expression Adi has, I wouldn't be able to stop myself from walking back and grabbing her as my own.

How noble. How ironic that moments ago, you were thinking of letting Adi lose herself into lust. My inner voice scolded. *What contradicting morals you have.* I internally shook the thought out of my mind, not wanting to have this conversation right now.

"Wha –?" Exasperation was evident on Adi's voice. "What the heck, Alex?" I was walking towards the kitchen when she caught up to me.

"You're not in the right head space tonight," I tried explaining as I began clearing up the plates. "I don't want you to do something you're not even sure you want to do."

You are more than a good fuck. I wanted to tell her.

Adi let out a disgruntled growl, then grabbed my arm to turn and face me towards her. The frustration was painted all over her face. "I am tired of people trying to tell me what I am and what I am feeling! I am not someone so fragile that you have to put up your safety nets for me! I am a grown ass woman, and I know what I want!"

I stepped a bit closer, now towering and trapping her with my body against the kitchen island. "Then tell me, Adi," I lowered my face closer to her ear. "What do you actually want from me?"

Her breath hitched, but her face was petulant as a kid. "Tell me your wish first." She crossed her arms, trying to intimidate me.

"I kissed you, right?" I straightened as I turned back to the dishes. "Wasn't that enough of an answer?"

"Well… I thought you wanted to fuck me," Adi answered, trying to be nonchalant as she could but I could hear the shakiness of her voice.

I chuckled as a response. She didn't need to know that I've been wanting to hold her body against mine since that night she threw herself on my lap. The way her skin felt under my palm and the way her body sang to mine was something that has haunted me ever since. Even when I was holding another woman's body under mine, it was hers that was in my mind.

Sorry, Summer. No offense to you.

Nevertheless, this was not the right time. I wanted to do it with her once she could decide with a clear head.

"What? Are you scared to fuck me?"

I faced her again, trying to show that I did not appreciate being taunted when I was barely hanging on the thread of my control.

"Adi," I smiled slyly at her. "Don't threaten me with a good time."

Chapter Thirty-One

RECKLESS! YOU *are such a reckless asshole!* I have been scolding myself for the past thirty minutes as I cleaned up after our dinner. To Adi's annoyance, I almost pushed her in the washroom after enticing her with a bath to soak for a few minutes before we continue setting up her home office, leaving the conversation of fucking her ignored. *For now.*

She obliged without complaint after smelling the lavender bath bombs I used to draw the bath.

I thought you wanted to fuck me. She didn't know how much. My morality was in a tether that was about to break. I promised myself that I would not do anything with Adi during this vulnerable phase yet the moment she asked me what I wished for, I couldn't help myself but give in just a little and have a taste of her. The scent of the sweet wine still lingered in her mouth, making me want to throw sense out of the window and devour her right there and there—down south, if I could. And I have to thank my self-restraint for not failing me when my rationale went out the windows as soon as I felt Adi's soft skin under my lips.

By the time I finished cleaning up, I could still hear Adi's phone playing music in the washroom. *It has been more than thirty minutes. Should I be worried?*

I was about to knock on the door to check when it opened, revealing a flushed Adi with only a small towel covering her body. Droplets of water visible on her shoulders, and my mind was consumed with the overwhelming anticipation of having my mouth explore every nook and crevices her body has.

"Oh!" Adi's surprised voiced pulled me out of my unclean thoughts. *Not yet.* I had to remind myself. "I'm sorry, did you need to use the washroom?"

As speechless as I was, seeing her with almost nothing, I forced my expression hopefully into nonchalance because I could feel my hand itching to touch her blushing face and pull it against mine. "Yeah, I just need to use the toilet." I closed the door without looking back.

The universe was really toying with me at this point.

Instead of just taking a leak, I've decided to go straight into shower to hopefully help wash the train of thoughts my mind kept pulling me into. I turned the shower dial into scalding hot, stealing my thoughts away from Adi even just for a minute. The hot water cascaded into my body, untangling the wired muscles from my back. Today was such a long day.

I heard the TV sounds as soon as I stepped out of the washroom, towel in hand, drying my hair out. I was stunned to see Adi in her boxer shorts *that was too short for my self-control*, and a green hoodie. She has a plate of cake in one hand and a glass of wine in the other. She grabbed the blankets from her room and made space for a mini picnic set up. I looked at the TV and I heard an all-too-familiar soundtrack.

"*Princess Diaries* on a Monday evening?" My brows raised in question. "You have work tomorrow, right?"

Adi tapped at the seat beside her. "I called my manager and told him I needed a day off." I was amazed. This woman has a lot of time off available. *Maybe I should apply at the company where she is working.*

"Aren't you gonna get fired from missing too much work?" I asked as I sat down beside her, grabbing the cake from her hand.

"No, I did a lot of overtimes during Q1 and instead of paying me overtime, I opted to accumulate the hours, so I can use it as my paid time off." She took a slice from the cake in my hands. "It's a better option for me since I was saving it up to travel."

Adi beamed at me. The candidness of her innocent smile while having cake stuck on her teeth, made my heart feel a bit lighter. "We're gonna wait until midnight for your birthday." She started settling in with the fort of pillow behind her back. "Just like old times."

"Yeah, just like old times." There was a tug in my heart; an overwhelming feeling that wasn't supposed to be let out yet. I distracted myself by looking at the plate in my hand and something click at the back of my mind.

"You remembered..." I whispered. I glanced at Adi, now giving me one of her toothy grins.

"Of course, I remembered! How you won't have anything other than this chocolate mousse cake when we used to celebrate your birthdays. *Tita* Marian used to say that you would throw tantrums if you had a different cake."

The longing I felt from the uncovered memory was not something I was expecting. Adi used to sleep at my house every year to celebrate the first few hours of my birthday together. Regardless of if it was a school night, we would spend the night watching movies until it was midnight. And she would sing me a happy birthday despite her eyelids already dropping and her wits already flying to dreamland.

I have not celebrated my birthday like this after. I was always drowned with schoolwork when I was in university, and that didn't change when I got to work my first few years in the corporate world. I even forgot that tomorrow was my birthday.

"Thank you," I said, barely a whisper. "You didn't have to."

Adi turned to me and beamed as a response. I forgot how I missed that smile. "Of course, I have to!" she beamed and turned her gaze back to the screen.

For the longest time, all I remember was the incident that tore us apart. And I forgot all the good years we had before that. All the times we slept over at my or Nico's home; the time we got an earful from Nico's mom after drinking beer when we were still underage. I forgot the mundane things that I enjoyed doing with Nico and Adi when we were at school. I forgot how much I loved seeing Adi's carefree smile, the determination in her face during exam and deadline week. But also, just being in her presence. I thought I was indifferent. I convinced myself that I didn't care. Yet the moment I laid my eyes on Adi, a storm of emotions shoved its way into my carefully built walls, removing it brick by brick, until I was left bare.

We let the silence settle as the movie started playing, sitting shoulder to shoulder, with blankets covering our legs. Despite the years that have passed, it was so easy to fall back into the rhythm of *us*, just like how we were before. The realization that struck made me sneak a glance at the woman beside me, enjoying the warmth of her blanket and the wine in her hand.

Adi was no longer the young woman she was. She used to be so bubbly like a sunshine one prays for on a rainy day, yet now there was a heavy energy that surrounded her. Her gaze often felt distant and when she smiled, its as if it never reached her eyes. It was too selfish of me to think that I was the one only suffering after that incident yet here she was, still haunted by the ghosts of her past.

Adi's eyes were trained at the TV with a child-like concentration—the perfect chance to look at her, and hopefully not get caught. She always told me when we were young that she never found herself too pretty, and that was primarily because of the puberty spurt and the acne that came along with it. I have always reminded her that she was beautiful, despite the belief she has of conventional standards. And until now, I believed that. I have seen a lot of women who were the epitome of beauty standards yet the moment I saw her in that black dress at the club, my eyes could not look away, even if I willed it to.

She definitely had outgrown the short bob that she used to have during high school. And now all I could imagine was how my fingers would tangle in that long dark mane of hers. Or how that mouth, which have always worked its way almost out of anything when we were young, would feel like gliding across my body.

I was lost in my thought when Adi reached out for the plate in my hand and placed it at the coffee table. She paused the movie, and I noticed that we were at the part Mia and Michael were about to kiss by the fountain.

"Alex." She scratched her neck, her voice a bit shaky. "I have a question." I nodded, unsure what to make of it. "If you were standing in front of me in that garden, what would your answer be if I ask you 'why me'?" Out of all the questions that she could ask under the sun, I didn't expect it to be this one. "or 'why me' when we were still young?"

Adi was looking at me, patiently waiting for an answer. I paused and gave it a thought. *Why her?*

I didn't know what to say.

I could remember how she wormed her way into my life – greeting me with toothy grins, making me laugh with her innocence, and just making me feel safe and accepted. What could an eighteen-year-old ask for more? When I thought love looked like that.

When love looked like her?

Before I could delve more in depth into the thoughts my mind steered me into, Adi grabbed both of my hands and held it entwined with hers. "Alex," she said barely above a whisper. "I need to tell you something."

The internal panic ensued after hearing those six words.

Not before my birthday, please. A silent plea of my subconscious. 'We need to talk,' and 'I need to tell you something' were sentences that I did not wish to hear as it mostly ends up with terrible news. Bad news just before my birthday, and right after kissing Adi, would be the most ironic cherry on top. Yet I pulled my mental adult pants on. I could imagine my inner self picking up the blocks, starting to build that wall again.

It ended right even before we could start again.

I saw Adi close her eyes and release a huge sigh. *Here it goes.*

"I like you," her voice so low, I almost did not catch it. I was about to waive the news off, trying to show the nonchalance I have so overly practiced. Yet I had to stop myself to rewind the words that she just said. "And if you're gonna ask me the same question, I know that I would answer the same – 'cause you saw me as me. Nothing less, nothing more."

I like you. Three words. Three words that left my mouth hanging slightly opened, words failing to come out of it. Three words to put an end to the silent suffering that I have been pushing to the side. Yet despite the relief of finally hearing the three words that I have been waiting for since a decade ago, there was a tinge of uncertainty growing in my stomach.

"Are you sure?" I asked.

Adi's brow shot up as if surprised with the question. "Am I sure about what?" she retorted a bit confused.

I could see where she was coming from. She just confessed her affection yet here I was, being a skeptic to dampen the mood. And as much as I loved her, I needed to protect myself, too. I could not go through that pain again.

"Are you sure that you like me?" I asked. "That you *really* like women?" The unsaid implication grew heavy in the air; my aired doubts rooting itself once again as Adi looked down at her hands, choosing to stay silent.

As much as I wanted her to be mine, I cannot let her silence ruin me again.

Adi finally raised her gaze. "*Lexie...* I'm sorry." She held my hands in between hers. "I was young, and I was scared. I didn't have the power to fight for you back then." My heart broke in a thousand pieces for the two young woman who just wanted to be with each other but was forced to be apart because of societal expectations and reputations.

"I would understand if you can't accept my apology just yet. I'm here to try and make things right." Adi dropped her hands to her lap. "I came here, not expecting anything. I was just hoping for the best, hoping to win my best friend back."

We were young. We were scared. We didn't have the power to fight for each other back then. Adi was not only speaking for herself, but for me, too. And that was the straw the broke the camel's back. We were not the young women ten years ago. We were the same but so, so different.

"I think it's time we forgive our younger selves." I wiped the tears that had started running down Adi's face and smiled at her. "We didn't know any better."

The relief in Adi's face was tangible as she grabbed my face in between her hands, also wiping the tears that have started brimming my eyes. "You are the embodiment of the things I lost because I didn't stand up for something that I love. Whenever I looked at you, all I could feel is my overwhelming regret—regret that I didn't fight for you. I was so scared... scared that now I'm starting to accept who I am... *who I was*; that I wouldn't have the chance to make it right with you anymore." We both started sobbing, letting the burden of the past ten years, fully disappear in the air. "And after that night... After I saw you with Summer... I thought my fear had finally come true to slap me in the face as my karma. I thought I lost you that night just because I was scared ten tears ago, and I was scared until now..."

"But not anymore," I finished the sentence as it rang true to both our truths after the longest time.

Chapter Thirty-Two

WE FINISHED the night the same way as we did when we were young—Adi sleeping halfway through the movie and me turning off and cleaning up everything before I turned in. The sun has not risen just yet when I decided to peel away from Adi's arms and legs that were wrapped around mine. The urge to just stay and cuddle with her was far too tempting, yet I knew I had to do somethings that were too important than sleeping with the person I loved.

Love. The conversation last night played over and over in my head—three words that were on repeat until I could barely open my eyes anymore. *Is this what it is?*

I grabbed my phone and walked towards the washroom after tucking Adi in for a few more hours of sleep. The buzz from my electric toothbrush was enough to shake the sleepiness from my eyes as I started looking at the notifications on my screen. One from Scar and one from... *Summer.* My heart dropped from anticipation as I clicked the banner.

Three words. It was just three words: *We got him.* I almost dropped my phone from relief. She did it. She actually did it. And it was the last puzzle piece to put this issue to rest.

I tapped on the phone button, unable to contain the buzz in my nerves. After the sixth ring, Summer answered the phone with a very sleepy voice.

"Alex, it's...." Her voice faded for a second. "Five in the fucking morning. What do you want?"

"Did you do it?" With the rustle in the background, I assumed she got out of bed. And that made me feel a bit guilty but not enough to end the call right away. "What happened?"

"Get me coffee, you woke me up anyway." I could hear the annoyance in her voice, but I couldn't help myself but smile as I gave her the name of my favorite coffee shop.

The anticipation to finally end *this* was humming in my veins that half an hour later, I opened my door to the brisk November morning, almost running on my way to the coffee shop.

I WAS greeted with a grumpy Summer, wrapped with multiple layers of clothes and a touch of a heavy wool scarf and shades to finish the look. She plopped at the seat in front of me, hot coffee, and pastry already in front of her.

"I am not a morning person, Alex. You know that." With an annoyed grunt, she started stripping away her layers and finally rested her hands at the side of the mug with a sigh. "I am not a *fall or winter* morning person, Alex. I'm not made for this weather."

I wanted to get right into the conversation, wanting to know what happened, and wanting to return to Adi who I left sleeping still. I left a note at the fridge, letting her know that I would be grabbing breakfast for us and will return in a few hours.

Adi didn't need to know what this conversation was about... for now. And it was better if she didn't know just yet.

"So, what happened last night?" I asked. "I hope it wasn't as bad."

"You were right. He was around the clubs last night. He was just drinking at the bar and wasn't really looking out for women." Summer paused, a mischievous smile on her face. "But what you said worked. I styled my hair like hers and that black little dress. It took a few minutes for him to warm up to me. But I got him."

A relief that nothing bad happened to Summer was a thorn of my chest. "I tried *so hard* to be the submissive little girl that you wanted me to be. And it worked like a charm. By the end of the night, he has his hand on my thigh, my back, and my arms, asking me to come home with him."

A spark of anger, flared inside of me, knowing that *that* man had laid those filthy hands again on someone I knew. I didn't realize the reaction was evident in my face until Summer reached out a hand across the table to cover mine.

"It's okay," she reassured me. "It was not the first time I experienced unwanted touches in my body. And to be fair, this was for a worthy cause."

It was not okay. I squeezed her hand. That was the main goal of starting *Club Tala*—for everyone to be able to express their own selves without thinking of their safety.

"Alex," I heard Summer called out.

"Alex?" Followed by another voice that was too familiar, had pulled me out of my simmering thoughts. I turned my head to see Adi, standing in her joggers, eyes at the holding hands on top of the table. I quickly drew my hand away, hiding it in my pocket. "Uh… I saw your note. And I thought I'd join you… but it seemed that you already have someone to accompany you."

I could see confused hurt in her face, her body angling towards the door, ready to run. I stood up to reach out and stop her, but Summer had beaten me to it.

"Adi, right?" Summer stood up and grabbed another chair from the table next to ours. "Why don't you join us? I'm sure we have a lot to talk about."

Adi looked conflicted but decided to grab the chair that Summer offered and sat down in the middle of us. An awkward silence settled at the table.

"Here, let me grab you something. Hazelnut Latte?" I offered.

She nodded.

I was by the counter, waiting for the order, when I heard a laugh from where we were sitting. I sneaked a glance at the two women, Summer talking animatedly and Adi was just looking at her with a huge grin on her face. *Well, that was unexpected.* I left them alone for ten minutes and now the animosity was gone and they're acting as if they were besties.

"You seemed like you're having fun." I placed Adi's coffee and pastry in front of her. "You want to let me in on the laugh?" The two women gave each other a secretive smile.

"If your girl decides to tell you."

My girl. That has a good ring to it. Yet before I could bask in the moment of hearing those words, unwanted thoughts have started clawing its way back up, the trigger pulled.

Will she deny me again?

Will she say that it's nothing like that again?

Will she be scared to stand by her actions, again?

Will she hide me again like a dirty, little secret?

The thoughts were running wild in my head, thinking of all the possible worst-case scenario that may happen again. I promised that I would never let myself experience the same pain again and here I was, playing with same fire.

All of my thoughts were squashed when I felt a small, warm hand grab mine from under the table, giving it a squeeze. I looked up and saw Adi smiling at me. And a small ray of possibility cleared the clouds of my doubts, that maybe this could work.

We could work.

I squeezed her hand and returned the smile. The silent agreement that we have, an anchor that I would be holding on.

By eight in the morning, the coffee shop had started to get busy, and we took that as our cue to leave and let other customers use our table. Adi excused herself to use the washroom and left me and Summer outside, saying our goodbyes.

She stepped in for a quick hug. "She seemed like a nice woman. No wonder you looked so distraught that night." I knew the night that she was referring to and the conflict that had cause between me and Adi. "Don't think about it, anymore. It was a night of fun, nothing more."

"Summer, thank you again for last night." I never thought that I would be able to trust this woman to help me in my time of need. "You were the *perfect* woman for the job, I couldn't deny that. Let me know how I can repay you."

"One night," she smiled at me coyly. My eyes widened, assuming what she was implicating. Summer guffawed after seeing the expression on my face. "Not that kind of night, Alex. I need one night with you and Scar to hear me out. I have a proposition for you."

I was curious but I held my questions and told her to come tonight at the club for a meeting since it was a Tuesday night, and we were not expecting as much customers as the weekend. I needed to know the rest of how last night went as well.

Adi stepped out of the coffee shop as she was pulling her toque down.

"Ready to go?"

Adi nodded and gave Summer a quick hug before saying our goodbyes.

We settled into a comfortable pace, walking side by side with our hands in our pocket. "Did you mean it?" Adi asked. I didn't have a clue what she was asking about. "You told Summer I was your girl?"

Oh. I stopped walking and turned to Adi. "No, I mean… Summer just assumed that we were together when I told her that you were staying at my place. We'll have a meeting tonight; I'll straighten it up." The panic had risen in my face. She was right. Why didn't I correct Summer right there and then?

"Don't," she said barely above a whisper. "You don't have to. Only if you want to."

Huh? It seemed like my brain had stopped working for a quick minute before I realized what Adi was implying. She took my hand and held it between hers, a small smile playing on her lips. "I'll be yours, if you take me."

The only thing I could think and do was grab her face and kiss her like it was a lifeline. *She's mine. Finally mine.* Despite all the fucked-up things that have happened between us, fate had given us a second chance I didn't even knew I needed. I convinced myself that it was the perfect moment to finally reveal my hand, to finally tell her all the things I wanted to since we were young—how pretty she was when she laughed, how it made my heart skip a beat whenever she looked at me from under her lashes, and to allow her to touch me now, without holding back. *Finally.*

Yet as I basked in the moment of overwhelming affection, I realized that Adi's body was as rigid as a rock under my touch, her lips not as welcoming as I thought it would be. Her eyes were darting everywhere. Except mine.

And one thought kept repeating in my head.

I knew it.

I knew it. I knew it.

It was the same fucking thing all over again.

The dread had started its way in my gut again, knowing full well where this was going. "I'm sorry, I didn't mean to force you to do that." I stepped away and started walking away, the heaviness in my heart starting to weigh me down. *I knew it.* I scolded myself. *How stupid can you be?*

I could hear footsteps following me, but I chose to ignore it. *Not this time.* I kept reminding myself as I try to walk as fast as I can, close to even running, just to get out of wherever she was.

Not this time. Not anymore. Flashbacks reran in my head like a broken film, repeating the scene where Adi's mom slapped me in the face and Adi silently sitting at the corner.

Not this time. Not again. The whispers that surrounded me for the last two weeks at school, and all I could do was pretend that I was not affected.

I'm done. It was clear as day how I came running home to my parents telling them that I wanted to leave. They never knew what happened, but I could see in my mother's eyes that her heart was breaking for the daughter she wasn't able to protect.

"Lexie…" Adi called out to me after we have reached the apartment. "I'm sorry…"

"It's Alex." I stopped walking. I had to take a deep breath to maintain the composure that I had so perfectly practiced. "Sorry? You're sorry for what?"

"I—" Adi tried to step closer, but I put a hand put up and made her stop. I couldn't have her anywhere near me right now. "I was just surprised that you kissed me… Out in public." The last three words barely a whisper.

"Out in public?!" I finally welcomed the flare of anger. "Adi, do you remember last night? That you were asking me—no, begging me to fuck you?! And now you're scared that people out there saw us kissing?" I could see her flinch from the truth that was thrown at her face. And the guilt in her face was the final plug that was undone as my heart spilled its pain for her to witness.

"What? Are you embarrassed by me?" My voice almost breaking. "Are you ashamed that a *woman* kissed you out in public? Are you so repulsed by me?!"

"Alex... I—" My heart felt tug of worry when I saw tears started falling from her eyes. *I would not be shaken,* I remind myself.

"No, Adi. You tell me that you're mine yet the moment that there are other people involved, you fold as easily as a paper." I remembered the relief when she held my hand at the restaurant then I realized that it was under the table. *No one saw it.* "You say you like me, but only when it's convenient for you, right? When no one else is around so no one can judge you and ruin your reputation." *Just like before.*

"If that's how your love is going to be," *Not this time. Not anymore.* "you can keep all that to yourself."

Chapter Thirty-Three

THE NIGHT couldn't get any faster for me to have a reason to get away from this wretched apartment. So here I was, at four PM, sitting at *Club Tala's* bar, reviewing reports that I already looked at, at least four times. I called Summer to move the meeting up by a few hours and instead of her usual complaints, she agreed a tad too excitedly.

I heard the back door opened with a clank. "Never thought I'd see you when the sun is still shining, boss." Scar teased. When I didn't answer, I heard scurried footsteps until I saw Scar in front of me, brows scrunched in worry. She knew there was something wrong right away when I didn't even spare her a single glance. "Hey, what's wrong? Are you okay?"

"*Okay* is a relative term," I answered quietly, not trusting my voice not to break. I gazed up at Scar and saw her concern. And that look broke something inside of me, finally letting the dam of tears flow freely. "But no, Scar. I'm not okay."

She wrapped me around her arms, allowing me to let it all out without questions. She drew circles in my back, reassuring me that she was there for me.

I didn't know how long it took before I finally calmed down, ready to revert to the old self I carefully crafted. A glass of water stood in front of me, untouched. "Are you ready to talk about it?" Scar asked.

"There's nothing to talk about, Scar." I tried putting steel in my voice. "It was a moment of vulnerability that backfired at my face. Nothing more." The imbued tone of finality, hoping to make Scar stop prodding the wounds I was trying to hide.

Scar stared at me. "There's a lot to talk about, Alex. And you hiding beneath that *'I-don't-care-I'm-Alex-Johnson'* attitude isn't gonna help you deal with this issue." She extended a hand for me to hold. "What is it, Alex? I know you. You don't have to hide from me."

I reached out a hand and grasped hers. I often forget that I have people around me that loved me, who were not ashamed of me, and had fully accepted me as who I was. But the deep-rooted insecurity still lingered, hoping for validation to cure its pain.

"Scar," I continued to gaze at our hands. "I know we see each other at work more than outside, but do you feel embarrassed to be seen with me, thinking that people may mistake us as a couple?"

Scar gave me an understanding look, as if knowing where this question was coming from. "No, Alex," she reassured me. "It would be the opposite of that. If I were your girlfriend, I would feel so lucky and show you off to everyone I knew." She gave my hand a squeeze and smiled at me proudly. "You have gone through a lot most especially when you were young. You embraced the scars and the hurt, and it turned you into this strong woman who have tried to heal and forgive herself for things she didn't know how to cope with.

"Besides, who am I to complain? I have the Alex Johnson as my girlfriend? Have you seen her dress and strut her style at the club while I labor away making drink?" she teased. "Never a sweat on her brow, always clean and crisp. Even after having sex with a woman in her office, she has new pants ready." She side-eyed me. "Don't think I didn't notice."

A laugh bubbled out of my chest. A feeling of overwhelming gratitude to one of the people who was always there for me, swelled in me. Yet the reality of the current situation bore its way down, and tears had started blurring my vision again.

"Why does she, then?"

Scar paused for a good minute before answering in a quiet voice.

"I love you, Alex. You've always known that. You are so strong headed and so goal-oriented but sometimes you fail to see that some people are not in the same timeline or pacing as you." She gave me a sad smile. "You had years to explore your sexuality, but she had just started. Almost 30 years of conditioning and mindset are not easy to switch off."

And as much as I hated to admit it, she was right.

"There is no denying that she hurt you. She did. But if you really want her, *really love her,* you would give her time to heal. I'm not saying you should fix all her problems for her. But be a helping hand, ready to hold hers during times she cannot do it alone anymore."

"80/20," I whispered.

Scar smiled and nodded.

"You do it for your friends—being their eighty when they were only at their twenty. Why not extend it to her?" She dropped my hands and turned around to start brewing coffee. "But then again, it would always be up to you—whatever decision you make that you think will be best for you. And we'll always be here to support you."

Scar placed a cup of steaming black coffee in front of me, knowing full well that I haven't slept a wink to prepare for tonight's meeting and work. I offered her a grateful smile.

"*We* as in you and Eli?" I asked with a side-eye, grateful for the changed topic for once. "*You think I didn't notice?*" mocking her with the same tone she just used on me. She shot me a look and rolled her eyes.

As I was about to take my first sip, a knock at the main entrance echoed through the empty club. Scar waived me off to stay seated while she ran over to open the door. I tried fixing myself the best that I could, even if it was Summer, it was still a business meeting. And looking like a bee stung my eyes was not a good impression. I took the glass of water and pressed it in my eyes, praying for a miracle that she wouldn't notice.

I turned around on my seat and plastered a smile I have so carefully crafted and was surprised to see Summer out of her usual outfit. She was donning a tailor-fitted suit with a skirt, matching with very bright red stilettos that can almost be considered as a deadly weapon. She marched towards me and leaned over to give me a kiss on both of my cheeks.

"Seemed a little too formal?" I asked.

"I want you to take me seriously. I am here not as a friend but as a prospective investor or if this conversation goes well, a partner." She took the chair beside me and had pulled out her laptop with her presentation and offered us a physical copy of it as well. It was like seeing a stranger in front of me. Summer has always been playful and flirty at best whenever she was around me or the club but now, she looked like she really meant business.

I browsed through the papers and saw that it was reports of the performance and trends of the club that was within the vicinity of our location. Rankings, number of customers, ratings, and customer feedback all consolidated in visual representation.

"So, I know you've only known me as a regular at the clubs around here," Summer started. "But I was actually doing research in which business to invest for the next five years."

I couldn't hide the surprise on my face. Not once did it ever cross my mind that Summer was actually doing business during the months that she had been coming here. "I have hired people to do the market research for me, but I wanted to know the actual situation and the people who operate the business behind closed doors—to build connection and of course to truly know the people who I will be working with potentially."

Scar and I were staring at Summer as if she was talking gibberish. It was a total one-eighty change from what we have known her for, and connecting the two persona was a bit of a struggle for me, considering that at one point, she was on top of my office table, grinding her hips against my hands.

"I was planning to build my own club but seeing how it was becoming saturated in this area, I thought that my best recourse was to invest for the time being while doing additional research for different locations that I could start my own." She smiled at us. "I know you're thinking that I will be a competitor—yes and no. I am planning to build my club in a different location, and more likely in a different province, and no, the reason why I'm choosing to invest for now is because I want to learn it from the ground up. As much as I have my people to do the work for me, I still want to be involved in everything. And I think that learning from you is the best option for me."

"So, sleeping me with was a ploy for me to agree?" I teased.

"No Alex," Summer teasingly grazed her hand across my chin. "You just seemed so... distant and cold, that I needed to know what makes you warm. I was merely curious. No offense to you."

I knew that it was nothing more than a hook-up. "I hope the experience had satisfied your curious mind."

"Oh, very much so!" she exclaimed. "Definitely recommend!"

Scar made a show of gagging, making us laugh. "Please don't. I don't need to know my boss' sex life, or how good she is. This room might not be enough for her ego."

I almost smacked Scar playfully which she returned more viciously. It was nice to feel like myself again, even just for a couple of minutes.

Summer continued to discuss in detail the amount she was willing to invest and if she became a partner, the projects that she wanted to propose to attract more customers. It wasn't a bad idea, and me and Scar had been running the place with as minimal employees as we could. The additional budget could let us hire more staff and hopefully improve the quality of the overall business. This would also give me time to focus on the new business I was planning to undertake.

An hour later, Summer was shaking our hands, thanking us for the time that we have given to hear her proposal out. And that sixty minutes completely changed my perspective about this person, finally understanding that the Summer I knew barely scratched the surface.

"We'll give you a call after I discuss this proposal with my *partner.*" I closed the door behind after seeing Summer's car drive away. I looked at Scar, still as a statue with her mouth hanging agape.

"Partner?" she asked. Incredulity evident on her voice. "How? Why?"

"I'm promoting you, isn't it that obvious?" I mirrored the growing smile on her face. "You deserve it." I continued walking to the office, grabbing the folder that has been sitting on my desk for a few weeks now. And when the footsteps behind me stopped by the door, I turned around and handed her the folder. "Here's the contract for the partnership. I had my lawyer draft it up for your review, and you can have yours review it as well. Let me know if there's anything you want to change or negotiate, and we can set up a meeting with Eli to discuss it."

"But… I don't have the money to invest as a partner." Her smile losing its brilliance with the realization.

"Remember the contract we had before, or did you just sign that without even reading it?" Scar looked at me sheepishly as if caught red-handed. "There was a clause there for deductions. Retirement, Employee Insurance, Enhanced Benefits and the last is…?"

"Company investment," Scar finished, finally recalling.

"We're not a big company, I know. But I am a strong believer that I shouldn't be the only one profiting from this business and I want you to grow with me as well." I sat on my office chair, firing up the laptop to start the workday ahead. "Think about it and if you can let me know your decision as soon as you can, so we can discuss Summer's proposal."

Scar sat in front of my table and had started reading the contract. We continued working in silence for the next thirty minutes as I went through the business emails for invoices and pending bills that we had to pay as it was nearing the end of month.

The monotony of the tasks was the perfect distraction from this morning's incident.

Before seven PM hit the clock, Scar asked for a pen and signed the contract.

"That's probably a stupid idea," I scolded her. "At least, have a lawyer look at it first."

Scar stood up, dismissing my suggestion as she handed me the paperwork. "I trust you." I rolled my eyes at this. Even if she trusted me, legal stuff was a different conversation. "I had nothing when you took me in. I was contented with working in this club, grateful for the paycheck that I know pays more than the clubs at this block. If you wanted to take advantage of my ignorance, you could've done so right from the start."

She continued, "You treat me as an equal whichever circumstance we're in. That's far more than the people I used to be with, had given me." Scar walked towards me and wrapped her arms around me. "And as I have trusted you, you have to trust me, too. That I will not take advantage of this opportunity and will do my best to do this."

"As you should." My sarcastic tone resulting in Scar's laughter.

"So, yes to Summer?" Scar nodded.

By the time we have finished the proposal as outlined by the presentation Summer sent, there was still a separate inner folder containing additional papers. I pulled it out for me and Scar to look over, thinking it might be additional research to back up the proposal.

But when we saw the first picture printed on the front page, grim reflected on our faces, both determined to finish this once and for all. She nodded and grabbed the folder from my hands, a purpose evident on her strides.

CLUB TALA was a bit quiet, considering it was a Tuesday evening. As expected, this was the time to do the inventory and project purchases for the next two weeks. Scar was going through her list, while I was in my laptop, sitting at the corner of the bar, third cup of coffee in hand.

"No wine tonight?" I was surprised with the voice, not expecting him to pass by at a weekday. Nico sat beside me, asking Scar for a glass of beer. "I heard what happened this morning. Adi's asking me if she could come back and stay at my place."

The thought of Adi, ready to run away was a stab in my heart. What did I expect out of this, when one of her feet was already outside the door even before we even started? "Did you help her pack?"

"Lex…" Nico offered his hand. "I'm sorry you have to go through that… Again."

I took his hand. As much as I wanted to hide and run away to deal with this on my own, these people have been extending their hand to reach out and be with me as I suffer this torment again. "She made her stand truly clear. I am done forcing myself to people who can't accept who I am." My words were starting shake, the emotions that I have been pushing down since this morning ready to pounce outside again.

"I am done," I continued, tightening my grasp on Nico's hand, letting it be the crutch that I need to ground myself again. "I don't want to live in a world where I'm always reminded that who I am and who I love, is sin; that embracing my true self and choosing to love someone regardless of their gender is an immorality so unforgivable."

I could see the tears in Nico's eyes. It was the truth of our choices. People would always look down on us and spite us merely because of who we are and who we choose to love.

"Who would want to live in a world where strangers would tell you that you would rot in hell just because of who you are? They don't even know me, at best just my name. Yet the judgment and hatred that they pass comes from somewhere so deep-rooted, as if they knew me to the core. I didn't hurt anybody, Nico. I didn't spread lies. I didn't covet anyone's wife. My faith is strong, and I have been kind. I just loved... just loved someone who has the same gender as me. How could that be so wrong? How could that be so evil and vile?"

He held my hand, silence enwrapping the truth of our existence.

"She had always hidden us, Nico. Right from the start."

PART VI

They say love is blind.

I beg to disagree.

Love is not blind.

It could see,

But it does not mind.

And maybe that's a human flaw.

But isn't that beautiful?

To love someone beyond the imperfections.

To forgive someone who deserved another chance.

To fight for a love that was so consuming.

Because we are all learning along the way.

And it would be a life content,

To have a hand to hold,

Until we are gray and feeble.

Wrinkly and old.

And that would not matter.

Because love is not blind.

It could see,

But it does not mind.

It could feel,

Despite the flaws.

Perfectly imperfect,

Just for each other.

Chapter Thirty-Four

ADI

I FUCKED up. Yet again. There was no other way to describe it other than that. *I fucked up, again.* The though of losing Lexie again has come to its fruition and why? Just because I was so vigilant that someone I knew might have seen her kiss me on the lips. And for what? Alex was right. At the core of everything, there was still a part of me that wanted to hide this. And the same face always crossed my mind. Mom.

I packed my bags, ready to leave. There was no reason for me to stay here anymore. The only chance I got, not only reconciling with my best friend but hopefully having her as I have longed before, was thrown out by my single mistake—a single repeated mistake.

I have never learned.

Nico and Amanda had agreed to pick me up after I begged them to let me stay for a few more weeks as the application from the apartments I contacted, were still processing. I have a few more hours to remove my existence from Alex's space, hoping that I have not violated and tainted one of the safe places she has for herself.

What is wrong with me? I continuously asked myself as I shove the clothing I have already arranged in the dresser Alex has specifically bought since I was moving in. *She had put in all the effort, helped you without asking for anything in return. You kept on throwing yourself at her, even saying that you are hers, then not have a backbone to stand by it.* I took a pillow to scream my frustration away, the realization of her selflessness a continuous stab in my heart.

Alex saved me. Time in time again. She came in swooping to save me when I was almost kidnapped. She came running to my office, knowing I wasn't safe. She offered me a glimpse in her new life, despite the mistakes I have committed from the past.

A dawning memory had me sobbing against the pillow. When my mom had slapped her, she was looking at me. *At me*, wanting to run towards me and protect me from my mom. And I have always left her, alone to deal with all the aftermaths. No self-loathing was enough to make me feel at least a bit okay. But I knew what I needed to do, once and for all.

I grabbed my phone and dialed the number. It took only one ring before the call was answered.

"Mom, I need to talk to you. Meet me at Palace in the Sky at eight PM tonight. Bring dad. Only *dad*." I didn't wait for a response before I cut the call off.

I WAS fifteen minutes early and was already sat at the reserved table with wine in my hand. I did this out in a whim, knowing that if I thought more about it, the anxiety and fear would grow more, and I would just push it back and probably would never be done.

It had to be done.

I looked at my watch. *Ten more minutes.* Ten minutes before my truth would finally be revealed. A secret that I held on for more than ten years and I was expecting nothing less of the worst-case scenario when my parents finally hear that their only daughter was doing everything against their values and beliefs.

I scrolled through my phone before a hand gripped my shoulder, making me jump from my seat. I turned around and familiar, green-tinged eyes stared back at me, a huge smile across her face.

"Adi!" Eli greeted. "What are you doing here?" Her gaze wandered, probably hoping to see who I came with. As much as I loved seeing her here, this was not the time to chatter. My nerves were already frayed from the dread on how this meeting would go.

"What are you doing here?" I returned the question.

"Meeting up with clients. I just returned from visiting my family, and it was work right away when I got home," she answered as she pointed at the table at the other side. "I almost didn't recognize you. You look so... formal?" I chuckled. She was right, though. I chose to wear the only three-piece suit that I have tailor-fitted for a friend's wedding. At best, I looked like the one meeting with a client.

"Oh, I'm meeting with my parents." The answer was greeted with a grim smile.

Eli didn't prod anymore and walked away back to her table.

A few minutes later, the two faces that I known since I was a kid, walked towards my table with huge grins on their face. My mom kissed me on the cheek with giddiness, and my dad offered his hand for me to take and *mano*. We all sat down as we browsed through the menus.

As I raised my hand to get the attention of the server, my mom pulled my arm down. "Don't order yet. We're still waiting for Damien. He's just looking for parking."

Damien. It was as if an ice bucket was poured over me, my body almost giving in to the shivers of fear. "Why did you bring him along when I specifically told you that it's just for the two of you?!" The anxiety and anger in my chest were starting to comb its way around my spine and gut. "When did you ever respect what I request of you?" The tears were already threatening to spill.

"Amy?" My dad turned to her with a questioning look. My mom waved her hand. "Oh, don't be so dramatic, Adalia." She merely returned to the menu in front of her. "Damien's your fiancé and he should be here for the wedding planning."

My heart continued to shatter as if arrows were buried deep into it. She would never see me as an adult. She would never respect my decision. "*Mom, I am not getting back together with Damien,*" I gritted. "There is no wedding."

"Such a joker, this one." I heard a familiar voice behind me. My body straightened up, palms sweating and my heartbeat already starting to get erratic. "That's one of things I love about her. You never know if she's kidding or not. Keeps me on my toes." He draped his arm around me and pulled me closer to him. He acted as if he was going to kiss me at my cheek but lingered a second longer to whisper the words that would destroy my resolve. "*You couldn't say no, remember?*"

The fear that was instilled in me started slithering up as I felt the grip on my shoulder, tighten and tighten, as if it was a threat. I stood up, not knowing anything else to do. "I'm just gonna use the washroom. Just decide what you're getting, so we can order when I come back." I forced a smile.

I almost ran to the washroom as tears spilled down my face. I sat in the cubicle, trying to even my breathing and remove any traces of crying when I heard the washroom door open, a soft voice calling out. "Adi?"

I forgot Eli was here. Why was she here to witness the greatest failure of my life? I took up the courage and decided to finally speak up for it to be crushed by the one person who wanted me caged and obedient to his whims and desires. The realization that I might not be able to escape this cycle had me sobbing more.

"Adi," Eli's voice calling out right in front of my window. "Are you okay?"

The irony of the question almost had me laughing. "I'm crying in a stall and you're asking me if I'm okay?" A few moments of silence before Eli chuckled, realizing how stupid the question was.

"I saw the motherfucker out there." There was a tinge of fury in Eli's voice. "Do you need help for a way out? I can have you sit with my clients for a bit."

The offer was tempting. Run away from this trap, knowing that they would manhandle the decision out of me to marry Damien. In their eyes, he was the perfect son-in-law, and I was the one who was making everything difficult for this to go through and blocking them in achieving their wish of grandchildren running at their backyard.

Could I live with myself if I said yes to this marriage? Knowing that I would be miserable yet my parents and husband happy? Could I live with myself knowing that I had to offer my body to this man who had never respected me as a human being and only saw me as possession? Would they love me more, if I say yes to the very thing I wanted to run from?

You are not the young girl from ten years ago. My inner voice reminded me. *You have the right to decide for yourself and your happiness.* I could sense the anger rising from my gut, my resolve steeling bit by bit as I was reminded of all the things I had to endure to make the people around me happy, even at the expense of my own. And yet I hurt the only person that was willing to give me everything just for me to be happy and safe.

"Uhhh…" Eli gave a soft knock at the door. "You're awfully quiet there. You okay? Are you still conscious?" I could hear the slight panic in her voice despite trying to mask it as a joke. I opened the door and revealed my tears-stricken face, a smile formed in my lips as I saw how worried Eli was.

She straightened up and offered me a paper towel. "You have a snot line across your cheek." She shielded her face as I teasingly smacked her.

After washing my face and retouching my make-up, I faced Eli with a new determination on my face. Eli's lips started pulling up until a full-blown grin was on her face. She opened her arms and engulfed me in a tight hug. "Attagirl."

I stepped out from the washroom with a new sense of identity and resolve yet I still couldn't erase the feeling of dread as I walked closer and closer to the three figures that had had their power over my life for the longest time.

And it was time to take it back.

Chapter Thirty-Five

ALEX

MY BLOOD ran cold as I heard the voice at the other side of the phone.

"He's here, Alex. I think she's trying to confront them." I could hear the concern in Eli's voice. "But she's outnumbered. I saw the fear in her eyes as soon as that motherfucker sat beside her."

It wasn't my place to intervene, not anymore. But deep in my heart I knew that I couldn't let her face that battle alone. I called Nico back from the dance floor and explained what happened. Scar heard everything Eli said, and she knew what was needed to be done.

Scar nodded and her eyes spoke more emotion than words can: *save her.* Because she knew what would come after. Her scar was a testament to that.

Chapter Thirty-Six

ADI

DINNER WAS served to each of us, my mom talking excitedly with Damien. My dad has been distant to the group right after I returned to the table, not knowing the full reason if it was something discussed when I was not there. I concentrated at the steak and mashed potatoes in my plate, deliberately chewing slowly so I wouldn't get pulled in the conversation. When mom tried asking me a question, I pointed in my mouth and shrugged. My dad looked at me curiously, as if catching up on what I was purposely doing.

I signaled for the server. I was planning to talk about things during dessert. "Order what you like for dessert, I need to talk to both of you about something." I was ignoring Damien intentionally, not acknowledging the side comments here and there.

The server arrived and had started getting mom's order. And when it was my turn, "I'd like to get the strawberry—"

"No," Damien cut me off. "She will be getting the carrot cake slice." He turned to me with a menacing smile. "You have to watch your calorie intake, sweetheart. We don't want you getting too big for the wedding."

It was an awkward moment where the server's hand was paused midway from writing the order, her eyes darting from me to Damien, and my mom laughing forcefully to hide the embarrassment.

"No," I said a bit firmer this time. "I'm gonna get the strawberry shortcake please. Dad, how about you?"

Dad merely shook his head and the server, to her relief, walked away from our table.

"Adi," My mom reprimanded me. "Damien's just concerned with your health. Why did you have to embarrass him like that?"

Time to call out this hypocrisy.

"So, you're saying," I started. "That it was okay for him to embarrass me, yet I am getting scolded for embarrassing him?" My mom looked taken aback from being called out for her bias. Her eyes were starting to redden, and I could see the anger starting to simmer underneath her skin.

"Adalia, how disrespectful. When did you start learning how to answer back to your parents?" she scoffed.

Damien placed his hand on top of mine at the table. "Mrs. Castillo… Amy," Wow. I didn't know they were on first name basis already. "Adi is just under a lot of pressure right now. Work, wedding… me." He flashed an arrogant smile my way. "So please, don't take it against her. Eating can be her way of destressing. I'm sure that after the wedding, we'll get our bearings."

And as usual, my mom gobbled up his attention like a piranha hungry for meat.

"There will be no wedding," I finally said out loud. "I broke up the engagement months ago and that did not change." My mom was staring at me as if offended with what I was saying. "Damien is not needed here so respectfully, if you can leave now while I'm still civil, I will appreciate it."

Damien's madness was dancing in his eyes, yet I knew he couldn't unleash his violence because of my parents. He grabbed my hand under the table and started pushing his nails against my skin as a retaliation to the restriction he has. I didn't let it deter me nor let him see that I was affected.

"Stay, Damien," My mom stared at me as she commanded Damien. This was her power play. For the longest time I had bowed to her wants and needs, never thinking about what I wanted. *Just hers and hers alone.*

"Okay," I smiled sweetly to my mom. "Stay, then. So, you could hear all the things I needed to say, once and for all." I pulled my hand away from Damien, seeing the indented, almost bleeding marks on my arm.

"See this?" I pulled my arm away from his clasp and showed

it to the two people in front of me. "This is what he does to me. It's not even the worst." The shame I felt for letting this happen to me finally out in the open for them to see. "Is that what you want? Mom? Dad?" I watched both of them, eyes widening in shock.

"Mr. And Mrs. Castillo," Damien started as he pulled my arm back. "I only got carried away. I forgot how fragile your daughter is." He was trying to talk in his soothing voice, the one I often heard whenever he talked to my parents, but I could hear a small tremble in his voice.

"Carried away." I laughed to myself. "You were so blinded by your desire for me to marry him, that you didn't even realize that you were giving your *only* daughter away to someone who intentionally hurts her."

Mom's mouth was slightly agape, my dad has his brooding stare at Damien's hand holding my arm.

"I mean…" My mom blinked far too many times for it to be considered normal. "You know people in relationships have problems and a foundation to a good marriage is trying to work things out." She smiled at me and Damien. "This was just a lover's quarrel, right?"

I was too stunned to even respond to what she just said. *Work things out?* "So, mom, *again*, you are telling me," I didn't even care that my voice has started to tremble and the apparent wetness in my cheeks. "that you don't care that I come home to you bruised black and blue, as long as we work things out?"

My mom closed and opened her mouth for a few seconds before adding salt to the wound. "Don't be so dramatic, Adalia." She turned to Damien. "Damian, dear. Tell me that's not true." She smiled expectantly.

Damien, taking advantage of the moment, "No, Amy." He reached out a hand across the table and my mom took it with eagerness. "You know us men, sometimes we get carried away. I'm just sad that Adi thought that I was doing it on purpose. You know *I'll never let her bleed.*" The promise was too much not to notice.

My heart broke as I saw my mom beamed empathically to Damien but not to her daughter. This was a lost cause, and I had no way to win. The people that I thought would at least give me a sparing glance to save me from a fate so dark, ignored me. What did I expect? That something would change?

I quietly let the tears fall, hopelessness an abyss that I was starting to drop into. Maybe I should just accept the fate that I was handed. Maybe this was my karma from the universe after what I did to Alex. Or maybe I have to cut two of the most important people in my life to be able to live my own.

"Amy," My dad rarely spoke against my mom and never called her out in public. But his tone was dead serious, making my mom drop Damien's hand and hold his right away. "Are you so enticed by Damien that you will ignore the suffering your daughter is enduring when she's pleading right in front of you?"

My mom was taken aback. *"Darling,"* she had put all the sweetness and yet full of warning on her tone. "Damien is a really good fit for our Adalia."

"Says who?" I could feel trouble brewing. They had never shown their fights, especially right in front of me. I had always thought that mom wore the pants in this relationship but looking at her right now, and the subdued annoyance on her face, I knew that mom weighs dad's words more than I realized. "You?"

"Darling, are you saying that you're siding with Adi on this?" She tried acting coy and hurt, masking the embarrassment of being called out in front of us. "We know what's best for her, as always. Right? And Damien is one of those decisions."

My dad was starting to visibly get upset. "If you like Damien so much, why don't you marry him, instead?" The deadpan tone made it hard to decipher if this was a sarcastic remark or a serious suggestion.

"What are you saying, Philip? I'm married to you."

Dad laughed sardonically. "That's your issue? That your married to me? Not that the man your eyeing is more than half your age?"

"Uh… no. I mean—" Mom's mouth closed and opened, but no coherent words came out.

"Don't worry, as soon as we're home, *darling*, I'm moving out." Dad stood up, ready to leave. "Better find a good divorce lawyer." And it was the perfecting timing when the server came back with the cakes we ordered for dessert. My dad let out a small cough and sat back down as the food was put in front of us.

I looked at my dad, overwhelmed with gratitude that *finally*, someone stood up for me in this circle.

He gave me a small smile as he took a fork out of the cake I had. "Calories," he scoffed at Damien.

Damien looked pissed but he knew he couldn't do anything to my dad, most especially not in public. Yet the words he uttered next sent shivers down my spine. *"Be careful,* Mr. Castillo." He smiled innocently to my dad.

"Is that a threat, young man?" Dad casually asked. Damien shook his head with the same menacing smile as he had given me before. "Don't hide behind your words and tell me like a man."

Outsiders would think that we were a family having a casual conversation about the most nonsense things in our life. Yet the words that were being said were full of weight, that one misinterpreted word could blow up our table.

"I'm not hiding, Philip," Damien continued playing with his food. "You would definitely know if I was threatening you."

My mom was looking frantic between Damien and dad, not knowing which to deescalate first. And I knew that I wouldn't have another chance once things blew up, considering how volatile the environment at the table was.

"Stop it," I demanded. Three heads whipped in my direction. "I'm not done talking."

I was glad the decision to do this in public was favoring my intentions. Looking at what was happening right now, if we had this talk at home, I could already imagine the screaming match that would have already ensured as soon as I said no.

"The main reason I wanted to talk to you was," I heaved a gulp of air and released it with a sigh. "I wanted to tell you that... I like women." A few seconds to let that sink in. "I'm gay."

There was a moment of silence, then my mom left out a hearty laugh as if I was telling a joke that was too funny for her. Her eyes gradually widened when I held her gaze, not uttering another word. It was then that she realized that I wasn't kidding. The visceral reaction of my mom standing up and making a sobbing sound made the other tables look at us.

"Amy, stop being *dramatic*. Sit down," my dad sneered to my mom.

Before mom could open her mouth to react, I continued, "I have known for a long time. And I chose to hide it from the both of you because you had instilled it in me that it was wrong. I never wanted to feel that who I was, was wrong—a sin." I looked at mom, her face masked with rage. "You have pushed away the only person who allowed to be myself, and accepted me as who I am. But I'm not blaming you. This is all on me. I could have fought for what I wanted long before. The grasp you have in my neck had suffocated me to the point that I almost settled in a relationship that would eventually kill me." Her eyes darted for a moment to Damien. "This is all on me, 'cause I let you. And now, I'm done. I'm taking back the decisions you have made for me."

"If you both cannot accept me as your daughter anymore, I will respect that." My voice broke. "If your love was measured by how much I do what you want, I couldn't blame you. All I craved for was your acceptance, your love without conditions. And if that is too much to ask, I will respect that. My only option if that is the case, is to leave so as not to be an embarrassment and tarnish *your reputation*, mom."

The silence was as loud as music blasted right by my ears. Dad's eyes were shining, tears almost spilling down his face while my mom's rage could be felt viscerally. To let it sink in and give them more time, I raised my hand to ask for the bill.

"So, no, mom," I broke the silence. "I will not be marrying Damien and if worst comes to worst that you cannot accept me, then I will leave, and you won't hear from me again."

"*Be careful*, Adalia," Damien muttered under his breath. "Don't forget what happened before when you tried hiding form me." The fear in my body had me standing up, ready to run.

"Adalia, sit down." My dad said, oblivious to the threats that were whispered in my ear. "Are you sure about what you are saying?" he asked with genuine concern in his voice.

"Obviously, she's not," My mom scoffed. "We've talked about this before Adalia, don't think I forgot the bargain that we had. *You promised.*"

"Bargain? Before?" Dad asked. And basing it on his reaction, he didn't know what happened ten years ago. And before mom could manipulate the story to side with her, I started explaining to dad what happened—the bargain I have made for her not to file the complaint, and the threat that she had made to Lexie that made her run away.

Dad stayed silent. No reaction, no emotions. He was just staring at mom as if looking at a stranger.

"And speaking of the devil," Damien clapped his hands, excited at the turn of events.

I saw the familiar dark hair and brown eyes, walking towards our table.

Chapter Thirty-Seven

ALEX

I THOUGHT I was not going to make it. Fortunately, the traffic had just started dissipating and thankfully, parking near the restaurant was not as full. Nico kept reassuring me that it was all going to be okay. The way his voice was shaking seemed that he was convincing himself more than me. I get it. After reviewing the folder that I have handed him, he knew we have to get there as fast as we could.

By the time we have reached the restaurant, it was almost an hour later from the time Eli had called. She was waiting by the door, expecting our arrival. We walked towards the lounge, trying to figure out how to tackle this.

"I have tried asking them to move my table after my clients left," Eli explained. "But there's someone occupying it already. I heard some loud voices here and there, but they haven't caused enough ruckus to be thrown out."

Nico had started talking to Eli about the possible ways we could approach the group yet all I could see in my mind was Adi all alone, cowering to the pressure of the people around her.

I have to get to her.

"Ms. Johnson!" the restaurant manager greeted. "I didn't know you would be visiting the restaurant today. We could've prepared the usual for you."

As thin as my patience would allow me, I turned to him and smiled. "Barry, I appreciate the gesture. Don't worry, this is not my usual visit anyway. But would you be so kind to prepare a private room for me... good for eight?"

I have to get to her.

"Of course, Ms. Johnson!" Barry walked towards the hostess.

I have to get to her.

And I knew I couldn't wait any longer. I stalked towards the dining hall where Eli pointed the table where Adi and her family were sitting at.

The first thing I saw when I stepped in was Damien with a smug look in his face. I would pay thousands just to know what he was thinking right now, and another thousand to have his reaction recorded once we reveal everything in front of them. I felt a twinge of victory swelling in my chest, knowing that we could finally show his true colors to the people who have been forcing Adi to marry this asshole. But it didn't lessen the urge to punch him right now—really tempting, and maybe I could put the years of kick boxing into action.

I turned to the person beside him, and my chest tightened. The moment my eyes connected with Adi, her gaze softened, relief visibly off her shoulder.

I have to get to her.

The need to wrap her in my arms to finally protect her from these people, was all I could think of right now; to whisk her away and get out of this place, away from these people.

Mrs. Castillo was startled when I dropped the folder at the table with a thud. It took a minute, but her eyes widened as familiarity took over. "You!" She pointed her finger at me. "Why are you back? Didn't I tell you to never show your face in front of us again?!" she almost spat the words out.

"I don't care what you say to me," I dismissed her sputtering anger. "All I care about is for the both of you to read the content of this folder. I'll leave you *all* alone once I know you opened your eyes and realize what kind of person you keep pushing your daughter to marry."

The implication was something I knew I needed to throw out there. There was no pressure for Adi to confess whatever she felt for me, nor what happened between us. *But sometimes you fail to see that some people are not in the same timeline or pacing as you.* Scar's word echoed in my mind and as usual, she was right. I didn't have the right to force Adi to be at the same pacing or timeline as I have. *She needed to come to terms about her sexuality, in her own time.*

I offered Adi a sad smile, knowing that this might be the last thing I could do for her. I turned to the two parents in front of me.

"We don't need you here," Damien sneered. "You keep on latching to Adi as if you're a leech. Are you that desperate to get into her pants?"

"Enough, Damien," Mr. Castillo said with a tinge of annoyance in his voice. "What is this, young lady?"

I almost laughed at Damien's face.

"That is the background check of this man who you're marrying your daughter to." I pulled the paper from the folder to show the complaints that he had over the years. "He has been cited and detained multiple times for reports sexual harassment and domestic battery."

Damien's eyes bulged. "Those are not true!" he almost shouted.

The employees have started whispering, throwing concerned looks in our direction.

I ignored Damien. "If you don't mind, I have a more private room reserved for us to continue this discussion." I looked around and saw that almost all the patrons were now gawking at us. "We don't want to get kicked out in this freezing evening."

Mr. Castillo stood up, but Mrs. Castillo remained in her seat. "I actually do mind," she answered with the most condescending tone she could muster. "I don't want to get involved with pariahs like you. A private room? I doubt you're *that* rich," she scoffed.

I could engage and flaunt all the things that I have accomplished just to throw them at her face. As much as I hated the woman, she was still Adi's mom and the least I could do was not embarrass her in front of this crowd.

"That's enough. Can you please let the young lady talk?" Mr. Castillo interrupted her scorn.

It was so satisfying to see him just call out everyone to shut up. A small smile played in my lips. Something changed. And I hope it was for the better.

"Lead the way, young lady."

We walked in silence. I could see in my peripheral that Nico and Eli had came up to hug and walk with Adi.

The manager led us to the private room, plates ready if we want to order. "Just a bottle of iced tea," I said before he left. No need to fuel this confrontation with alcohol.

The room was large enough to accommodate at least fifteen people. It has a long table in the middle of the room with soft yellow lights enveloping the walls. Everyone started to sit but I have opted to stand up.

Damien drew closely to Mrs. Castillo, a taunting smile across his face. "These are lies, Amy. A fabricated story to earn your favor."

I scoffed. As if I wanted her favor. "We have hired a private investigator to monitor Damien's movements and possibly uncover his motives for pursuing Adi. The PI was able to figure out that Damien has a... *type.*" I pulled out all the pictures of the exes who reported abuse from him. They almost all looked the same. Long dark hair, brown eyes, shy disposition. "He only moved back to the mainland four years ago. The reports that we were able to uncover was from the east provinces. Almost all women had been scared to report him since he stalked them after. Most of these reports are weeks or months or even after the relationship is over. Since there are no more physical evidence and no medical reports, more often he was let go."

I glanced at Nico holding Adi in his arms. "I have a friend test him out last night." I turned to Damien. "Do you remember the woman you've been wanting to take home last night?" Damien's fist tightened, and I knew if it were just us, he would have already thrown that punch. "You were literally telling Adi's parents that the wedding was back on but what were you doing at a club last night, asking another woman to come home with you?" I turned my gaze to her parents, and as much as I detested her mom, I had to try my best to make them see reason. "He was ready to cheat on your daughter, and they're not even married yet."

"Is this true, Adi?" her dad asked. Out of Adi's parents, it seemed that her dad was more receptive to the idea that something bad was really happening. And I could only thank the gods for that.

She's not alone anymore. A reassuring thought.

"Yes, dad," Adi's voice was above a whisper.

"Tell me what happened, honey."

So, Adi did. Adi recounted the times she could remember when she got a beating out of the simplest things, the moment Damien forced her to have sex, and the moment he stalked her at her office. All throughout, no one interrupted her. We knew how difficult it was to relieve a year of memories full of pain and anxiety.

We could see Damien making faces, scoffing to himself as if what Adi was saying was ridiculous. Her mom, an unexplainable twist in her face. And Mr. Castillo had silent tears streaking his cheek, the pain of not being able to protect his daughter evident on his face.

Adi finally stopped, unable to continue as she sobbed uncontrollably. *It's the pain you can't talk about and be okay.*

I stepped out to request for water for less than five minutes when I was greeted by a loud crash inside the room. I ran, panicking that that son of a bitch might have done something to hurt Adi, again.

The dread of realizing that I left her there with that man was a clutch in my heart, constricting bit by bit. To my surprise, and *to my delight,* Mr. Castillo was on top of Damien, trying to pound his face. Damien covered his face to shield, his arms getting brunt of the punches. Mrs. Castillo was shrieking, trying to make her husband stop while the three others were just watching the circus.

As much as I wanted to help Mr. Castillo with a few kicks, conscience won, and I pulled him off of Damien. "Sir, please calm down. We don't want you getting arrested tonight." He was huffing and puffing red all over the face. *"Your daughter needs you tonight."*

He paused, clarity starting to reflect in his eyes.

He turned around and put a hand on my shoulder before walking where Adi was. I turned back to Damien, getting up from the floor, wiping the blood that has started dripping off his nose. "You're lucky I don't want to press charges," he sneered.

I was glad Mr. Castillo was able to get some punches in. "Go on," I dared. "Press charges. Let's see who ends up behind bars." I had Eli call security to escort Damien out while Mr. Castillo was given a bag of ice to put on his knuckles. He winced as the cold penetrated his broken skin.

"Are you not running after him?" he spatted at his wife. "We don't need you here if you're gonna take his side." Despite the anger that made him shake, it was evident in his eyes that the hurt and betrayal were the ones making the tears fall from his eyes.

Mrs. Castillo looked at her husband, and we could all hear her heart shattering in front of his husband. "Philip…" she whimpered. "Don't leave me like this… I love you… How can you leave me like this?"

"Go home," he dismissed. "You've done more than enough to hurt Adi." Mrs. Castillo's face fell as she gathered her things and started walking out. "We'll talk later."

Adi was now in his father's embrace, weeping her eyes out—for the pain that she endured all alone, and maybe the relief that was unburdened by this confrontation, and the reprieve that she may not have both of her parents to open their eyes to the suffering she had wholly accepted to seek their approval, but she has her dad now.

I smiled at Nico. A silent message. *We made it.*

He stared right at back at me. *We're done now. Are you sure?*

I nodded as I walked to the table and gathered the papers. Eli came up to help. "Is that okay?" she asked. "We're just letting him go?" As much as I didn't want to, and just have him thrown behind bars, we were not the victim of this situation. It would be up to Adi to decide what she wanted to do next. It was her choice, *from now on.*

I motioned for Nico and Eli to come about, to give space and time for Adi and her dad to have a moment. There were a lot of things they needed to talk about that doesn't need an audience.

I started walking out, hoping to ask for leniency for the ruckus we have caused. *William would be so annoyed.* I made a mental note to send the restaurant owner a message and apologize to Barry as soon as possible.

"Alex!" A voice called out from behind.

Here we go.

I was expecting that Adi might want to talk to me at some point specifically about the report we have pulled to show them. I probably could recite the information on the report as if it was a graded recitation.

But I wasn't ready for any confrontation about *us*. I yearned for her to be mine, the longest I could remember. Yet I realized that the trauma that it has caused was something I was still trying to heal from. I didn't want to blame her anymore. I was tired of being trapped in the past, unable to move forward. Just because we didn't have the power to fight for each other back then.

My heart is breaking for the younger us.

My heart is shattered for this version of us.

I turned around and held a smile on my face, ready to recite the PI report to whatever she has questions about. She has her hand clinging to his dad, both of them standing in front of me.

"I never got the chance to introduce you to my dad." She gave me a sad, little smile.

I extended my hand to his. "Alexandria Johnson, sir." He squeezed my hand in acknowledgment. "I was in school with Adalia before."

"You have a strong handshake, young lady," He smiled. "Philip Castillo."

Before I could release his hand, he pulled me into a hug. "Thank you for saving my princess," he whispered. "Thank you for being there when I failed to protect my daughter."

Chapter Thirty-Eight

ADI

THE TURN of events was something I had never expected. The apology my dad kept saying over and over again as he held my face in his hands, had my heart breaking for him. He never knew what my mom was doing behind his back, and everything had been dumped right in front of him without warning. I always thought that both my parents were in on it, making me feel all alone throughout my life. Dad was always working, and the assumption that he just didn't care devastated the fragile heart of young Adalia.

"Why didn't you tell me?" Dad kept asking. "I thought you liked him that's why I didn't say anything."

I shook my head vehemently.

"It's okay, dad." Now that I know where he stood, a thorn has been plucked from my heavy heart. *I have him back.* "What matters is now you know it." My tears had not stopped pouring. "I only wanted to make you proud of me," I whispered.

I looked in his eyes and I saw this man's heart break for his daughter. He pulled me into a tight embrace, feeling the silent sobs in his chest. "I am always proud of you, my baby." He kissed me on top of my head. "Never think otherwise. You always come first."

We spent the few minutes in each other arms, silence speaking more than words could. When he pulled away, he motioned to the trio that was talking to each other by the table, arranging the papers to its folder. "Friends?"

Friends? Yes. "Best friends." But not one.

Alex was right. I was always afraid of what the people around me would think. Other people. *Strangers.* I cared more for their perception of me more than my happiness and the people I loved.

Why?

Societal standards?

Taboo?

Judgment?

Acceptance?

Was this more important than having the person I love beside me?

I knew the answer to all of those for the longest time. I was just afraid to accept it.

It has always been her.

"Best friends," I repeated to my dad. "Except one."

He looked at me with brows raised. Curious at best.

"That person?" I pointed at Alex. "I had loved her since I was young, dad." To say it out loud to one of the most important people I looked up to, and confessed who I truly was, felt like chains falling off from my hands and feet. *I'm free.* "She has always been there for me, even if I had been not the best person for her." I proudly told dad all the time Alex had protected me, and was just there for me. His eyes started getting teary again and before I could tease him a bit for it, he pulled me into a tight hug.

"I'm glad someone's been there for you, Adalia" he said barely above a whisper. "She was there for you when I failed you."

"I have you here now."

Dad smiled. "Whatever makes you happy, my princess."

When we finally calmed down, dad asked me to introduce him to Alex.

Meet the parent. My heart leapt in my throat, realizing how big of a step this was. And I wasn't even sure if we were in good terms or not.

My hands started to get sweaty, and my heart was beating a bit rapidly than normal, as I walked towards Alex. But this time, not for the wrong reasons and all the *right ones*.

Alex was about to step out of the room when I called her name out. She stopped and turned around us. A timid smile on her face.

"I never got the chance to introduce you to my dad." I said tentatively. She extended her hand to reach out for my dad.

"Alexandria Johnson," she introduced herself as if she was meeting a client though I could see the nervousness dancing in her face. "I was in school with Adalia before."

My dad looked at Alex, an affectionate smile on his face. "You have a strong handshake, young woman. Philip Castillo." And to both of our surprise, dad pulled Alex into a tight hug. Her eyes bulged in shock for a moment but was immediately replaced by a soft grin. Dad pulled away but they stared at each other for a bit longer before breaking away.

"I'll go home for now," he said as he grabbed his stuff. "Your mom and I need to have a much-needed talk." The dread in his voice didn't go unnoticed.

He turned to Alex, "Take care of my princess, for now." He put his hand on her shoulder and gave it squeeze. "I'm hoping to talk to you again soon."

Alex was left with a bewildered face as my dad walked out the room, leaving us four in an awkward silence. I turned to them, "Thank you for being the rescue team I never knew I needed. You're missing one musketeer, though. Where's Amanda?" I joked. Nico smiled at me knowingly, Eli with a smug look in her face, and Alex with relief on her face. "Please order whatever you want, it's on me."

"Amanda checked in a few minutes ago. She's in Hawaii and will be back tomorrow to join in on this ruckus. She's mad she didn't get a punch in on Damien," Nico stepped in and enveloped me in a tight hug. "Also, can you refer me to your company? You're missing a lot of work, yet you still have a lot of money. I need to get it on this scheme."

I hit his back softly and was returned by a laugh. "It's called 'saving,' ass."

Eli stepped in next for a hug and before she could utter a word, I cut in first. "I knew you were the one who told them I was here," My tone, scolding. "If it weren't for you, I don't know what could have happened." I tightened my hug. "Thank you, Eli."

Realizing how lucky I was to have these people around me had me clutching my stomach, stopping a sob to come out. I have cried enough tears tonight.

Eli pulled away. "I told you, Adi, ladies usually cry out because of happiness when they're with me. You keep on breaking the streak, Adi." I smacked her playfully as a response. She pulled away and gave me and Alex the eyes. *Very subtle, Eli. Very subtle.*

Nico and Eli excused themselves, saying that they were going to ask for the menu outside, even though there's eight lying at the table inside the room. I rolled my eyes at them. Despite the not-so-discreet set up, I have to thank them for it as it removed a bit of anxiety in my heart.

I approached Alex, ready to accept whatever happened after this.

We both could not deny, this was long overdue. We've been holding out in this thug of war of who was going to make the first move first yet pull away when the other had shown their hand. I was tired of playing this game, and I knew she was, too.

Whatever happens in this conversation would make or break the possibility of us.

"Alex," I asked her to come over to the seat beside me. "Lexie… I need to tell you something."

Lexie released a huge sigh before seating down. "Let me go first?" She offered her hand out. I took it without hesitation. "I'm sorry."

Sorry? I should be the one sorry.

"I'm sorry that I wasn't any better to the people who have forced their way, and made you do what they want. All I thought about was the hurt I felt when I assumed that you might be ashamed of me." I opened my mouth to assure her that I was not, but she put a hand to stop me. "Let me finish first. I failed to consider that you have just started accepting this part of you and you might not be ready for the things that this world, this relationship, with yourself or with another woman, would entail. It is your timeline. It is your pacing. And I failed to realize that. I had expected you to run at the same pace as me, right away; pressuring you to be okay to do the things you're not yet ready for."

She tightened her grip on my hand. "I'm sorry." The anguish in her eyes was enough to break the control I have been holding on since she entered the room.

"I am no way perfect, Lexie." I held her face in between my hands. "I have lied to my younger self for years, denying that what I was feeling for you before was not just as best friends; the realization that I might actually like women had shaken my being to its core. And my fear had come true, that I didn't have choice but to run away." The things I have been hiding since I was young, pouring out with no stop. "I have a lot to learn… and a lot to unlearn. I am broken in different aspects of my life… my body, and I do not know if I would ever be whole again. Damien had taken a piece of me that I might never have back." She stared at me, tears brimming at the corner of her eyes. "But I will work on it, to the best I can. To be a better person for myself, for the people I love… most especially you."

Her eyes widened, realizing what I have confessed. "Yes, I love you, Lexie." I thought I couldn't shed anymore tears but here they were, falling freely again. "And it took me losing you twice, for it to wake me up from my stupor and finally fight for what I wanted and what I loved. I was ready to confess it all to my mom, even if I thought we were done." She wiped the tears on my cheek. "You deserve more than that, Lexie." I pulled her into a hug. "You deserve more than what this cruel world could offer."

Lexie pulled away, tears and laughter stained our faces. "I loved you then, Adi." She pulled my face for a peck. "And I love you now."

"I'm yours to take." I stared right straight into her eyes. Channeling all the emotion words could not describe. "If you'll still have me."

I could feel her slow ragged breath. "*Always*," she whispered against my lips. I closed the distance and welcomed her lips into mine, our tongues dancing with emotions we could not describe to each other.

I knew it was love. More than that; a lot more than that. It was love and a lot more things —the good and the bad.

We rested our foreheads against each other, basking in how surreal this moment was.

"I have a lot to learn," I whispered. "So, please be patient with me."

Lexie closed her eyes; a soft smile was playing in her lips. "As long as you're trying, Adi. That is more than enough."

I was about to close the gap between us again, to taste her again when I heard a grunt by the door. A stupid smile spread across my face.

"Eww." I heard Nico say. "Not here, please. I don't want to see that."

"Then, don't look Nico," Lexie said as she held my face in my hands and pressed her lips on mine again.

"I can't not look. I have nowhere else to lay my eyes on. You're the only thing that's interesting here." I heard his voice getting closer.

"Adi and Alex, sitting on a tree. K-I-S-S-I-N-G!" Eli sang.

I pulled away from Lexie and was ready to throw my shoes at them with a laugh when I saw what Eli was holding. Lexie also turned around and was shocked to see a cake with candles on it.

"Happy birthday, *biatch*. It's still your birthday. Thought we forget?" Eli almost shoved the cake at Lexie's face playfully. "Make a wish."

Lexie stared at the cake for a second longer then blew out the candles.

"What did you wish for?" Nico asked as he laid the plates and fork by the table.

Lexie looked at me with a twinkle on her eyes, her lips pulling from side to side. "I think my wish had been answered already." She squeezed my hand.

"Ugh. So cheesy."

I could see Eli and Nico mockingly gag at Lexie. We laughed our hearts out at the duo as they started retching for real. And as they recovered, the cake-smearing party began. By the end of the evening, we were like four little kids, belly stuffed with sweets, dying of laughter from our shenanigans.

It wasn't my birthday. But I knew my wish has been granted, too.

No more regrets.

Epilogue

ADI

THE SWEAT rolled in my bare back, the feeling of anticipation coiling in my stomach as a hand grazed the skin on my shoulder, sending jolts of electricity in all ends of my body. Never in my life had I imagine I would be in this position. If I asked the Adi from a year ago if she would see herself in this situation one day, she would vehemently shake her head and say that what I was suggesting was insanity.

But I was not the same Adi from a year ago. A lot has happened within the last year, that I felt like I was granted my chance to a second life. A small smile played in my face, looking back at the trajectory of my life; how I was able to reconcile my relationship with my dad, my mom, a working progress—not the best, still, it was progress.

"Distracted much?" I almost jumped out of my position as a low voice purred by my ear. "You're getting bored, Adi?" Humor playing in her voice.

I turned at her and shook my head. "How many more seconds?" I asked. She looked at her watch and gave me a proud grin. "Hold it for… 5, 4, 3, 2, 1… and you're done!"

I slumped on the floor, my core quaking from the plank. "God, I'm gonna die. Why do you this to yourself?"

Lexie sat beside me, offering a bottle of water. "You said you wanted to join my work out." She shrugged as if what we have been doing for the last thirty minutes had not siphoned the life and energy out of me. I didn't realize that attaining Lexie's body figure would entail sacrificing myself to the devil. I think that would have been easier than the workout routine she had made me go through.

"I'm so sore. I'm not sure if I would have the energy to celebrate Eli's engagement tonight." I groaned as I laid down at the floor in the middle of her apartment, the cold wood making me shiver.

Lexie looked down at me and lowered her face to give me a soft peck on the lips. I smiled, contented of just being here, regardless of how sweaty and probably smelly I was, with my best friend... *my girlfriend.*

"Can you imagine? Who would've thought that she would have the bone in her body to settle down." She lifted her finger and booped my nose. "I never thought that this day would come. But I'm happy." She sighed with content. "She deserves to be happy."

I never thought this day would come. I gazed up, staring Lexie's face. *So, who am I to question the universe?*

"Also, I don't know why you were so insistent to work out." I was pulled out of my musings as I felt her finger trailing across my moist chest. "You look perfect to me." Her eyes were lost in a trance, focused on the touch that was making its way to my body.

"You look perfect *for* me." She lowered her lips at my bare stomach, grazing her lips across. I could feel the need rising in my gut from even her slightest touch—always hungry for more, as if making up for all the time we let slip away. And as much as I wanted to give in, the insecure part of me overpowered the lust that had started creeping up.

I closed my eyes as I remember the first time we have allowed ourselves to bare even our most hidden sides to each other, not because of a call to a need, but knowing it was the perfect time.

"You are more than a good fuck," Lexie kept whispering in my ear. A reassurance that I was more than my body, not just a means to a physiological release. "You told me that you always give. Have you ever asked or given something back to yourself?"

I shook my head.

"Have you ever touched yourself?" she asked.

I knew that it was not to mock but a genuine question to know. I shook my head again.

"So selfless," she whispered. I wasn't selfless. I was scared—it was a taboo. "Twenty-eight years, Adi, and you've never even wondered how it would feel to pleasure yourself. Come on, show me what you know." She sat by the chair at the corner of the room, observing. I was left at the foot of the bed, staring at my naked self at the mirror in front of me. "Take your hand and show me."

I opened my legs, hand slowly creeping down my stomach, and to the space between my opened legs. My eyes darted to Alex who suddenly stood up and stalked towards me. She held my face in the middle of her hands and slowly lowered her lips against mine.

"You're beautiful," she whispered. "And you must also learn to accept and love your body, no matter how imperfect you think it is."

She straightened up and crawled up at my back, taking my hand in hers. She guided my hand all throughout my body, helping me explore the parts I never knew could give me pleasure. She gave the space in between my legs a gentle swipe, and I could feel my body coiling… anticipating for more. "And you have to know how to keep yourself happy and satiated… even without the help of another."

And that lesson opened my eyes to wonders I could not even fathom.

"Please, let me shower first." My voice barely audible from my heavy breathing. Lexie had started peppering the part of my breast that was visible from my sports bra, her hand playing at the insides of my thighs.

As startled as I was when she sucked the skin, leaving a barely visible mark, the feeling of her lips and tongues against my skin had me arching my back, asking for more.

"Come on." I could feel her holding on to her restraint. "I'll help you shower."

Lexie pulled me up and guided me to the shower. No words, just hands that were roaming our body, cleaning methodically. As soon as we were done, she pulled me towards the bedroom, not even bothering to put on clothes.

Despite the lust that my body had been yearning, I couldn't help myself but feel overwhelmed with how she had been treating me for the past six months. I had a lot to learn and unlearn—heal and build myself again. She had been my crutch, *like before,* during times that I needed to be grounded. She had always respected my decision, my requests, regardless of if she had to give way first. Just like a moment ago when I asked to shower even though both of us knew we wanted to jump each other right there and then, she respected my decision—*my body, my decision.*

The trauma from my ex-fiancé was a demon I had been trying to dance with, and Alex had been a supportive partner, always there to extend her hand if I asked for help. She always reminded me that I always had power over who I was, regardless of if giving away my energy to people, or my body itself.

"You could always say no, you know that right?" Alex said as she turned me around to face me. She bared her body in front of me, and every time I told her that I wish I had her figure, she always reminded me that my body was beautiful, and it was perfect in her eyes.

The need was pulsing in my core, seeing the glazed eyes roaming my body. I knew it was physiology calling out to release this need, yet I knew that above anything else, I was giving my body willingly to the person I love.

I took her hand and guided it to the middle of my legs, showing her that I wanted her as much as she wanted me.

"Come here, and make sure to fuck me out of my mind." It was supposed to be a joke, yet I couldn't mask the need tainting my tone.

She turned my around, giving me a soft push so I land at the soft mattress. Alex smiled at me, a promise of mischief and release.

"Adi…" She crawled over me, kissing me from my lips down to my body. And soon as she was in that space between my legs, she smirked at me and teased, "I told you. Don't threaten me with a good time."

My breath hitched and my eyes rolled back as I felt Lexie's tongue doing wonders I had never known. And before I could even finish, Alex straightened up, wiping the evidence of my need from her face.

Her eyes looked feral, blanketed by pure lust.

"Come on." She pulled me up. "Sit on my face."

Oh, the joy of being loved by *my* woman.

Acknowledgements

To my wife, Faith, who has been the inspiration to start this novel—thank you for your patience and allowing me to just be in my element despite the crazy year we had. The enthusiasm you show for all the things I do is beyond comparison. You are the best cheerleader that anyone could ask for. I am beyond blessed to have you as my partner in this life. Thank you for always being my 80/20. I love you.

To one of the people who had always supported and gave me the courage to write, my best friend, Patricia—I could definitely say that I wouldn't have finished this novel without you. Thank you for being with me chapter after chapter, revision after revision, until the completion of this work. I am excited for all the plans and more projects that we have in store. To more published books and the goals that come after!

To my beta readers: Ron and Camille– this was the first time I had ever tried beta readers, and you both have not failed me. I appreciate all the feedback and the recommendations to further improve this novel. Your kind words have been a crutch for me to hold onto, whenever the impostor syndrome starts to creep up again. I am forever grateful for your support.

To Tamara, my editor and beta-reader, (and my reading buddy, too!), thank you for all the back-and-forth memes about writing that helped ease the pressure of putting this out. You have always been there to give that motivation and push to finish this book. Thank you for sharing your editing expertise in making sure that this novel is ready for the public's eye. (I'm sorry for all the prepositions that were all over the place. Lol) And a special shout out to your assistant, Alister!

To one of the most artistic people I have ever known in my life, Dane—thank you for creating this book cover (and the character sketches) for me despite the late notice. I am forever in awe of your talent, and I truly hope this marks the beginning of your art reaching a wider audience. Know that I'll always be one of your earliest and biggest supporters.

To my family, thank you for always supporting me through all the weird and wonderful shenanigans I've taken on. I'm forever grateful for the safe space you've given me to express myself freely and be accepted for who I am. I am so lucky to have you as my family. I miss you and love you always.

To my friends, both online and offline, who have always provided support in your own ways, my heart is full of gratitude for having you with me throughout my writing journey.

And of course, to the 8Letters team and Miss Cindy Wong, participating in your challenge was the final nudge I needed to make sure that I finish this novel. I am forever grateful for the trust and opportunity that you have given me to reach out to a wider audience for the message I want to share.

And lastly to my mom, there's not one day that I don't miss you. I love you, always. Have fun up there!

About the Author

Anjel Reyes lives in a cozy apartment somewhere in California, with her wife and their two mischievous orange cats, Fred and George. She spends her days immersed in books, writing or staring at a blank page, or enjoying the delightful chaos of Ryan and Shane's shenanigans on *Watcher* (All hail the Watcher!) and true crime deep dives with Stephanie Soo's *Rotten Mango*.

When she's not glued to her laptop, she attempts (key word: attempt) to step outside and soak up some sunshine. Despite being a homebody, she finds joy in hiking, camping, and long coffee dates, preferably somewhere with good pastries and even better conversation.

A Pocket Full of Regrets is Anjel's debut novel, created in the hopes to shed a light on some of the not-so-easy parts of being queer—that coming out is just one foot out of the closet, and the journey to self-acceptance is never black and white.

She also co-authored a collection of poems with her best friend, titled Musings: Midnight Thoughts published under Ukiyoto Publishing. This anthology has been recognized as the *Parangal ng Gintong Pluma* 2024, Poet of the Year by *Ukiyoto Publishing* and *Scribblory*. A special edition has been published in partnership with 8letters Bookstore and Publishing.

Follow her on her social media accounts:

Instagram: *@am.reyes_*

Linktree: *https://linktr.ee/amreyes*

A Pocket Full of Regrets

is on Spotify

Listen to the some of the songs that were on repeat
during the creation of this book.

MUSINGS: MIDNIGHT THOUGHTS

BY ANJEL REYES & KATRINE MADAYAG

"Go through the pain, go through the loneliness –
Until you find yourself stronger than before;
Until you find yourself comfortable with being alone;
Until you find yourself smiling and laughing again,
Even without the company of another hand to hold."
—An Ode to the Fallen

In partnership with 8letters Bookstore & Publishing, Anjel Reyes and Katrine Madayag released a special edition of **Musings: Midnight Thoughts**. This edition follows the recognition of their first volume as *Poet of the Year 2024* by *Ukiyoto Publishing House* and *Scribblory*. This anthology combines the voices of two talented authors, each sharing their unique journey through love, loss, self-discovery, and healing. Their words offer an intimate exploration of life's challenges, with the hope of providing comfort and connection in a world filled with uncertainty.

Musings: Midnight Thoughts welcomes you into a space of vulnerability, reflection, and healing, where late-night musings and personal revelations inspire growth and understanding.

Available in paperback, hardbound, and eBook formats. Grab your copies now from the available platforms below!